We hope you enjoy this b
renew it by the due date.

You can renew it at www.n
by using our free library ap

vise you can a'

BOOKS BY CAROLYN ARNOLD

Brandon Fisher FBI series

Eleven
Silent Graves
The Defenseless
Blue Baby
Violated
Remnants
On the Count of Three
Past Deeds

Detective Madison Knight series

Ties That Bind
Justified
Sacrifice
Found innocent
Just Cause
Deadly Impulse
In the Line of Duty
Power Struggle
Shades of Justice
What We Bury
Life Sentence (prequel
romantic suspense)

McKinley Mysteries

The Day Job is Murder
Vacation is Murder
Money is Murder
Politics is Murder
Family is Murder
Shopping is Murder
Christmas is Murder
Valentine's Day is Murder
Coffee is Murder
Skiing is Murder
Halloween is Murder
Exercise is Murder

Matthew Connor Adventure series

City of Gold
The Secret of the Lost Pharaoh
*The Legend of Gasparilla and
His Treasure*

Standalone

Assassination of a Dignitary
Pearls of Deception

THE LITTLE GRAVE

CAROLYN ARNOLD

bookouture

Published by Bookouture in 2021

An imprint of Storyfire Ltd.
Carmelite House
50 Victoria Embankment
London EC4Y 0DZ

www.bookouture.com

ISBN: 978-1-80019-018-4
eBook ISBN: 978-1-80019-017-7

This book is dedicated to George, who always reminds me of the power and strength I possess and has been my cheerleader for over twenty years.

PROLOGUE

Atlanta, Georgia, United States
Five and a Half Years Ago, January

Her past didn't sit and stay like an obedient dog. It was more a wolf that stalked her every move, breathed down her neck, and inched closer with every passing second. The hundreds of miles she'd traveled or the state lines she'd crossed in the last five months didn't matter; her hunter was there and had her constantly looking over a shoulder. She yearned to stop and catch her breath but knew the second she did her life would be over. She'd be ripped apart by the unmerciful teeth of her history.

Casey-Anne was three minutes into her set and hanging upside down on the pole when she spotted him at the back of the strip club, leaning against the bar, no drink in hand. He appeared within a haze of cigarette smoke, giving the illusion of an apparition. But he was very much real, and his gaze was fixed on her. Not in the sad, pathetic, and predictable way most men ogled her at Georgia's Peaches, pinning her with their lascivious leers. No, he had something else on his mind.

He was there to kill her.

Her heartbeat thumped, its bass reverberating in her skull. She spun around and landed on the stage, feeling more vulnerable than she had since that night she'd run away. Performing had given her a sense of power and control. Men could look but not touch. But right now all that confidence had been stripped away. She was more exposed than ever—not because all she wore was a skimpy thong that left very little to the imagination and fine-pointed heels that added six inches to her height—but because of that man.

She carried on her routine, pretending to ignore him. She focused on her well-practiced moves and gave sultry pouts and seductive looks to every man who tossed a wadded bill at her feet. But the only thing she could think about was getting the hell out of there.

Her last song wound down and she rushed back to the dressing room. She'd have to leave the money from the stage behind. Small price if it meant her life.

Tessa, a fellow dancer who went by the stage name of Ginger and wore a wig of red curls that reached her ass, was applying mascara in a grimy, pitted mirror. "How's the crowd?"

Casey-Anne barely spared her a glance as she grabbed everything from her locker and stuffed all of it into her duffel bag.

"Hello? Ya hard of hearing?"

"I'm getting the hell out of here." Casey-Anne shucked the heels, slipped on a pair of blue jeans and pulled a sweater over her head. She pushed her feet into running shoes and threw on her coat.

"That bad, huh." Tessa exchanged her mascara brush for a compact of blush.

Without another word, Casey-Anne flew past her, out the back door and past the bouncer. She'd just swing by her apartment and pick up some things before hitting the road. She wasn't safe here anymore.

The streets were bare, and the January evening was cool for Georgia. It seeped through to her bones and turned the sheen of sweat on her body into a layer of ice.

She hustled, glancing behind her with attention on the shadows, the darkness the streetlights didn't reach. She didn't see anyone following her, but that didn't mean the man wasn't there. She could feel his eyes piercing through the night.

She picked up her speed. Her place was only a three-block walk from the club; a short distance but it always felt like a long way in the dark. Her skin pricked with goose bumps, but she couldn't give in to panic and hysteria. Or let her mind dwell on her nightmarish past.

There was the scuffing of shoes behind her and she spun around. But no one was there.

A half block to go. Maybe she was overreacting. Maybe there was no need to head out right away. She could wait until daylight. Tonight, she'd pour herself a glass of wine and take a nice, long hot shower and crawl into bed. Yes, that was a pleasant thought, and it spurred her forward. In this fantasy she could almost blink away the recollection of that man. Blank stare, hardened jaw, rigid body.

She took the stairs to her apartment building's front door two at a time and unlocked it. Once inside, she pushed against it to ensure it shut tight and the automatic lock was back in force. It was then she caught movement outside the sidelight. She jumped back.

A man was on the other side. There was a scratching noise at the knob.

She couldn't get herself to move toward the stairwell for her third-floor apartment. Her legs weren't responding.

The handle turned—the sound had been a key in the lock—and a man she recognized as another tenant stepped inside.

"Hey," he said.

"Hi." She could barely squeeze out the tiny word as she rushed to push the door shut again.

He took off toward his apartment, leaving her in the small entry, heaving for breath like she'd run a marathon. She jogged to her apartment, threw the deadbolt and linked the chain, and fell against the door. Safe. For now she had escaped the wolf on her trail.

She dropped her bag and jacket on the floor and rushed to the kitchen. A bottle of Cabernet Sauvignon had her name all over it. She guzzled some back, assuring herself that soon all would be better, and took some wine in a glass with her down the hall.

She ran the water hot, got undressed and under the spray, closed her eyes and let her mind drift to dreams of a future that didn't include dancing for money, and where her past was so far behind her she couldn't recall it. A time, flashing forward, when she obtained her nursing license and had a job in a doctor's office or a hospital.

A thud.

Her eyes shot open and she turned off the taps to listen. All was silent except for her breathing and the pounding of her heart in her ears. It had to simply be paranoia eating away at her sanity. She was, after all, in a locked apartment, in a locked building. But doubt gnawed on her. If someone were determined enough, they could find their way in. Pick a lock, come up with a ruse, or let themselves in on the heels of another tenant.

She squeezed her eyes shut, took some long breaths and calmed her nattering mind. There. All was better.

The shower curtain was ripped down, and the man from the club was standing there.

A scream curdled in her throat.

She scrambled to get around him but there was no way past. Her feet slipped on the wet surface of the tub and her arms sprang out to help her offset her balance, but he had a hold on her. He yanked her out of the tub and slammed her to the floor.

Her head smacked against the tile, and sparkles of white light danced across her vision.

He lowered himself on top of her, pinning her. "Where is it?" His breath smelled like stale cigarettes and whiskey.

"I…" Her eyes rolled back and there was brief, inviting darkness. A place where pain didn't exist.

He slapped her across the face and clamped her jaw in his hand. "Tell me!"

She wanted to fight, to show him that she'd learned her power since she'd escaped. But her mind wasn't working, and she didn't have the strength to move.

He stood and pulled a gun.

She couldn't get her mouth to work or she'd tell him where it was. That might give her a chance of survival.

"You want to die? Tell me where it is!" he roared.

Tears fell down her cheeks. "I—I—" Her mind went blank; her thoughts encased within a web of thick gauze.

"Stupid bitch!"

She barely had a chance to blink when the bullet hit, but her final thought was, *The wolf caught me, and now I can stop running and rest.*

CHAPTER ONE

Woodbridge, Virginia
Sunday, January 10th, 11:30 PM Eastern Time

Amanda Steele threw her legs over the side of the bed, grabbed her underwear from the floor, and stepped into them. In the dimly lit room, she followed the trail of clothing, collecting each piece as she went along.

"Where ya goin', darlin'?" the man, whatever-his-name, said.

First rule of one-night stands: no names.

She kept moving but pinched her eyes shut. It was January tenth, the start of a new year, and, while most people were still clinging to their resolutions, she'd resumed old habits: sleeping with strangers. But she knew better than to deceive herself into thinking she'd change. There was only one adjustment she was interested in making and it was outside of her abilities. It would require a time machine. Only she'd go further back than three hours ago when she'd picked up the handsome guy drinking beer in a Woodbridge bar.

"Come on, don't you want to stay? We can—"

"I don't spend the night." Rule two. She was surprised by how often she had to tell the men that. In fact, most begged her to stay. Some even tried to lure her with the promise of breakfast. Despite men being painted as philanderers, so many were desperate for a sole, meaningful relationship.

She had found everything but her T-shirt, and a bubble of panic started in her chest as she scanned the room. *Think, think, think…*

Her shirt had been the first thing he'd taken off her as they stumbled into the motel room. Her gaze went to the air-conditioning unit by the door and she was relieved to see her shirt in a ball on the floor next to it. She snagged the shirt and set out for the bathroom, hugging her clothing to her chest. She shut the bathroom door behind her with her foot and halted at the sight of herself in the mirror. The green of her eyes had dulled over the last five and a half years, a testament to the fact she was doing nothing more than walking through life, barely a shadow of her former self. But she'd lost everything one tragic, fateful night. Her drive, her purpose, her career aspirations about following in her father's footsteps and becoming police chief. The hardest hit: she'd lost her family—in one swoop. Her love and husband of ten years and her six-year-old daughter, taken out by a drunk driver.

She gripped the sink, her knuckles turning white. She'd been robbed—they'd been robbed. But she'd also been taught the harsh lesson that there was no point in making grand plans for the future. Clinging to optimism was nothing but a cruel illusion. Life held nothing but pain and sorrow. And emptiness. Hopelessness.

A single tear fell, and she swiped it away, angry at herself for bringing them into her melodrama again. As if their deaths had turned her into a woman who slept with strangers and had her popping sleeping pills every night. They were not to blame, and she didn't need to consider their feelings. They were dead. Six feet under.

Cold. Hard. Fact.

She snapped on her bra and put on her shirt. She was zipping up her jeans when the man knocked on the door.

"You sure I can't talk you into staying? It was pretty hot."

Every guy found it "hot." So many of them had bigger egos than they had—

"One more go?" he implored.

She swung the door open. He was standing there naked with one arm overhead, elbow leaned against the doorframe, his other hand positioned on his upper thigh in a cocky pose that would make most women weak in the knees. He was a handsome man—and he was right, the sex had been hot—and maybe in another life they could have been something, but she'd had the love of her life. He'd been taken away. Maybe that's why one-night stands had become her medication, her addiction, and her punishment.

The man smiled at her and moved in to kiss her.

She stepped back and held up a hand between them. "It was fun. Now it's over."

"I've got the room for the night." Spoken as if that made a difference.

"Enjoy."

His shoulders sagged. "Ouch, you're cold as ice. Can't I get your number at least? Maybe give you a call sometime?"

She laid a tender hand on his cheek. "Now, now. You're a big boy and you know how this works."

Rule three: keep anonymity in all respects. No names *and* no personal ties. That meant no exchanging phone numbers. It was also why they'd hooked up in a motel and not at her place or his. She viewed the detachment necessary to protect her emotions but also to keep them out of her personal business. None of the men needed to be privy to her past and the baggage she carried. She didn't want to be looked upon as some damsel in distress in need of saving, and she certainly didn't need anyone's pity. She got all she needed from them: a few seconds to feel something and a distraction from her grief.

"Well, I'm not really sure what to say then. Thanks?" He raked a hand through his hair and she almost felt sorry for him. Almost.

"Sure." With that she grabbed her coat and left the room.

The January night air was cool on her cheeks and nipped at her nose. Christmas lights still twinkled in the windows of the motel's lobby; any magic spells the season tried to cast were ineffective on her. Christmas was a representation of how sad and pathetic her life had become since the accident. She used to love it, but there was no point anymore. She'd lost too much, become too hardened. The only way she'd survived this past Christmas was due to the company of her best friend Becky Tulson. They'd drunk hot apple cider, shared laughter, and watched action flicks. The rest of the world could keep their seasonal feel-good movies with their carols, gingerbread, and destined soulmates. She'd had all that, but it was gone. Just like the season and any mirage of normalcy and joy.

She got into her Honda Civic, giving a quick glance at the black Dodge Ram pickup parked in the slot next to hers. It belonged to the man she'd just slept with. She could run his plate, find out his name, but there'd be no purpose. Whatever they'd shared was over.

She cranked the heat and was rewarded with an initial blast of cold air from the vents. It still wasn't warm by the time she pulled out of the motel parking lot.

She should just go home, have a shower and wash the sex off her. After all, her shift started at eight in the morning and it was going on eleven thirty at night. But the pain in her soul was so intense, it was like its own entity. She used to cry so hard after sleeping with a man, her body would heave. Now she stuffed any emotions way deep inside, did her best to shut them out completely. But tonight, she could use something stronger than a sleeping pill. And it wasn't just because she'd slept with a stranger. The drunk who'd killed her family had just been released from prison a few days ago, giving her that final nudge toward the precipice. Maybe now she'd finally have the courage to step further into the darkness.

She drove to a sketchy neighborhood with a smattering of lit Christmas lights clinging to the eaves on a few houses. The strings sagged as if begging for reprieve. Discarded trees were lined up at the curb awaiting pickup.

She parked in front of a rundown clapboard house. It wasn't advisable for a woman—or any outsider, for that matter—to come to this area unaccompanied after dark, but she wasn't entirely alone. She opened her glove box and took out her Glock. Her detective's badge slid to the front of the compartment, resting over the registration and insurance paperwork. She held it in her hands and traced her fingers over the eagle. This piece of gold used to mean so much to her, but when Kevin and Lindsey had died it was like the world had gone from color to black and white, and she wasn't sure how to reinfuse color.

She looked at the house—no sign that Christmas cheer had ever existed there—but couldn't get herself to step out of the car. She'd never been here before, but she knew who was inside. He went by "Freddy," but his real name was Hank Cohen. He'd turned to the streets at fifteen when his mother took up with an abusive man who'd slapped him around one too many times. He had been in and out of jail for dealing, but Amanda would guess his list of crimes was more extensive than that. The reasoning behind his handle was a mystery to her.

Now, all she had to do was get out of the car, walk up the cracked pavement to the door, and knock.

That's all, she coached herself. But it really wasn't "all." She was a detective in the Homicide Unit under the Criminal Investigations Division and Violent Crimes Bureau for the Prince William County Police Department. She was supposed to be a role model, to lead by example.

But Freddy could give her what she needed. He offered street drugs, but she was interested in getting her hands on some Xanax. After the accident, her doctor had prescribed it for a few months but then he had refused to renew the prescription. He'd told her it wasn't healthy to stay on the pills long-term and recommended she see a therapist. He'd referred her to one, who she saw a grand total of three times. It made her feel worse talking about Kevin and Lindsey to a stranger. Her internal dialogue nattered enough, and that's why she needed something to shut up the voices. The over-the-counter sleeping pills could only do so much. The Xanax helped her become so relaxed she didn't have the energy to feel or think a damn thing.

She gave another glance toward Freddy's house, then at the badge still in her hand, and blinked back tears. She'd already fallen so far from grace. Did it matter if she slipped further? If she took this step, would there be a way back? And if there wasn't, did she care?

She tossed her badge back in the glove box and reached for the door handle. Her cell phone rang, and her heart palpitated off rhythm. She took a few deep breaths. "Detective Steele," she answered, sinking lower in her seat and feeling shame.

"Amanda? It's Becky."

She'd known Becky since kindergarten, but now Becky was an officer with Dumfries Police Department, the small town where Amanda lived. Given that it was just after midnight now, she'd wager Becky's call was related to work as Dumfries PD turned suspicious deaths and murders over to Amanda's department at PWCPD for investigation, but Amanda wasn't on shift. "Is everything okay?"

"There's something you should know. Chad Palmer's been found dead in a room at Denver's Motel."

Amanda's throat constricted and her vision went black. Chad Palmer—the man who'd destroyed her world and taken her family from her. All because he'd gotten behind the wheel drunk and crossed the line in more ways than one.

She couldn't bring herself to talk. She was too busy processing this news. Denver's was a dive motel that catered to lowlifes. It was a fitting exit ramp for Palmer.

"I had to call it in, but I just wanted to give you a heads-up." Becky's voice was barely above a whisper.

"Was he murdered?" she squeezed out.

"I don't know. I'm here now, and it's not obvious exactly what killed him."

Chills shot down her arms, goose bumps rising in their wake. "Thanks for letting me know."

"Of course."

Amanda hung up but kept her grip on her phone tight and turned her attention to the glove box, her mind on her badge. She gave one last, desperate look at Freddy's and drove toward Denver's. Becky's call had saved her this time.

CHAPTER TWO

Amanda pressed the gas and made it from Woodbridge to Dumfries in less than the fifteen minutes it would normally take. Between the time of night and her speed, it took her under ten. But for every one of those minutes she was thinking about what she was going to find once she got to Denver's Motel. Was Chad Palmer really dead?

If so, he had finally gotten what he'd deserved after all this time. The law certainly hadn't doled out justice when it had given him five years, the equivalent of a slap on the wrist. Even tacking on the additional five months he'd spent behind bars during the trial was nothing. Call it karma that he'd just been released from prison two days ago and his undeserved freedom had been snatched from him so quickly.

Denver's Motel was a single-story establishment with maybe twenty rooms, laid out in a horseshoe around an inground swimming pool that had found a second life as a garden. Its clientele would have included the shadier types.

When Amanda arrived, there was no sign of the Crime Scene Unit, but two police cruisers were in the parking lot; both had their lights flashing. An officer was in one but shrouded in darkness, making it hard to distinguish if it was Becky. There was also an SUV marked *Police Town of Dumfries*, which would belong to a sergeant with Dumfries PD, likely Lisa Greer. Amanda only knew of her through Becky and hadn't met her yet, as she'd just transferred in a few weeks ago. Hopefully, that meant she didn't know Amanda's history with the deceased. But whether the sergeant was Greer or someone else, they'd leave once Amanda's sergeant from PWCPD arrived. Their immediate job was just to watch over the scene until it could be handed over.

Amanda parked, grabbed her badge and gun and set across the courtyard. There was a woman in slacks and a winter coat posted next to an opened door.

"Amanda," Becky called out to her.

Amanda shut her eyes for a second, then turned. Her friend's shoulder-length hair was in a ponytail, as it often was when she was on duty, and swinging side to side. She'd hustled to catch up.

"What are you doing here?" Becky asked.

"Where else would I be?" Amanda resumed walking, but Becky cut in front of her, blocking her path.

"You need to go home."

Amanda juked to go around Becky, but her friend moved with her. She was a couple of inches shorter than Amanda's five-foot-nine, but she was solid and athletic. Amanda stopped, let her arms dangle. "You had to know I'd show up."

Becky looked over a shoulder, and it had Amanda following the direction of her gaze. The woman outside the motel room was watching them closely, her brows pinched together.

"Maybe," Becky admitted, "but I'd hoped you wouldn't. Your being here really isn't a good idea."

Amanda tucked a strand of her ginger hair over her left ear and scanned the lot for any department vehicles from PWCPD. "I don't see any other detectives from Homicide on scene yet." The words were out before Amanda gave them much thought. Did she really want to get involved with the investigation, assuming Palmer had been murdered? When she'd sped over here, it had been an instinct, just to see the man who had killed her family dead, as if by doing so it would heal a part of her.

"No, but—"

"Then I'm the first homicide detective to arrive. That means I qualify to enter the scene."

The woman waved her over. Amanda pointed her out to Becky. "I'm guessing that's Greer?"

"Uh-huh."

"Well, your boss seems to think I'm here because I was assigned the case."

"But you weren't."

"Can't help what other people think. Besides, it's only a matter of time, and she's looking impatient." Amanda butted her head toward Greer. She felt like she was careening down a steep hill without brakes, unable to stop, only able to steer.

"Fine," Becky huffed out. "But, just so you know, seeing him dead isn't going to help. You might think it will, but it won't."

Tendrils of anger twisted through her, squeezing, gripping, like vines to brick, working to pry the stone loose and destroy the structure. "How could you possibly know? That man took my—" She couldn't bring herself to finish. There were times she battled with who was truly to blame for the accident. If she hadn't insisted that Kevin look at some stupid meme on her phone, maybe he'd have had a chance to react in time.

Becky put a hand on her arm. "I know." With that, she walked back to her cruiser to resume guarding the crime scene.

Amanda clenched her jaw and worked to calm her temper. She flashed a cordial smile as she approached Greer. "Sergeant," she greeted her. "I'm Detective Steele from Homicide with Prince William County Police Department." She held up her badge with a shaky hand.

"Sergeant Greer," she said stiffly, glancing past Amanda to Becky, likely curious about their interaction.

Amanda tucked her badge away and peacocked her stance. She wanted to give the absolute appearance that she belonged there. "Has the medical examiner's office been called?"

The sergeant's attention shifted back to her. "Yes, of course, and crime scene investigators from Forensics."

"Mind if I—" Amanda gestured toward the room. Number ten.

"Not at all."

Amanda stepped over an upturned running shoe just inside the doorway and stopped.

Chad Palmer was supine on the bed beside two empty handles of whiskey. A rigored hand was wrapped around one of them. His eyes were shut, but there was vomit around his nose and mouth. She turned away at the waft of stench hitting her nose, but otherwise she was unmoved. Numb, indifferent, as if she were watching a scene from outside of herself.

The man she'd villainized appeared vulnerable in death, soft, human… even harmless. A man of thirty-seven, only two years older than she. But she could never forget the evil he'd inflicted.

*

The black pavement is glistening from the rain, making it look like they're driving on a blanket of a million sparkling diamonds. Fat drops pitter-patter against the windshield and the wipers squeak on every other pass.

"I spy something that is… black," Lindsey says amid giggles.

I turn and smile at my baby girl. Her ginger curls fall as ringlets over her shoulders.

"Give me a clue," Kevin says, keeping his attention on the road. "Is it outside?"

"Yes." Another gaggle of laughter, the sound of a cherub.

My phone pings with a message from my sister, Kristen. I laugh and hold my phone up for Kevin to see. He starts to smile, but a blinding light is rushing straight for us.

Kevin torques the wheel, but it's not fast enough.

A deafening crash of metal on metal as two vehicles mangle together and spin.

Absolute darkness descends.

*

Amanda turned her back to Palmer, her heart hammering. What did she really expect by coming here? Closure? Redemption? Debt repaid? Ridiculous.

"Steele? What the hell are you doing here?"

She blinked as her boss, Sergeant Malone, came into focus. He was in the doorway, hands on hips. He was in his fifties with a receding hairline. What hair he lacked on the top of his head, he made up for with a full beard and mustache. All of it gray, supposedly to testify to his wisdom and experience, as he would happily point out. In her favor, he was looking more concerned than pissed off by her presence.

"I was nearby." She could still back away without inserting herself in this investigation, but something about seeing Palmer dead made her feel a modicum of control, something she hadn't felt in a very long time.

"Small town. Everywhere is nearby." Malone scowled and jacked a thumb over his shoulder to indicate Becky. "Your being here have something to do with—"

"It has nothing to do with her."

"Uh-huh. Detective Steele, I'd like to talk to you. Outside. Now." Malone curled his finger, signaling for her to go with him but, when he turned, he bumped into Detective Dennis Bishop a.k.a. Cud.

He was smacking gum, as he often was, much like a cow. Hence the nickname. Except Cud was a lean, muscled brickhouse, with not an inch of flab on him. "Oh, Steele, I didn't know—"

"She's just about to leave." Malone met her gaze and darted his eyes toward her car.

Sergeant Greer was speaking with Becky by her cruiser, and, given her friend's defensive gesturing, it would seem Malone might have mentioned something to the Dumfries sergeant about Amanda's connection to the victim. The touch of guilt she felt for showing up there and causing a problem for Becky still wasn't enough to make her leave. It was almost like she had something to prove now; though what that might be, she didn't quite know. "I'm not going anywhere," she stamped out.

"No?" Malone angled his head, challenging her.

"We don't know what happened to Palmer yet."

"And your point?" he countered.

What was her point? Again she faced the question of whether she really wanted to get involved in the investigation, but like that out-of-control car, she didn't feel she could stop herself. Like she'd already come too far or crossed a line just by showing up here and now she had to see it through. She gave Malone's question some thought, then said smoothly, "If he was murdered, I'm going to have the most motivation to find the killer."

"How do you figure that?"

Fair question as she didn't feel sorry for the guy—not at all. So what was her motivation here? The feeling of control was something that echoed back to her. She'd had none when he'd wiped out her family; by uncovering what happened to him, in a way she'd have some power over how justice was served.

"Palmer? As in Chad Palmer?" Cud interjected, bringing his chewing to a momentary pause. "The man who—" He silenced under her glare and paled.

That was the thing with small towns; everyone knew your story. It was also something that had her going to Woodbridge to meet men. "Don't you ever mind," she slapped back.

"I was just going to say you made a good point… You know, with what you said." Cud glanced at Malone, then back to her and added, "You would have motive."

She glared at Cud, hoping he received her silent sarcastic *thanks for your support, buddy*. "If he was killed, there's at least one other person with motive, because I didn't kill him."

"Hold up. No one's saying you did," Malone groaned but seemed to hesitate.

"You can't honestly be considering assigning her the case." Cud flailed his arm toward Amanda.

"Excuse me," she barked. "I'm more than capable of setting aside my personal connection here." But her internal voice was calling her out on that claim. *Did* she have the ability to set it aside?

"More accurately, conflict of interest," Cud volleyed back.

"Sarge," Amanda said, wishing Malone would step in. "Give me the opportunity here."

Malone rubbed his jaw.

Cud smacked his gum. "You can't really be considering letting her take the lead, boss."

"What's it to you?" Malone snapped at Cud. "I give it to her, and you and Detective Ryan catch the next one."

That would be Natalie Ryan, nicknamed Cougar, for reasons any knowledgeable adult could imagine.

"Whatever," Cud mumbled.

"Give us a minute alone." Malone snapped his fingers at Cud when he didn't move.

"Fine. I'll be over there." He walked about ten feet away.

Small flakes started coming down and Amanda glanced up: overcast and no visible stars. Nothing to wish on. Story of her life these days.

"You sure you could handle this?" Malone asked.

"Absolutely."

He leaned down, leveling his gaze with hers. "If you have any doubt about it, speak now. You know you can talk to me."

Scott Malone had been a good friend of her father's, and still was, as far as she knew, and it earned her special treatment. Other detectives under Malone couldn't talk as freely to him as she could.

"No doubts," she lied. How had things escalated to this point: her fighting for the case? Her heart wanted to run, but her legs wouldn't move.

He scanned her eyes and straightened back up to full height and rubbed the top of his head. "I'm probably going to regret this— And if I catch a whiff of drama, so help me, you'll be off the case so fast your head'll spin. Got me?"

"That means—"

"Yeah, I'm letting you work it." The way his mouth contorted, his permission must have tasted like bile. "If Lieutenant Hill finds out, my head will roll, so I'm being very serious when I say don't let me down."

The sergeant really was putting himself in a precarious spot, and a flash of remorse rushed through Amanda. Sherry Hill was no-nonsense and not one to mess with, and, as much as Malone was a fan of her father's, Hill was not. The lieutenant made no secret of holding a grudge against her dad. Keeping drama out altogether would be a challenge, but she'd do her best. "I won't let you down."

"Good. Now I have other conditions." Malone hooked his thumbs on his waistband. "You need to call your father, tell him that Palmer's dead. And who knows, maybe you'll—"

"No." She shook her head. "You don't get to tell me to talk to him and leverage this case to make that happen." She hadn't spoken to any of her family since not long after the trial had ended. Not her mother, father, her four younger sisters, or her older brother. It had been her decision to pull away from them, and even though they still reached out to her at Christmas and on her birthday, it just felt far too difficult. Being around her parents, her siblings, and her nieces and nephews amplified all that she had lost.

"It would just be nice, is all, if you could reconnect," Malone said. "I know your father would love nothing more."

She wanted to tell him he'd crossed a professional line with this request, but if she pointed that out, he'd likely reciprocate with the fact that her working this case was technically crossing that same line. Then he'd assign it to Cud, and now she'd been given the go-ahead, she wanted to keep it. "You said you had conditions plural?"

His face darkened, and she feared her effort to redirect the conversation had him changing his mind.

"What else?" she asked, afraid to take her next breath as if it would alter his response.

"You realize my letting you work this case at all is a huge conflict of interest."

"I do."

"For that reason, I can't have you working this one sol—"

"Oh no," she griped, dreading what was coming. He was going to give her a partner. "Haven't we talked this topic to death?"

"Yes, but apparently it hasn't sunk into your thick skull that it's happening."

She groaned. He was going to give her a partner, but every one she'd had pried into her business, thought they knew her, tried to mind-shrink her. To date, all of them had been homegrown and acquainted with her tragic story. They treated her with kid gloves, like she was some sort of fragile china doll about to fall off a shelf. They missed the fact that she'd already smashed into a million, indiscernible pieces. "Who?" she shoved out. "Don't tell me it's Cud."

"It's not Cud. It's a new guy." He added that tidbit under his breath.

"A new guy?" she parroted. Surely he was joking.

"And I suggest you make it work. You might be the former police chief's daughter—"

"And good at my job," she cut in, now longing to be out from the shadow of Nathan Steele. She'd kept her maiden name after marriage because for the longest time she'd wanted to be her dad, and his name was powerful as she worked up the ranks. After

Kevin's death, there had been many times she'd wished she'd taken his surname, James.

"Sure, but you need to play by the rules like the rest of us," Malone said, disregarding her interruption.

And he didn't need to lay them out to her. At every homicide it was desired to have a primary detective and a number two. Maybe she should be grateful she'd gotten along solo as often as she did. "Okay, fine, have it your way. But what am I supposed to do now? Sit around and wait for the new guy to show up?"

"His name's Trent Stenson, and you won't need to wait for long. I was going to tell you in the morning, but it seems like Christmas has come again, or early, however you want to look at it."

"Yippie," she mumbled, picturing some backwoods type in a cowboy hat and chaps with grass hanging out of his mouth, but a face popped into her mind. "Wait. You said Trent Stenson?"

"Uh-huh. You know him?"

To say that she knew him would be stretching it, but she'd met him at a barbecue Becky had hosted one summer several years ago. He had boyish good looks—blond hair, blue eyes—but his starry-eyed approach to life made him seem younger. He had been a uniformed officer with Dumfries PD at the time and had rambled on about how he'd helped the FBI with a serial-rapist-and-murder case. He declared then that he wanted to be a homicide detective for Prince William County PD one day. Guess some people had stars to wish upon and grant their dreams.

"Amanda?" Malone prompted.

"I've met him."

Malone smiled. "Yeah, small world, law enforcement is round here."

Trent had been so cheery and just the thought of being around that… "I don't know if this is a good idea. And you said he's new to the department."

"Sure, and as you just said, you're good at your job, so you'll be a good mentor for the kid."

She hardly felt qualified to be anyone's mentor, and "the kid" was probably only a couple of years younger than she was.

Malone went on. "For the record, Stenson is now officially your partner."

"Let me guess. He'll take over Turner's old desk?" Russell Turner didn't deserve the badge and had been a huge pain in the ass, though his true failing was his outright bigotry against people of color. There was no room for that in any capacity, on any force.

"Why not?"

Some days it felt like everyone was sitting on everyone else. "No reason," she said.

"Good, it's settled. And I also want to make it clear that I'm giving the lead on this case to Stenson."

"The lead," she blurted out. "To a rookie detective?"

He raised his eyebrows, the arches serving like upward-pointing arrows. "On paper," he added, holding eye contact with her. "It's the only way I can get this to fly. As it is, I'm not going to advertise it."

"You want me to be his number two? Report to him?" She didn't do well with being managed, let alone by an underling.

"You report to me. The rest is just on paper—for this case."

She took a few deep breaths. "Fine."

"So we have an understanding?"

"Yes, we have an understanding," she mumbled.

Malone turned his head and put his left ear near her mouth. "Can you say that again? I didn't quite hear you."

"I'm on board," she said, raising her voice.

Malone cringed and pulled back, cupping his ear. "No need for that. I'm doing you a favor here. And I'm not deaf—or at least I wasn't."

She mouthed, *Sorry.*

"All right, I'll call Stenson and give him the good news."

He pulled out his phone and headed for his vehicle but stopped after a few steps and turned. He looked at her for a long moment and said nothing. Whatever he was about to say was going to kill him if his sagging shoulders and hooded eyes gave any indication.

"In case this thing truly does turn out to be a murder, you need to get your alibi in order immediately. Without that… Well, I'm going to have to pull you from the case."

"Shouldn't be a problem." After all, she knew she hadn't killed him.

"One more thing, and I mean it. Don't touch a thing until your partner gets here." Malone pulled out his cell phone and put it to an ear as he walked away.

Amanda looked heavenward again. After losing her husband and daughter, she'd blamed God, but if there was any chance that He or She could intervene and give her strength to see this investigation through, she just might try prayer again.

CHAPTER THREE

The smaller the town, the harder it was to keep secrets. It had been the bane of Amanda's existence since she was a little girl, but she'd always managed to dismiss the murmurings and gossip. After the accident though, it came to define her. She was the "poor thing" who had lost her husband and daughter. She was marked, unable to escape the repercussions. While other people moved on with their lives, she was locked in the past. Even the rare times she caught a glimpse of the horizon, she couldn't seem to advance toward it.

She stood outside the motel room and blinked away snowflakes, gripping her coat to herself. They didn't get much snow in Dumfries and it was sort of magical when it did happen. Lindsey used to squeal with delight and come running to Amanda. *Mommy, Mommy, can I play outside?*

"Amanda? Hello."

"What?"

"Where's the sarge going?" Cud nodded toward Sergeant Malone, who was getting into his vehicle.

"Not his keeper," she replied as Malone drove off. He probably wanted to remove himself as far as possible from this investigation. Normally he hung around crime scenes longer.

"You get the case?" Cud asked.

"I did."

"Figures. And I'm your number two?"

"A shit? Yeah." She didn't really have a problem with Cud, not normally anyway. She just didn't appreciate him accusing her of being unable to remain objective with this case.

He frowned. "Very funny."

"And no, you're not the number two. I am." *At least on paper*, she thought.

"You—" Cud laughed. "I'll be. Steele's getting a partner. Still not me, I'm guessing?"

"Seeing as Malone never said a word to you? Wow, you should make detective."

"Whatever. Guess I'm out of here then." Cud trudged toward his vehicle, head into the wind.

Amanda walked over to Becky, who was stationed next to her cruiser. Sergeant Greer must have left while Amanda was talking to Malone.

"You okay?" Amanda asked Becky.

"Yeah, of course."

"It looked like Greer was laying into you a bit."

Becky rolled her eyes. "She can be a piece of work."

"What was it all about?"

"I left my post for a millisecond, but Greer overheard Malone asking why you were here and she got the sense you shouldn't be here, so she blamed me for letting you on scene. Anyway, enough about me. Malone give you the go-ahead?"

"If it's a murder."

"Can't say I'm surprised. You have Malone wrapped around your finger."

"Correction: my father has him wrapped around his. I just get to benefit."

"Whatever way it goes," Becky said. "I'm still worried about you."

"No need. I've been through more than this."

"I'm just afraid that 'this' is going to trigger the past."

Amanda didn't know how to respond. After all, what didn't trigger the past? She was mired there. But maybe by investigating Palmer's death, she could put all the guilt and the feelings of turmoil behind her and start to heal. What she knew for sure was there certainly wasn't any way she could watch the case from the outside. She'd go crazy wondering where things stood.

"Why aren't you in the room, doing your thing?" Becky asked.

"I need to wait for my partner to show—"

"Whoa, hold up. *You* are getting a partner?"

"Yep. Trent Stenson."

Becky grinned, showing teeth, the expression touching her eyes. "What a great break for him. He must have just been transferred to Homicide."

"He was." She couldn't conjure any enthusiasm at his dream coming true.

"He'll be great. You'll see."

"Maybe." She hitched her shoulders.

"Okay, what's the problem? I know you don't like working with a partner, but—"

"He's the primary on the investigation."

"Oh." Becky's mouth dropped open. "He's—"

"Yeah, new, a rookie. Apparently, he's the lead on paper. Only way Malone would let me work the case at all."

"I see."

"At least one of us does. So while I wait, I'm not to touch anything, but you can bring me up to speed. Who found him, for starters?"

"The hotel manager, guy by the name of Ronnie Flynn. He was headed down there"—Becky pointed to an ice chest against the motel—"for some cubes for his drink. He saw the curtains were open, said his eye was naturally drawn to look inside."

"Uh-huh."

"Blamed the flickering lights from the television. Anyway, that's when he saw Palmer lying on the bed, eyes wide open and unblinking. Called it in."

"He never went into the room?"

"Claims not."

"And where is he now?"

"With Officer Deacon." Becky pointed to the motel office. "He's giving his statement."

Two figures were inside, but the colored lights blinked in the window, taking her back to the Dreamcatcher Inn where she'd had her one-night stand. She really needed a shower. She'd speak with Flynn herself, but not yet. She turned back to Becky. "Anyone else staying in the motel tonight?"

"Yep. Five rooms were rented out in addition to Palmer's. Everyone's been asked to stay put and told to expect an officer to come by and question them, but that's about as far as that's gotten. I called you the minute I saw who it was."

"I understand. All good anyway, as I like to talk to potential witnesses firsthand."

Becky licked her lips, her gaze intent on Amanda.

"What?" Amanda asked.

Becky toed the accumulating snow on the ground with her boot. "It's just that a lot of people aren't going to be too thrilled you're on the case. It could cause some problems for you."

"I'm aware, but I can assure you no one wants this case wrapped up like I do." As much as she struggled with her personal feelings toward Palmer, investigating his death had to bring her some closure. If not, she was at a loss for what would.

Becky squinted, the snowflakes larger and more plentiful than before. Why it bothered to snow when it would be melted by morning was beyond Amanda.

"You want this case wrapped up?" Her friend put it out there gingerly, but the enclosed implication still stung. "Are you sure there's not a small part of you that might be happy he's dead?"

Amanda glanced toward the road. There was no way she could look Becky in the eye and claim that wasn't true. After the accident, she'd thought about his death a million times over, even contemplated taking his life herself.

"There is," Becky concluded. "How can you investigate—"

Amanda bristled. "I never said that I was happy about this. You're putting words in my mouth."

"Am I though?" Becky punched out and with that turned toward her cruiser.

Tears beaded in Amanda's eyes as she stared at the back of her friend's head.

"Here, you'll need these." Becky lifted a pair of gloves and plastic booties out of the trunk of the car. "Looks like you could use them," she said and pointed at Amanda's now-wet boots.

Amanda took them and offered, "Thanks."

"Uh-huh." Becky got in the driver's seat of the cruiser and shut the door.

Amanda felt her friend's judgment coming through, despite the nice gesture. But there wasn't time to dig into that conversation. She had a job to do and she was about finished waiting on Trent Stenson.

CHAPTER FOUR

Amanda stopped outside the door to the motel room. Malone had said not to touch anything; he hadn't said she couldn't look around. She slipped the plastic coverings over her boots and stepped inside.

She made a mental note of the upturned running shoe. The left one. She looked at Palmer to see the right shoe was still on his foot.

Had Palmer been so drunk that he'd tripped and hadn't noticed or cared that he'd lost a shoe? Had he just taken one off and stumbled to the bed where he'd proceeded to drink two huge bottles of whiskey? Or had there been someone else who had pushed him and caused him to lose his shoe?

But there were no visual signs of an altercation or that Palmer had any visitors. No obvious shoeprints on the carpet, although it had been dry until a bit ago. Two spindle-back chairs were tucked under a small round table under the window—unused or put back? Two drinking glasses with their covers still in place were on the table—untouched.

She reached into her back-right pocket for her notepad, but it wasn't there. She hadn't exactly needed it at the Dreamcatcher Inn or the bar where she'd picked up Motel Guy. But surely there was something on her person she could use to make a note. She tapped her pockets and felt her phone in her jacket. She pulled it out and opened the notepad app, pecking in *Ask the motel manager and other guests if they saw anyone come to Palmer's room*. One day she'd learn how to text like a teenager, but that day was likely a long way off; she had more important things to do.

Her gaze returned to the unused glasses. Palmer must have just drunk directly from the whiskey bottles. Not unheard of with hardened alcoholics, but Palmer had been sober for years. Albeit a forced sobriety. Had he been making up for lost time or had something specific made him start drinking again? Had it been guilt or had he felt anything at all?

*

The judge looks over his bench at Chad Palmer. "How do you plead to the charges of drinking and driving?"

"Guilty," Palmer responds like he's comatose.

"How do you plead to charges of DUI vehicular involuntary manslaughter times two?"

"Guilty."

A collective gasp comes from the gallery.

I am cold and barely feel Kristen's or Mother's hands squeezing mine.

Mother leans in and whispers in my ear, "God, let there be justice."

*

Amanda clenched her jaw, returning to the present, her gaze on Palmer's dead body. Maybe things had a way of working out and justice had finally been served. It certainly hadn't been with the measly sentence he'd received.

She walked over to the table and looked out the window that gave a view of the parking lot. The curtains were open, as the manager claimed to have found them. And further inside the room and across from the double bed, the television was flickering on the dresser. Its volume was so low it was hard to hear sober. Intoxicated, there would be no way Palmer could have discerned a word.

She made a note of that in her phone's app, then proceeded to inch closer to the bed. With each step, her heart pounded harder. As if he could somehow reach out from beyond the grave and hurt her more than he already had. Utterly impossible. In fact, his death, in a way, had lessened her pain.

She inventoried his wardrobe. White socks, one shoe on his right foot, blue jeans with a black belt, and a *Grateful Dead* T-shirt. The resting state of his face and mouth seemed to testify to some horror he had felt before his death, and her sense of justice warred against a dark part of her that found satisfaction in the hope that he'd suffered.

There was a gash on his forehead, which could be consistent with a fall. She looked to the carpet and followed along the floor, stopping her scan at the end of the bed. She put on the gloves that Becky had given her. What no one knew wouldn't hurt them. She lifted the comforter marginally and ducked down. Metal bedframe. But with the cushioning of the bedding it was unlikely to have cut flesh and there was no blood.

She resumed her full height and studied the room from where she was standing. Nothing within sight would explain the cut on his forehead. It could have happened elsewhere in the room or at another location altogether. For now, she'd look at the lost shoe and the gash as separate and unrelated incidents. She made a note of her observations.

Amanda carried on through the room, ignoring the form on the bed and went into the small bathroom. Green sink and tub. Ring on the floor around the base of the toilet. Rust marks in the sink and tub. There was a toothbrush, a tube of paste, a razor and shaving gel, but that was it as far as personal hygiene products. A motel-provided and now-lathered bar of soap sat on the corners of the tub and small counter.

On her return through the room, she stopped in front of a closet with bifold doors. She'd already broken Malone's direction not to touch anything so she slowly opened one side and peeked in. Empty. She eased the door back the way she'd found it.

Palmer could have items in the dresser, but maybe she should draw a line with her snooping, just in case Malone returned.

The only personal effects she could see in the main room were a jacket and wallet on the table. But what more could she expect when Palmer had only been released from prison a few days ago? He'd only have the clothes on his back and whatever had been taken from him at the time of his arrest.

She made a note to find out what that was.

She reached for the wallet. Had Palmer left it there or had Becky or her sergeant pulled it out to look for identification? Another possibility was a robbery gone wrong, but she dismissed the theory quickly. Palmer probably didn't have anything worth stealing. Also, if it was a robbery, she'd likely be looking at a stabbing, shooting, or beating. Not to mention she'd expect to see evidence of an altercation, but there was nothing to indicate that aside from the shoe and the gash on his forehead.

Amanda thumbed through the wallet. A ten-dollar bill and two credit cards. She extracted each, one at a time—both long expired—and slipped them back where she'd found them just as shadows darkened the room. She returned the wallet to the table and turned to see two female investigators from Forensics and a blond man she recognized as Trent Stenson.

The CSIs made their way into the room, booties on their shoes and evidence collection cases in hand. The older of the two, a slender woman in her fifties, acknowledged her with a bob of her head. The other woman flashed her a beautiful smile.

"Hi, Detective Steele," Trent said. He looked older and more mature than she remembered, but there was something else different about him. His hair. He used to have long bangs that fell over his eyes, but now his blond hair was groomed short. She didn't reply to his greeting but went to leave the room, pausing only to take off the booties.

"I hope I'm not being presumptuous to assume you remember me." He thrust out his hand. "I'm Trent. Stenson. Malone briefed me on the phone, but I was at Becky's barbecue that time and we—"

"I know who you are." She wondered just how much Malone had told him, and if Trent had been told to keep an eye on her.

"Oh, good." Her refusal to shake didn't seem to have any effect on his enthusiasm, but he lowered his hand. "How's it looking in there?"

"You should look for yourself. As the primary," she added, unable to keep the bitterness out of her voice.

"I'll need—" Trent looked around and his gaze landed on the booties in her hand.

"Here." She handed them to him. "You should come prepared." She felt a twinge of guilt at her hypocrisy.

"Sorry, yes, I know. Thanks." He went into the motel room without touching her dig about him being the primary. Spunky or spineless? Too soon to tell.

She bundled into her coat. It had stopped snowing, but it was cold. Guess she'd just wait outside while Junior looked at the crime scene. Becky was coming toward her, holding a steaming takeout cup.

"I come with coffee," she said, giving it to Amanda.

"How—"

"I had a fellow officer bring it to me."

Amanda looked at the cup. "It's not from Hannah's, but…" Hannah's Diner had the best coffee in Dumfries—in the county if you asked Amanda—but they closed at nine.

"Hey, if you don't want it…" Becky smiled and reached to take the coffee back.

Amanda held the cup out of reach. "Now, there's no need to do that. And thank you."

"I'm sorry about before. I shouldn't have implied—"

"Just forget it." Amanda flipped back the tab on the lid and took a sip. Perfect drinking temperature.

"So what way are you leaning? Do you think he was murdered?" Becky nodded toward the motel room.

"Too soon to say, but there are things standing out to me. Speaking of, did you put Palmer's wallet on the table or was it there?"

"Sergeant Greer took it out to confirm identity. I didn't need it to."

Amanda nodded.

"I see that Trent's arrived," Becky said.

"Yep." She took another drink of her coffee. It was exactly what she needed right now. "Should be fun," she added, with a heavy dose of sarcasm.

"Trent's a good guy. He'll—"

"Did I just hear 'Trent's a good guy'?" He came out of the room. Amanda regarded him. "That was quick."

"I'll revisit. I like to take it in, process it in my mind for a bit, then revisit."

"Huh. First day out and you've already got a method." Snarky and uncalled for, and it failed to garner any reaction. Disappointing.

"Well, I'll leave you to it." Becky gave Amanda a pleading look to give Trent a chance.

"So, what were your first impressions?" Trent extended the booties to Amanda and she dismissed him with a wave.

"Keep 'em." She started walking toward the motel office. "We'll chat later. Right now, we're going to speak to Ronnie Flynn. He's the manager here and who found Palmer."

"Sure. Sounds good."

Amanda stopped walking and spun. He was still moving, and she bumped her cup against his chest, spilling some coffee on his coat.

He pulled a tissue from a pocket and wiped at the mess. She'd apologize but it would weaken her position.

"You say 'sounds good' like this is an exciting evening out for you. Someone died," she ground out. It was hypocritical given how little she felt for the deceased, and she remembered how at the start of her career in Homicide, murder cases had got her blood pumping and her adrenaline rushing.

"I-I know that," Trent stuttered and stuffed the tissues back in a pocket.

She clamped her mouth shut. She'd been prepared for Trent to spout off something smart-ass, maybe bring up her connection with Palmer; as a local he had to know the history there. She resumed walking.

"I didn't mean anything by what I said." Trent sounded apologetic, but there was also a note of confusion in his tone. He likely didn't understand her strong reaction.

But unless a person had suffered the loss she had, how could anyone appreciate what she had gone through—*was going* through? The man who had birthed her living nightmare was back. Dead, but no less real. And as much as she looked to this case to help her heal, it just may take her down if she wasn't careful. That's why she had to stay focused and serious.

"Let's just talk to the manager." She got the door for the motel office for herself and didn't bother holding it for Trent. It wasn't personal—at least not yet—but partnerships had a way of morphing into that territory if the boundaries weren't clearly defined from the start. And she wasn't about to let her wall down for one second.

CHAPTER FIVE

Amanda stepped into the motel office, noticing the security camera mounted outside next to the door. A chime sounded and Officer Deacon got up from where he'd been seated next to a forty-something male with greasy dark hair and a pockmarked face.

The fluorescent lights were harsh and assaulting, as was the dilapidated Christmas tree drooping in the corner; its fake branches finished with the season and some of its baubles reaching the floor. The lights were also unplugged, making it look that much more depressing.

"Mr. Flynn?" she asked the stranger.

"Yes." The man's eyes shifted to Deacon, almost as if asking permission to speak.

"I'm Detective Steele," she said, wresting back his attention.

"And I'm Detective Stenson," Trent offered after a couple of beats.

"We'd like to ask you a few questions," Amanda said.

"I just told him everything I know." He flicked a finger toward Deacon.

"We appreciate that the officer here has taken your statement, but we have some questions of our own." Amanda glanced at Deacon, who dipped his head and left in receipt of her silent message for him to leave them alone. "Let's start with how you came to find the man in room ten."

Flynn scowled and clenched his jaw. "Why must I keep reliving it?"

"We understand this may be difficult for you—"

"*May* be? I found a man. Dead."

It was strange how someone else died and people could still make it about themselves. "Yes. Sadly, it happens all the time."

"Maybe for you," Flynn spat.

She took a long, deliberate sip of her coffee. When she lowered the cup, she met Trent's gaze. Was he judging her, waiting for her to slip up so he could report her? "You're right, I've seen a lot of death." Her voice cracked ever so slightly on *death*. She refused to look at either Trent or Flynn for a few seconds. "You have the chance to help us figure out what happened to your guest."

"Was he murdered? I mean, I suppose so given you guys are here."

"It's an open investigation at this time," she said. "All I can tell you is his death is deemed suspicious, which simply means for his age he shouldn't have—" She almost said *kicked the bucket.*

"Okay, okay, I'll rehash it all," he whined. He went on to relay exactly what Becky had told her. He'd gone for ice, saw the flickering TV, looked in, and spotted Palmer on the bed.

"Then you entered his room?" she asked, remembering clearly from the account he'd told Becky he hadn't gone inside.

"I knocked on the window and called out. He didn't respond, and as I said, something about him just didn't look right. So, yes, I went in his room."

So he'd lied to Becky. It was creepy to think of the motel manager watching his guests through the windows but not the end of the world. "Did you touch anything in the room?"

"Nope."

She noted how quickly he'd replied—the honest truth or was he hiding something? "You told our fellow officer you never went into the room."

Flynn's eyes darted to Trent, then back to Amanda. "Just must have slipped my mind. Not every day I find a dead body."

Amanda wasn't sure she believed that was all it was. "Did you check the man for a pulse?"

"No need. He had—" Flynn pointed to his mouth and traced a finger around it, clearly indicating the vomit. "And I could tell his chest wasn't moving."

"Then what did you do?"

"Called the police."

Amanda nodded. She'd get to the tidbits about when Palmer checked in and if Flynn had any other interactions with him, but first she wanted to be clear on something. Flynn's wasn't a face she recognized, but it was very possible Flynn was aware of Palmer's past and her own. "Did you know the man who died?"

"Nah. Well, not really." Flynn shook his head.

"I'm not sure what you mean by 'not really.' Can you clarify that?"

"I just know his name was Chad Palmer because I checked him in. That's all."

"How long have you been working here?" Amanda was tiptoeing around what she really wanted to know. If he knew of her connection with Palmer, the entire investigation could blow up in her face before it really got started.

"For a few months."

"I see, and where were you before that?" Amanda could feel Trent watching her, but she refused to acknowledge his gaze and kept hers on Flynn.

"Florida." Flynn narrowed his eyes and glanced at Trent, then back at her. "Not sure what that matters, but I followed my college girlfriend there and finally, after marrying her, then divorcing her, I had the good sense to part ways and come home last year."

So he would have still been in Florida at the time of the accident. She felt herself relax. "When did Mr. Palmer check in?" It seemed strange referring to Chad so formally.

Trent coughed, probably to get her attention, to remind her that he was the primary detective, but when she looked at him, he mouthed an apology. That surprised her. He certainly wasn't anything she had expected so far. She leveled her gaze at Flynn.

"Friday night," he said.

That was the day Palmer had been released from prison. "Three nights ago. You're certain?"

He scrunched up his forehead. "Yeah. The wee hours always mess with my sense of time."

"So he checked in at night; what time?" she asked.

"Around eleven? Should be in the logbook." Flynn pointed to an open book on the reception counter.

Trent beat her to it. "Ten fifty-five," he said.

Palmer would have been released from prison in the afternoon, so she was curious how he had spent the time between then and checking in. One thought crossed her mind, and it had her clenching her right hand into a fist and sinking her nails into her palm.

"Was he drunk when you checked him in, or intoxicated?" She didn't need to look at Trent to know he was watching her closely.

Flynn didn't respond.

"Was he drunk?" she pushed.

"Maybe."

"Maybe?" she shot back.

"Hey, wait, am I in trouble here?" Flynn's cheeks flushed red.

Amanda tilted out her chin. "We're just trying to figure everything out."

Flynn shrugged. "He might have had something to drink before coming here. His words were a little slurred."

Amanda squeezed her fist tighter. The bastard had the audacity to waltz out of prison and pick up a bottle like no time had passed—as if his doing so years ago hadn't met with any consequences. Just like he'd walked away from the accident scene, unscathed. Meanwhile everything she loved the most had been—

"When he checked in did he have anything with him?" Trent asked, giving her a moment to get her temper in check.

She released her fist and downed some coffee, trying to calm herself.

"Heck, I dunno." Flynn mussed his hair, dropped his hand. "A duffel bag."

That got her attention. There'd been no sign of one when she'd worked through the room, so, unless it was stuffed into a dresser drawer, it was unaccounted for. She pulled out her cell phone, and, after trying to balance it and her coffee, surrendered the cup to the counter. She tapped *duffel bag* into the app.

"He paid cash, in advance," Flynn volunteered.

That wasn't unusual if Palmer had wanted to stay under the radar, but he'd provided his name so that didn't jibe. It also begged an answer for where Palmer had gotten the cash. It was entirely possibly he'd had some when he was booked, but this tidbit seemed worthy of note enough for Flynn to mention it. "For the night or was he planning to stay longer?"

"It's in the book." Trent traced a fingertip across the page. "Until the end of the month."

Palmer must not have had a place to call home to wind up here. It also seemed he'd had immediate plans to stick around Dumfries, so that was a point against suicide. That manner of death also didn't fit a man who'd just regained his freedom, though some ex-cons had a terrible time adapting to life on the outside again. So, really, it was too soon to conclude anything. She keyed into her app *Suicide?* then looked up at Flynn. "How much money are we talking here?"

"Fifteen hundred."

She whistled. "Never would have expected that."

Flynn glared. "I know it's not the Ritz, but we've got bills to pay."

She held up a hand in surrender to calm Flynn, but she was more interested in how Palmer had that much cash. It was more walking-around money than most people had, but Palmer had been a part-owner of a pawnshop, so maybe it wasn't outside the realm of possibility. Still, she added *Source of cash?* into her app.

"And he, what, had this cash in his jacket pocket or...?" she asked.

"His bag."

With that admission, something flicked across Flynn's eyes and his mouth twitched like he couldn't quite settle on an expression. The topic of the bag made him uncomfortable, possibly fearful. A weapon inside it, perhaps?

"Did he make you feel threatened?"

His gaze snapped to hers. "No."

A bald-faced lie. "No weapon in his bag then, or anything else that had you spooked?"

"I didn't really get a good look," he rushed out.

"Okay," she said, backing off just a tad, but his lack of a denial confirmed that Palmer's presence had caused him anxiety. "You do realize, though, that we're trained to read people and tell when they're lying to us?"

Flynn worried his bottom lip.

"You're not going to tell us," she concluded. "But it's not like he can hurt you."

Flynn's gaze hardened and he ground his teeth. "There was nothing else in the bag, okay. Just the cash he paid with."

"You're sure about that?" Amanda pressed, curious why he was getting defensive.

"Yes," he seethed.

"Besides the bag, did he have anything else with him?" Trent interjected, and she could have smacked her new partner upside the head. He'd given Flynn exactly what he'd wanted: a shift in direction.

"Not that I recall."

Amanda glared at Trent. "You're doing good; this is very helpful," she praised Flynn, certainly undeserved, but she had to do something to salvage the situation and get Flynn talking. "What you probably didn't know is Mr. Palmer just finished serving time in prison." She was trying to feel out Flynn and get a sense of what had him clamming up about the bag.

Flynn swallowed roughly. "I didn't know that."

"And if he had a weapon on his person, it would be helpful to know that." She tossed this out nonchalantly, trying to gauge what could have been in the bag that had him so worked up.

Flynn held up his hands. "None that I saw."

She nodded, finally assuaged that it wasn't Palmer himself or the contents of the bag that had Flynn worked up. That left one other possibility she could think of. Maybe the fear originated from someone Palmer had been with or who had visited him. "When Mr. Palmer checked in, was he alone?"

"Yes."

"Did you happen to see if Mr. Palmer had any visitors or left with anyone between his checking in and last night?" She resisted the urge to say *checking out* even if it was accurate.

"No, I didn't."

Again, she got the sense Flynn was withholding, but there was only so much she could do. The military would waterboard people to extract information, but that method was a little extreme for this situation. "Does that mean you didn't see anyone or you're just not saying?"

"I don't know when the guy died, but I'm not the only one who works here," Flynn huffed out.

"Fair enough," she said, though she felt there wasn't anything fair about the way he was shifting the onus to his employees. "Who else worked between Friday night and last night?"

"Lorraine covered Saturday and Sunday during the day, clocked out at six in the evening each of those days, and David worked Saturday night. I finally had a night off."

"Their last names?" she asked.

"Lorraine Nash and David Morgan, though I'm not sure I should be telling you all that."

"Let me assure you that you should," she said, making a note of the names in her phone. "And when are they expected for their next shifts?"

"Lorraine at nine this morning, and David later at six."

"Thank you. Now, I noticed a camera on the way in here. Does it work?"

"Nah. It's just there to keep the clients in line. The boss is too cheap to get a working one."

That answer didn't entirely surprise her, though it was disappointing. This area of town and this dump specifically would attract shady people. She went to fish one of her cards from a back pocket of her jeans and remembered that she didn't have any on her person.

She gestured toward Trent. "Detective Stenson, if you could give Mr. Flynn one of your cards." That's if he had any yet…

"Ah, sure." Trent pulled one from his jacket and handed it to Flynn.

Huh. Malone must have known about his transfer into the department for a while.

She drew her gaze to Flynn. "If anything else comes to your attention or your memory, call Detective Stenson day or night."

Flynn pocketed the card but made no promises.

"There's one more thing we'll need before we leave." She looked at the pegboard and the hooks. Six keys were missing. One was room ten where Palmer was, and the others were numbers two, three, seven, twelve, and fifteen. She gestured toward them and said, "Those the rooms currently rented out?"

"Yes, ma'am."

"Thanks." She put her phone back in her pocket, grabbed her cup and left. Outside, she gulped back the rest of her coffee, not bothered by the fact it was now tepid. She'd drink the stuff cold. She just about tossed the cup in a garbage can next to the office door but stopped herself. It was possible that something in there pertained to Palmer's death. She'd make sure the CSIs collected the bag.

"Everything all right?" Trent bobbed his head toward the garbage can.

She leveled a glare at him. "I had everything under control in there."

"I never said—"

"You didn't have to say anything," she said, talking over him. "And you let him steer the direction of the conversation."

"I just thought—"

"That I report to you?" she spat.

"Not at all." Trent diverted his gaze over her shoulder, then moved it back to meet her eyes. "I should have stayed quiet in there, listened and learned from you."

"Are you bullshitting me right now?" Did he really think that by sucking up to her he would gain her favor?

"What?" His cheeks turned bright red. "No."

She studied him. Was he still that eager-to-please Dumfries PD officer? He had to be thinking she was born yesterday to consider his speech was sincere, but by all accounts that's exactly what she'd say it was. Either that or he was a good actor, and she had met her fair share of those in her life.

"Malone explained the situation to me," Trent started.

"How I have history with Palmer," she ground out as iron walls erected and *clunked* into place around her.

Trent shrugged in his coat as it seemed a chill ran through him. "He told me that I'm the lead on paper. He stressed '*on paper.*'"

The temperature was still below zero but her core warmed. She'd given him the opening to dissect her past and he hadn't taken it. "And you're good with that? Being the lead on paper?"

"Absolutely. I can learn a lot from you. You've been at this— what?—thirty years?"

"Hey."

He smiled.

"Detective for seven." Her fellow officers would talk and say she'd only advanced so quickly because of who her father was, but she'd worked her ass off every step of the way.

"That's more than me. I'm on the ground floor here."

"Glad you know where you stand. Tell you what: you go talk to the guests in rooms two and three, and I'll hit seven and twelve. Whoever finishes first wins room fifteen. They might not like us knocking on their doors considering it's after"—she looked at the time on her phone—"one thirty in the morning, but we need to find out everything we can tonight. Ask them if they saw anyone go into or come out of Palmer's room in the last twenty-four hours or heard anything."

They weren't armed with a time of death yet, but she'd worked enough death investigations to know that rigor, as a general rule, took twelve hours to set in and started in the extremities such as hands and feet within an hour or two of death. Palmer's hand had definitely been in a state of rigor.

"Sure." Trent grinned, likely gushing at this opportunity to branch out solo and probably just about to thank her for the opportunity.

She turned before the conversation could become any cozier. It was a little uncomfortable as it was, and she had to draw the line. Besides, this little arrangement with Trent was only temporary, regardless of what Malone might think.

CHAPTER SIX

Amanda grabbed some business cards from her car's glove box before hitting her first room. Even with the pit stop, she beat Trent to room fifteen. Lucky her. The renter was some pothead who had no idea what day of the week it was and probably didn't know he was on planet Earth, but he did tell her he'd checked in last night and offered up his sob story. He said he was only there because his old lady had kicked him out—as if he'd had no part in that happening.

She finished up with him at the same time Trent left room three and headed toward him.

"How did you make out?" she asked him.

Trent consulted his notepad. "Room two were two men—'married to women,' they stressed. Not sure why."

"Guilt, shame at being caught, any number of factors." She rolled her hand to hopefully encourage forward movement. When he didn't seem to pick up on the visual cue, she said, "I'm more interested if they saw or heard anything that relates to our case."

"Nothing."

"And room three?"

"It was a lady who checked in a couple of days ago. She's hiding out from her abusive husband."

She tapped a foot. "Sad, but again more life story than I need."

Trent scanned his notepad, flipped the pages. "She said that she kept her curtains closed and stuck to herself."

"So she saw nothing?" Amanda pushed out.

"No."

"So how did it take you so long to walk away with so little?"

Trent tucked his notepad into one of his back pant pockets. "Showing a personal interest can go a long way in getting people to open up."

"Sure. About things that don't matter."

Trent clenched his jaw but didn't say anything.

"Just remember with a death investigation we're working on a fine timeline. The best chance of catching a killer is in the first twenty-four hours."

"I'm well aware of that—" Trent clamped his mouth shut and stared off into the distance. His eyes held more embarrassment than anger, and she actually felt a twinge of remorse for talking to him like he was a child.

"You know that," she shoved out, hating that she cared an iota about his feelings.

Trent simply nodded.

"I didn't get far either," she started. "Four people between the three rooms, but the guy in seven saw a short, squat man hanging around in the parking lot yesterday afternoon. The two in room twelve couldn't agree with each other, except for the fact they didn't see any men. One of them insisted they saw a thin woman, while the other described her as obscenely overweight. They couldn't agree on the time either but thought it was Saturday afternoon or evening—they couldn't decide. The guy in room fifteen was too busy carrying on a conversation with his invisible best friend while I tried to get him to talk to me. Apparently, his *friend* saw a tall, lean man."

Trent's lips twitched as he resisted a smirk. "We're not getting anything from these people. They don't want to talk to the cops."

"Safe to conclude, Captain Obvious."

The sound of a vehicle coming into the lot took her attention. It was a van with *Office of the Chief Medical Examiner* stamped on the side.

"Look at the timing on that," Amanda said. Though it would have been more ideal if they'd arrived already and had updates such as time of death, manner of death, and speculative cause of death so she and Trent could get on with their next order of business and dig into the last few hours of Palmer's life.

As the ME parked, Amanda went over to Becky and got another pair of plastic booties for her shoes. Trent had probably stuffed the ones she'd given him into a pocket. Then they headed to Palmer's room to check in with the crime scene investigators.

The smiley CSI was just inside the door working her magic with an apparatus that magnetically charged a sheet of mylar. The process would attract any dirt particles and, if there were shoeprints to find, make them plain to see. A forensic investigator once told her that shoeprints are almost as distinctive as fingerprints, each one unique. Numerous factors such as brand of footwear, weight of the wearer, gait of the wearer, history of the shoe made each sole different. Lifting prints in a place like this would be hell though. Amanda couldn't imagine the cleaning staff was too thorough.

The investigator stood and smiled at Amanda and Trent. "Want back in?"

"If it's not too much trouble," Amanda replied, and the investigator stepped aside. "Actually, while I'm thinking of it," Amanda started, "it might be a good idea if we collect the garbage outside the office too."

The investigator poked her head out the door, followed the direction of Amanda's pointing finger, and said, "You got it."

"Thanks."

Amanda and Trent put on their plastic booties and gloves and entered the room.

The slender and older CSI was taking Palmer's fingerprints. Trent looked at Amanda.

"It's procedure," Amanda started, about to explain the CSI's purpose for doing it.

Trent took over. "It's to verify the deceased's identity and it tells investigators right away if he has a history with the police."

She'd obviously misread why he'd looked at her. Regardless, if Trent had been her pupil, Amanda might have patted him on the back and given him a gold star. But he wasn't, and for some reason his knowledge and brown-nosing ticked her off.

"Did either of you find a duffel bag?" she asked, moving farther into the room. "Maybe in the dresser or the closet?"

"Not me," the investigator near the door answered.

"Me neither, but CSI Donnelly's been working on the room, while I've been tending to the deceased," the slender CSI said, nodding toward the investigator who had been searching for shoeprints.

"Donnelly?" Amanda said. "I'm Detective Steele and this is Detective Stenson."

"Nice to meet you," Donnelly said.

"I know who you are," the other CSI mumbled.

Amanda bristled. "I don't know who you are."

"Emma Blair."

There was an electric charge to the air, far more powerful than any forensic apparatus could be, and Amanda wondered why Blair seemed so hostile.

"Some *body* called?"

Amanda turned and was pleased to see Hans Rideout. With numerous qualified personnel at the Office of the Chief Medical Examiner in Manassas, a town about a half hour from Dumfries, it was a crapshoot as to who would be sent out. Rideout was one of the best. He had morgue humor down pat and, for a career built on death, he had quite the zest for life. In his forties with a full head of gray hair, he had deep smile lines around his mouth. Sometimes his cheeriness was almost too much to handle, but Amanda was more concerned by the fact he'd know who Palmer was to her.

"Hi," Amanda said to him.

"Hey-lo." Rideout's greeting came out in two parts, with the latter in a baritone. He waved one hand toward Palmer; the other held his case. "You do know who that is?" He looked directly at Amanda.

"Uh-huh." She drew up tall, ready to defend herself.

He held eye contact with her and eventually said, "All righty, then," and got to work.

She went straight to Palmer's wallet, more than ready to return to what she'd been doing when Trent and the CSIs had shown up. So, he had a couple of expired credit cards, a healthcare insurance card, and a ten-dollar bill. She rattled that inventory off for Trent, then pulled out two photos from another partition. One was of Palmer with a woman, both smiling, probably taken around the time of the accident given Palmer's appearance. They were standing rather close, which indicated a romantic relationship, though they weren't touching. If she was a girlfriend, Amanda didn't remember her face from the trial. The other picture was of a teenage Palmer next to two other boys about the same age, each of them holding bicycles at their sides. She flipped each picture hoping there'd be names, but no such luck.

She passed the photos to Trent. "We'll want to find out who they are." She wasn't hinging much hope on their identities having much, if any, bearing on the case, but it was still a matter that needed to be explored. If Palmer had been targeted, the more they found out about his life before prison the better.

"Possible one of them is Palmer's next of kin," Trent said.

"Could be," she replied.

Rideout lifted his gaze from Palmer's body to her. His frown said it all: she shouldn't be working this case. But damn it to hell, she could compartmentalize the personal from the professional. She'd had years of practice as a cop stuffing her feelings down deep, keeping the recommended emotional distance from the cases she worked and the families she had to deal with.

"Whoever they are, we'll find his next of kin." Her words circled back to her ears with far more confidence than she felt. After the accident, she and her father had pried into Palmer's life. The intention had been to build a case for the prosecution, to establish a pattern of behavior—Palmer had always been a drunk—but during the process they'd found out his parents were both dead and he didn't have any siblings.

Trent handed the photos back to her, and she looked at the one of Palmer with the woman again. If she had been his girlfriend, they could have broken things off before the case went to trial. She returned the photos to the wallet and in exchange fished out a business card. She angled it for Trent to see.

"King of Pawnshops," Trent read out.

"It was located in Woodbridge," Amanda said. "Place is out of business now, but Palmer was part owner there before he went to prison."

"We should reach out to his partner then," Trent said, not questioning for a second that Palmer had been to prison. He'd definitely been read in and knew Palmer's history.

"You said King of Pawnshops?" CSI Blair stopped whatever it was she was doing near the closet.

"Yeah?" Amanda angled her head, not sure where Blair was headed.

"Oh."

"Not following," Amanda said.

"The owner of that pawnshop was murdered. Brutally. It was one of the nastiest crime scenes I've worked in my career."

Amanda tried to recall the name of Palmer's partner. It was Jackson something, but his last name wasn't coming. "You remember his name?" she asked the CSI, curious about her change in attitude. She'd been so hostile up until now.

"Jackson Webb. I'll never forget. He'd been tortured. His fingernails were removed, and he had cigarette burns all over his body." Blair consulted Rideout. "Do you remember that?"

"Lots of bodies visit my table," Rideout said, "but I'm guessing someone else was assigned that autopsy."

"Signs of torture…" Amanda's gaze went to Palmer. Could it be that whoever had killed Webb was responsible for Palmer's death? But there were no signs of torture present here—at least not visible ones. After the sentencing, she'd let her obsession with Palmer go, choosing instead to wallow alone in her grief and anger. "When was this?"

"Easily five years ago or so. As I said, it was a memorable crime scene."

The skin tightened at the back of her neck. The accident was five and a half years ago; six this coming July eighteenth. Turnaround time from trial to sentencing was five months, twenty-six days, six months. But no wonder she didn't know about Jackson Webb's fate; she'd been out of touch for a couple of months after the accident. Hospitalized and monitored. An internal bleed had made an operation necessary, and that surgery had repercussions of its own. Long-lasting, life-altering ones. She did her best not to dwell on them. She had enough to deal with when it came to losing Kevin and Lindsey as it was. Only she and her doctors knew the full cost of that fateful day.

They needed to dig up the Webb investigation. Could it be that the same person who had killed Webb had come for Palmer? But then what motive could have bridged the stretch of time? Could the only thing that had kept Palmer alive been the fact he was behind bars?

"Did they ever solve the case?" she asked.

"I dunno." Blair hitched her shoulders. "I probably should have followed through, but then the next case comes up, and the next…"

She was dying to know if there'd been any leads, namely suspects, but she could dig into that back at the station. "What else do you remember?"

"The place—the vic's house—was an absolute disaster, and not just because of the blood. It had been tossed, no doubt of it."

Judges liked to pick apart the word "tossed," saying that without knowing the state of a place before the crime, it was impossible to conclude, but the word was still widely used outside of the courtroom.

Blair continued. "Drawers and cupboards were emptied out onto counters and the floor. Cushions and pillows were shredded, most likely with a knife."

"What was the cause of death?" Trent asked.

"Gunshot to the head—and between us, I'd say the bullet would have been welcome by the time it came."

"What's it looking like, Rideout?" Amanda asked him.

"It's too early to say, but normally when I see this, it's accidental not homicide. Suicide's also very unlikely."

"Cause of death being?" Amanda moved closer to the bed.

"Death by aspiration."

Could that be all they were looking at here? For some reason, that possibility made her feel gypped. The case would be closed before it really began.

Rideout lifted one of Palmer's eyelids. "As you can see, petechiae and hemorrhaging in his eyes." Rideout pulled down on Palmer's bottom lip. "Petechiae's also in his gum tissue."

Just like with his eyes, little red dots marred the pink flesh, which she'd learned years ago was an indication of being starved of oxygen.

"He choked on his vomit," she concluded.

"Yes, and my guess would be due to ethanol poisoning."

"Ethanol poisoning?" Trent said.

"Layman's terms, alcohol overdose. It would have hindered the area of the brain that controls life-support functions such as breathing, heart rate, and temperature control." Rideout stopped there and looked down at Palmer. "It is strange that he's on top of the comforter."

"Strange, why?" Amanda pressed.

"As I was just saying, his temperature would have been affected. He would have been very cold."

"So what are you saying? Someone set this up to look like he drank himself to death?" She could be reading too much into Rideout's words about the bedding, but she was a homicide detective and wired to rule out murder first.

"Never said that. He could have just been too drunk to bother getting under the comforter. I'm not ready to conclude the manner of death just yet." Rideout paused and chewed his bottom lip. "What does bother me, though, are the two perfectly empty bottles of whiskey."

The skin tightened on the back of Amanda's neck. "Why?"

"If he overdrank himself, it would make more sense to me that there'd still be some booze left in one of the bottles. But they're both completely empty. There's also no sign of spillage on the bedding or in the room."

Rideout stood back, stared at Palmer, then eventually shook his head and looked at Amanda. "Just let me get him back to the morgue before I make any calls on manner of death. But you should know that if someone did force-feed him alcohol with intent to kill him, it's quite an iffy murder, and the person would have had to stay around for hours, not a matter of minutes."

"Yet no one saw anything," she lamented. "Nothing useful anyhow."

"I wish I had something more conclusive, but until I get him on my table…"

"When do you figure that will be?"

"I'll keep you posted, but I suspect today for sure."

Amanda nodded. Though she'd heard what Rideout had said about this cause of death often being accidental, she couldn't dismiss the empty bottles *and* the murdered business partner. Webb had been tortured, and if Palmer had been murdered, as Rideout had noted, it would have required his killer stay around for hours. That would have been nothing short of torture. Did that mean Webb's killer was back or was she seeing ghosts where there were none? But there was the as-of-yet unexplained gash on Palmer's forehead. She pointed it out to Rideout and said, "Are there any defensive wounds?"

"Not that I've seen so far, but you can trust I'll do my diligence. Scrape under his nails and—"

She held up a hand to him, not needing the entire rundown. "I trust you. How's it looking for time of death?"

"Based on several factors, I'd estimate any time between six and eleven last night."

"You… ah… sure?" She rubbed her throat.

"I wouldn't have said it if I wasn't. You're looking pale, Detective; are you all right?" Rideout took a step toward her.

"Yeah, I'm fine," was what she said but she was far from it. During the time-of-death window, she'd picked up Motel Guy and climbed into bed with him at the Dreamcatcher Inn. Sergeant Malone had made it clear he required her alibi if she was to stand any chance of working the case at all.

She checked the time on her cell phone. It was just after two AM. "I've gotta go." She snapped off her gloves and brushed past Trent. "There's something I need to do," she told him.

He moved to go with her.

She stopped walking and spun. "It's personal." When Trent didn't say anything for a few beats, she considered the scenario.

Securing an alibi meant by its very nature it would become known, but she'd get it lined up first, then deal with that.

"It's far too early to start knocking on more doors, but we can't just sit on our asses either. I need you to go back to the station and find out everything you can on Jackson Webb's murder and see if there's any reason to suspect Palmer's death is connected."

"You think they are?"

"Don't know. That's why I want you to do a little digging. We cover all the angles with a suspicious death. We rule out murder first."

Trent flushed, glanced down, then nodded.

"Also, look for next of kin."

When Trent didn't move, she said, "What are you waiting for?"

"You going to be all right?"

"Don't ever worry about me," she shoved out and hustled to her car. She just hoped Motel Guy was still languishing in the afterglow.

CHAPTER SEVEN

Amanda pulled around Dreamcatcher Inn to where room eight was nestled. No sign of Motel Guy's Dodge Ram, but she got out and banged on the room door anyway.

"I just need a freaking break," she called out to the night.

No answer from the room or a greater being—not that she was certain one even existed.

She drove around to the inn's office and swung open the door so hard it hit the wall. The clerk's head shot up like he'd been asleep.

"I'm here about your guest in room eight," she told the dopey-eyed clerk.

"Okay, and who are you?"

She leaned on the counter and grabbed his name off his badge. "Bobby, I need the guest's name in room eight."

"And I need a million dollars."

"Don't be a smart-ass."

"Me? You come in here making demands. You need to cool it, lad—"

She pulled her badge and Bobby's eyes widened, and he held his hands up.

"I don't want any trouble with the law."

"Then you're going to be cooperative."

He kept his arms in the air. "As much as I can be, but I can't just be handing out guests' names, even to a cop. Shouldn't you get a warrant or something? And I'd still have to clear it by my manager."

"For God's sake put your hands down."

He lowered them incrementally.

"I'm here about an open investigation," she said, which wasn't entirely a lie but a complete diversion to the clerk's question.

"You have the paperwork? The go-ahead from my boss?"

"Nope."

"Then I'm sorry but I can't help you."

Amanda stood there staring at the clerk, tapping her foot, wishing she could exert some sort of power to make him comply. But she was in this mess all because of her stupid rule: no names.

"If you want to come back with a warr—"

She barreled out into the night air. She wasn't going to get anywhere with Bobby, but now what was she supposed to do? All she knew about Motel Guy was what he drove. That was hardly enough to narrow down a search with the Department of Motor Vehicles. And if she couldn't track down her alibi, she was screwed. Malone would pull her from the case. Then again, if Palmer hadn't been murdered, she wouldn't need one.

She drove home for a long, overdue shower. Trent would just have to wait for her; she'd get to the station when she got there.

She pulled into the driveway of the gray brick bungalow she'd shared with Kevin and Lindsey. They'd made a life and a slew of memories here. For the longest time, she'd look at the house and just sit in her car and cry before going inside. Then she'd gone through a phase where she'd stopped looking and crossed over to a numb indifference, doing her best to set aside the happy times because they didn't possess the power to rise above the pain.

Today, she was feeling different yet again. The man who had killed them had left this world—either assisted or due to his own dumb addiction.

There was a single garage, but Kevin had been a bit of a pack rat and it was piled high with stuff. She hadn't been able to bring herself to touch any of it, let alone clear it out.

She unlocked the front door and dropped her keys in the bowl on the hall table in the entry. The house was thirty-five years old, but she and Kevin had renovated and made it open concept. There was a tiled patch of flooring to distinguish the square-shaped entry. It butted against the wood laminate flooring of the living room to the left. The kitchen was beyond that, and to the right was a hallway that went to two bedrooms and a bathroom. The basement wasn't fully finished and was mostly neglected except for the laundry room that shared its space with the furnace and water heater.

She went right for the bathroom, craving a hot shower to wash off the sex, and stayed under the spray until the water ran cold.

She slipped behind the wheel twenty minutes after going inside and set out for PWCPD Central District police station in Woodbridge. But on her way out of Dumfries she found herself driving past the cemetery where she'd laid Kevin and Lindsey to rest. She was turning in before she could talk herself out of it.

It had been a while since she'd visited. Months maybe, but she'd started feeling so foolish talking to them as if they still existed on some plane. It hurt too much to think they were "out there" while she was stuck here.

She drove through the twisty roads in the cemetery, her memory recalling well where the family plot was that she'd bought so they could all be laid to rest together. At some point she'd join them, and often it didn't feel like that reunion could happen soon enough.

She got out of the car and suddenly felt unprepared to be here. She should at least be armed with flowers or something, but her family would hopefully understand—if they had any way of knowing.

She pulled her phone and used the flashlight to illuminate the shadows that the pale moonlight failed to penetrate. She walked through the forested graveyard, the trees' branches acting like arms and fingertips reaching out to the night sky. She crested a knoll marked by a magnificent oak tree. Kevin's and Lindsey's graves were just on the other side, on a slight downslope.

She hunched next to the graves, positioned between the two of them. Stacked in front of the headstones were a couple of snow-dusted bouquets of flowers and an unlit candle in a glass dish. Two cards rested against each stone. Amanda picked up the ones for her daughter. They were wet from snow, but she gently opened the envelopes.

The first was addressed to Lindsey in her mother's handwriting.

The card read, *To my sweet, sweet granddaughter, You brought so much light into this world, and I can only be saddened by what the world has lost. But I will always carry you in my heart and soul, my beautiful girl. Keep shining, angel. Merry Christmas and love, Grandma Steele.*

Tears stung Amanda's eyes and she sniffled. Her mother had been here—recently. Amanda felt a rush of guilt for her negligence in visiting the graves.

She didn't readily identify the handwriting on the second card marked *Lindsey.* She scanned to the bottom of the card and saw it had been signed by Kevin's mother and father, Maria and Solomon, her in-laws. Though were they still? Kevin was dead, and they had shied away from her after the trial, just as she'd backed off from her own family. Kevin's mother had written a poem by the looks of it, but she respected the woman's privacy in her words to her only grandchild and returned it to the sleeve.

Amanda palmed her cheeks and set the cards back on the ground. The words weren't for her.

She closed her eyes. What the hell had she been thinking to step forward for the Palmer case? What did she care that the man who killed her family was dead? Good. On. Him. He deserved it, and if he'd met his death at the hands of a cruel killer who made his leaving this world painful—well, he only had himself to blame.

"Why?" she cried out into the night.

She pictured the tiny coffin holding her precious daughter being lowered into the little grave, her love, her heart going into the ground. She had to force herself to remember her daughter as she'd been—a light, as Amanda's mother had described her, with a smile that lit up a room. As time passed though, the images of Kevin's and Lindsey's faces faded, graying around the edges with indistinct features, leaving behind more a whisper of a memory than a clear picture. She had photographs, but it was still hard to fully recall their appearance. She feared that as their faces obscured, she'd somehow forget them. But how was that possible when not a day passed that they weren't in her thoughts?

Amanda sobbed, her chest heaving, and her eyes blurred from tears. She blinked them away and, as her vision came into focus, her gaze was upon Lindsey's gravestone.

Lindsey Julie James, beloved daughter, granddaughter, precious angel.

Beneath the inscription were the dates of her birth and her death. She'd been alive for six years, one month, and eight days.

"Oh, my baby girl, I miss you so much." Amanda swallowed the rest of the words that came to mind, the heartfelt sentiments such as how great it would have been to see the woman she'd have become if only given the chance. She and Kevin had always instilled etiquette into their little girl and taught her how important it was to stick to her word. Something Amanda had gotten from her mother.

"A person's word is all any of us have or can truly control," was something Amanda had heard a lot growing up. It was a motto that had become the backbone of how she lived her life. It had come to define her relationships and her career, and had always served her well. And now it gave her perspective on how to handle Palmer's case.

She got up and put a hand on Lindsey's gravestone and said, "Thank you for helping me to remember. And if you're listening, sweetheart, send Mommy the strength to keep her word this time."

She blew a kiss to her fingertips and pressed it to the cold granite of Lindsey's headstone and then repeated the process with Kevin's. "I will love you forever, Kev."

She walked back to her car, her spirit lifted, while at the same time she could feel her body dragging. She'd give anything if it meant they'd return to her, but, until they met again, she'd do her best to make them proud.

CHAPTER EIGHT

The man who had killed her family was D.E.A.D. It should be easy to accept, but her mind was working overtime and nipping at her resolve. After all, no one would question her decision to back out. Not Malone, Becky, or Trent. That's even if Palmer had indeed been murdered and the investigation continued in earnest. Still, she found herself headed toward the station in Woodbridge, but she took a detour in the direction of Freddy's house. Sure, she'd managed without Xanax, but with Palmer's release, now death, the drug called out to her. Was it enough to risk her badge? But she wasn't even sure that meant as much to her as it once had, and her judgment may have been clouded by the memory of how just one pill could calm her nerves and silence her mind.

It was almost four in the morning by the time she stopped in front of Freddy's and punched the steering wheel. The better part of a couple of hours had passed since she'd left Trent at Denver's. If she took too much longer, he could call wondering where she was, though he probably didn't want to prod her given she was really his superior.

"What am I doing?" Again, she spoke out loud as if some greater being would reply. But she had no reason to be struck by some sudden pang of guilt. She could justify her intended actions. Steeles kept their word and saw things through by whatever means necessary. And what Freddy had could help her live up to her promise to Malone not to cause drama.

She got out of the car, keeping her badge where it was, clipped to her waist, and her gun in its holster on her person, and hurried up the front walk. She banged on the metal of the screen door, and the top half kicked against the frame. She tried a couple more times and was just about to walk away when the light turned on.

The interior door opened, the person inside obscured by a nasty glare across the glass. "Whatcha want?" He was groggy, half-asleep, and pissed at the interruption.

"I'm here for Freddy," she said, punching it out with authority.

The person stepped more into the light and she got a good look. Damien Rodriguez, street name Rat, and he was all of five-foot-five. She'd encountered him years ago when working a homicide and knew from then that his rap sheet showed he'd served time for dealing. She was quite sure he was guilty of far more than that, but she'd make peace with that if he could overlook her pending transgression.

"What business ya got with—Hey, I know you. You're that lady cop."

This had been a mistake. A part of her mind was screaming at her, but it was too late to turn back now. She was full speed ahead like a train on tracks. "Not here on police business."

"To hell you're not. Get outta here!" He pulled on the door, but she stuck her foot in to stop it from slamming shut. His face gnarled up. "What do you think you're doin'?"

"Look." She moved slowly and tucked her badge into her jacket pocket.

"If you ain't here to arrest us, why then?" Rat sucked his bottom lip in, then shoved it out.

Her skin was crawling like eyes were on her, but she had to keep her focus on Rat. A brief glance over a shoulder could prove deadly. "Let me inside, and I'll tell you."

He studied her and didn't move.

"Hey, you have no reason to trust me. I get that, but I'm here for personal reasons and I'm not about to conduct business out here, so either you let me inside or I'll take my money elsewhere."

Rat stared her down for quite some time before withdrawing into the house and leaving the door open. She took that as an invitation to enter.

There was a narrow staircase immediately inside to the right, and to the left was a living room that appeared to be busting at the seams, full of overstuffed and cracking leather couches and bulky end tables with pockmarks in the veneer.

"Freddy!" Rat yelled, and pounding footsteps sounded overhead and hit the stairs.

Freddy jogged down and scowled. "What the hell?" He glared at Rat, obviously recognizing Amanda too.

"She says she's here for personal reasons." A smirk played at the corner of Rat's mouth.

"Really?" Freddy rubbed his jaw and circled her. "That true?" He stopped mere inches in front of her, his nose to hers.

"It is," she confirmed.

A light brightened Freddy's eyes and he smiled. "How interesting. What is it I can do for you, Officer?"

"I need some…" She was tempted to leave it open for Freddy to make the determination based on her desired results, but it was best she stuck with what she knew. "Looking for some Xanax. I trust you can help me with that?"

"Maybe." Freddy let his gaze linger over her body.

"Don't waste my time. You have it or you don't." She was shaking inside but hoping that she was doing a convincing job of projecting herself as brave and in control.

Freddy clucked his tongue. "Feisty. I like it."

"Like it less and get me the pills."

He put his hands on his hips and angled his head. "Normally I'd say the first taste is on the house, but you're a cop. You pay. Five for fifty."

She fished into a pocket and pulled out cash. "Only have three twenties."

"I don't make change."

"Make it six pills then." She wasn't about to get into negotiating with a drug dealer. She just wanted the business over with.

Freddy snapped his fingers and Rat set out into the bowels of the house, leaving Amanda alone with Freddy, who was still ogling her.

He ran his tongue along his top lip. "What makes a cop—"

She narrowed her eyes. "Like you really give a shit."

Rat returned with a small baggie, which he gave to Freddy, who in turn extended it toward Amanda, but then drew his hand back. "Nuh-uh, money first."

She slapped the bills into his open palm, and he gave her the pills.

He sniffed the cash. "Nice doing business with you."

She left as fast as her legs would take her. She never should have come. Never. She sure hoped the benefits outweighed the assumed risk.

She got into her car, slammed the door, and eyed the pills in the baggie. *Just one*, she told herself, *that's all it will take to ease the pain*. Besides, it was too late to turn back now.

She unzipped the baggie and had one capsule pinched between her fingers when someone banged on the driver's window. She jumped and the pills flew everywhere.

Rat's face was pressed against the glass, and he was pointing his finger down. She lowered the window a crack.

"Don't be showing up here again. You want more, you call, and we'll arrange a meet." He slid a card through the opening and waited for her to take hold of it, which she did with a trembling hand.

"Just remember. We know who you are, Copper—Civic six four six."

Her stomach tossed. That was the car model and part of her license tag.

He tapped the roof of her car and left with a smug smile on his slimy face.

She put the window back up and looked at the empty baggie still in one hand, the card in the other. A simple card that could have come off Freddy's home printer. It just had *F* and a phone number. She stuffed it into her console and set about searching the floor for the pills. She collected three from around her feet, but the others must have fallen under her seat. She bent forward and reached blindly beneath her but came out empty-handed.

"Damn it all!" She got out of the car and searched using the flashlight on her phone. She found them, along with a plastic water bottle on the back floormat. She lifted it up. Empty. Just great. She'd never mastered swallowing pills dry and as she got into the driver's seat again, she caught the time on the dash clock. Quarter past four. She really needed to get to the station. She sealed the pills in the baggie, zipped it in her coat pocket, and headed for the station.

CHAPTER NINE

Prince William County Police Department had about seven hundred officers and three stations, as well as seven other facilities for things such as public safety training, animal control, and licensing. Homicide, under the Violent Crimes Bureau, worked out of the Central District Station in Woodbridge. The building had opened a few years ago and was marked by a grand opening to the public. It was mostly a single-story redbrick structure with the exception of one second-story office tower, sided with formed aluminum panels and situated on a country lot surrounded by trees. It would have been a serene setting if not for the nature of the investigations that went on inside the station's walls. In addition to Homicide, there were bureaucratic offices, including the one that belonged to the police chief.

Amanda was ravaged by guilt and paranoia as she made her way through the front doors. As if everyone in the building would know that she'd just scored illegal prescription drugs—that they were on her person, no less. She watched people she passed for any tells they were onto her, but she was aware it had to be her imagination working overtime. After all, they'd have no way of knowing what was in her pocket. She still felt eyes on her though, but that was probably because Cud had opened his big mouth and anyone working already knew about Palmer's death. No one could claim PWCPD's rumor mill wasn't functioning.

The homicide detectives were set up in low-walled cubicles to encourage ease of communication. She found Trent sitting at the desk in the space next to hers. He was absorbed reading something on his computer. She sat down at her desk and said to him, "How did you make out?"

He slowly looked over at her, taking his gaze from his monitor. "I've uncovered a lot."

"Hit me." She leaned back in her chair and swiveled. Nerves. She grounded her feet and stopped the rocking.

"Where to start?"

"Webb's murder." By far that was what she was most curious about, followed by what Palmer'd had on his person and immediate possession at the time of his incarceration, and then next of kin. She'd take whatever he had.

"Open case." Trent pushed back from his desk and joined her in her cubicle. "As CSI Blair told us, Webb was taken out by a gunshot, but not before he was tortured. All of his fingernails were removed, and he was burned with a cigarette on his chest and arms."

Trent gave her a few color prints of the crime scene. She'd never been squeamish, but CSI Blair had been on the mark when she said the crime scene was a bloody mess.

"Looks like a slaughterhouse," she said as she shuffled through the images, taking in the slashed photos and cushions—unmistakably tossed. "I'd say whoever killed Webb was definitely after something, and the knowledge of whatever that was might have gone with him to the grave. Who were the detectives on the case?"

"Bishop and some guy named Jonah Reid."

"Bishop?" she pushed out. Cud. Unbelievable. Had he purposely not mentioned Webb's murder at Denver's Motel last night or not seen the connection? She popped her head up, but Bishop wasn't at his desk. If he were, she'd be asking him why he'd failed to share that tidbit of information. "I don't know Jonah Reid."

"Looks like he just had a brief blip with PWCPD. He was only here for a few months and then transferred out not long after Webb's murder."

It must have been during the time she'd been healing and isolating, but cops came and went all the time.

"Were there any suspects in Webb's case?" If the two did turn out to be connected, it might give them a place to start.

"No, but you'll find this interesting. Webb's murder is connected with another one. Ballistics matched to another cold case in Atlanta, Georgia, which took place a few days before Webb's."

She straightened up. "Georgia?"

"Yeah. A twenty-one-year-old stripper by the name of Casey-Anne Ritter."

She got up and rounded her chair. "So two murders… or three?"

"Well, technically we don't know the manner of Palmer's death—" He stopped there under her gaze.

"Was this Casey-Anne tortured too?"

"Not exactly. Now, the medical examiner concluded that she'd hit the back of her head, likely from a push to the floor. She was found naked in her apartment bathroom."

"Was she raped?"

"No evidence to confirm that, but she was shot point-blank to the middle of her forehead, just like Webb."

"Huh. Both shot execution style. Not exactly matching what happened to Palmer," she said, deep in thought. Maybe she really was reaching to see a link between the cold cases and Palmer's death.

"Not entirely, I agree, but what about Palmer's bag? We can't dismiss that someone was looking for something from this Georgia woman and Webb. Maybe it was in Palmer's duffel?"

"So does Ritter tie back to Dumfries or just to Webb?" Amanda was still intrigued by the murders.

"I don't know, but I did a database search for Casey-Anne Ritter. No hits that are remotely close to matching that name. There are other Casey-Anne Ritters out there, but none line up for age."

"Okay, that has my attention. She must have been—what?— using a fake name and living off the grid."

"My guess."

"Still doesn't give us any sort of link to Dumfries." Her mind was spinning, and she grabbed onto her next thought. "Was Ritter's apartment rummaged?"

"Can't say. Guess her place was rather sparse."

"Hmm. Let's say the killer was after something. Question is, did they return because they're still after whatever-it-was? They couldn't get to Palmer in prison and came after him soon after his release?" She was trying to figure out how those cases could possibly tie in with Palmer's—if they did. Really all they had was the fact the former business partners were both dead. Palmer hadn't been shot. But, as she'd thought earlier, if he'd been murdered by being force-fed alcohol, that would have been torturous.

"It is possible."

"Except for the undetermined manner of death," she grumbled. If she listened to her gut though, it was telling her Palmer had been murdered. But it was the cause of death that was wreaking havoc on that theory. Rideout had said death due to alcohol poisoning was normally accidental, but it could have been the work of a psychopathic killer with time on their hands.

"Yeah, well, I placed a call to find out what was taken from Palmer's person at the time of booking. I wrote down what they told me. The official list will be forthcoming, but I asked specifically about a duffel bag. Well…" Trent paused there, and his eyes widened.

He was going for dramatic effect, but she'd never been a fan of suspense. "And…"

"He had twenty-five grand in cash in the bag when he was booked."

"Twenty— Wow. So where the hell is the money now?"

Trent certainly had a way of burying the lead, and maybe the manager, Flynn, had noticed all the cash and that's what had made him uneasy.

"Good question, but so is: What was Palmer doing with all that money? Did the money have some nefarious purpose or was it simply earnings from the pawnshop that he was on the way to the bank to deposit the night of the accident?"

She shook her head. "The crash happened on a Saturday night. All the banks would have been closed. Some institutions have a place to drop off deposits after hours, but I doubt anyone would use it for large sums of cash."

There was a brief period of silence, then Trent said, "Curious if Palmer's missing money might be what Ritter and Webb's killer was after, and, if so, did that person come back and take out Palmer? Then again, we may be jumping to the assumption there's a connection between the three deaths."

"Add all that to the list of questions that need answers. We'll need to dig into Palmer's life before prison. And speaking of, did you have any luck finding next of kin?"

"None. Parents have been dead for years and he was their only child. The closest blood relative is Rick Jensen, his cousin, who lives in Henderson, North Carolina, a three-hour drive away."

"Too far," she said. Technically notifying next of kin was limited to the immediate family: spouse, children, brothers, sisters, parents anyway.

"Thinking we might be best having a talk with Palmer's former landlord, Jerrod Rhodes, and seeing if he can direct us to anyone. A girlfriend maybe?"

Amanda recalled the girl in the photo from Palmer's wallet. "We should definitely do that, but first I think we need to focus on Palmer's last hours alive and speak to anyone that might help us with that."

"The Denver's Motel employees then?"

She nodded. "Makes sense. We should also find out where the whiskey was purchased and see if we can confirm it was by Palmer."

Trent pulled out his notepad and scribbled. She assumed he was making a note to visit nearby liquor stores.

"Before we go though," she said, "call the prison and ask for Palmer's visitor list. An amount of cash like that, it's possible Palmer could have owed it to someone, and they might also have shown up to try and collect from him at the prison."

Trent returned to his cube and placed the call.

Detective Natalie Ryan walked past and offered a basic greeting of, "Hey." All Amanda heard was, "*You buy from a drug dealer.*" Beads of sweat rolled down her back and she bounced her leg.

Trent hung up. "The visitor list will be coming over."

"Great. You ready to go?"

"Ah, yeah, sure. Lorraine Nash or David Morgan?"

"Let's start with Nash as she worked Sunday, the last day Palmer was alive."

"Sure." Trent flicked his monitor off.

Amanda spun and bumped right into Sergeant Malone's chest. He held up his hands to brace her and stepped back.

"Sorry," she offered quickly, blushing.

"No one was hurt." Malone let his gaze go over her to Trent. "You two headed out?"

"Yeah, have a couple of people to question," Amanda said.

Malone nodded. "Great. It sounds like you two have it all under control." He met her gaze, and with the last two words, a sliver of remorse wormed through her.

I have nothing under control! But as far as the world knows…

"We do," she said and tossed out a smile. She did her best to have it reach her eyes, but it was unlikely it had, given the suspicion reflected in Malone's eyes.

"Great," he said.

Trent started walking toward the hall and she followed.

Malone said, "Just before you go, Detective Steele."

Trent turned and she held up her index finger to let him know she'd be there in a minute.

"What is it?" she asked the sergeant.

He leaned in and hunched to reach her ear. "Do you have your alibi?"

She let out the breath she hadn't known she was holding, but it was shallow regardless. "The ME hasn't ruled that Palmer was murdered yet…"

Malone shook his head. "Doesn't matter. Get out in front of this or—" He ran a finger along his neck.

"I will."

"See that you do."

She held eye contact with him for a few seconds longer before hauling ass down the hall to catch up with Trent. With each step, it just sank in more and more the mess she was in. For one, she was in possession of illegally obtained drugs, and two, she had to manifest an alibi from thin air. But maybe she could return to the bar where they'd met and use her badge to whittle information from the woman who'd served them. If she went that route though, she could never return to the bar for risk of her name and her history getting out. But what was the lesser of two evils: the need to find a new place to pick up men or getting benched from the case? And the latter came with potentially worse consequences still. She could be assigned desk duty for the rest of her career or given the cases no one else wanted to touch. If things really spiraled out of control, she could be defending herself against murder charges or lose her badge. Some days she wasn't sure if finding a new path in life—away from Dumfries, away from Prince William County PD and the county itself—was that horrible an idea. She could start fresh and rebuild her life. Then only she would truly know the hole that existed in her heart.

*

They were headed to Lorraine Nash's home in Dumfries, Trent at the wheel, but Amanda requested a brief detour to Denver's Motel first.

The Forensics van was still in the lot, but Rideout's vehicle was gone. She booted up and stepped into the room. Palmer's body was gone and there was a different feel to the space, but she could still feel his presence. But there always was that tingling, tangible feeling where a person had died that stuck to a person's skin.

"Detectives? You're back," Donnelly said pleasantly.

"We're just finishing up here," CSI Blair said.

"Just on our way past and thought we'd drop in," Amanda said, trying to lighten the mood in the room. "Anything you feel like sharing?"

"I found a lipstick under the bed," Donnelly volunteered.

"May I see it?" Amanda asked.

Donnelly rummaged in her collection case, pulled out a sealed evidence bag, and passed it to Amanda.

She read the label on the bottom of the tube. The brand could be purchased at any beauty counter in any department store, and the shade was Ruby Red. She gave the bag to Trent for him to do his own inspection.

"I wouldn't get too excited about it." Blair pointed at the bag. "It could have gone under the bed at any time. Doesn't mean it was during Palmer's stay."

"A fact we'll squirrel away," Amanda said drily. She'd wanted to say *an obvious fact...*

Donnelly returned the lipstick to her kit and Amanda noticed a sealed bag with Palmer's wallet enclosed. *The photographs.*

"Actually, if it wouldn't be too much trouble," she started and cringed, because she could feel Blair's hostile energy from across the room. Apparently, anything Amanda requested was too much trouble as far as that CSI was concerned. "The wallet… it had a couple of photos. It might prove useful to get a copy of those."

"Sure." Donnelly smiled at Amanda and took the necessary steps of removing the wallet and the photos and redocumenting and sealing after Amanda took pictures of the photos with her phone.

"Thank you," Amanda told her and let her gaze drift over to Blair. The two investigators weren't just physical opposites; their personalities were polar to each other too. Donnelly was kind and accommodating, Blair a bit of a grouch, with the bedside manner of a bad doctor.

"Just one more question and we'll be out of your hair," Amanda began. "Before Rideout left, did he happen to say any more about where he was leaning for manner of death?"

"No," Blair said curtly.

Donnelly chuckled. "He mumbled to himself a lot."

"That's never good," Amanda said. Rideout only mumbled when he was puzzled. "And you got the garbage outside the motel office?"

"Yes, ma'am. We'll work through it back at the lab."

"Thanks."

Blair shot Amanda a cold look that said they didn't need to be micromanaged. What the heck was her problem?

Amanda and Trent saw themselves out, and Becky came toward them. Amanda gestured for Trent to carry on and get into the car, which he did. Amanda shook her head.

"What?" Becky smiled and glanced at Trent, then back to Amanda.

"He's like a puppy."

"Could be worse. Puppies are cute and—"

"They can get underfoot."

"I'm sure it's not that bad," Becky countered.

Amanda couldn't argue, but she wasn't about to defend Trent either. Their relationship was far too new for that.

"So, how are you doing?" Becky asked.

"Peachy."

Becky burst out a laugh. "Okay, now I know I need to worry."

Amanda smiled. "I've had easier cases, and Rideout's not even sure Palmer was murdered."

"But you think he was?"

"There are unanswered questions. Like Palmer's former business partner was murdered."

Becky's mouth formed an O.

"And his murder, the partner's that is, was linked to one in Georgia." She gave Becky the brief overview of the Webb and Ritter cases.

"Wow."

"Yeah. Thrilling. But regardless of how that part shakes out, I need to secure my alibi. Part of the terms of working this case."

"That going to be a problem?"

"Might be."

"Why? What is it?"

Amanda opened her mouth; shut it. She shouldn't have brought it up. "I'll figure it out."

Becky narrowed her eyes and tilted her head.

Amanda touched Becky's upper arm. "Everything will be fine. I promise."

CHAPTER TEN

Lorraine Nash lived in a small two-story house. The place was well maintained from the outside, despite forgotten unlit strings of Christmas lights that still clung to the eaves. It was just after six in the morning when they pulled up front and there was a light on inside. Amanda took that to mean someone was awake. She knocked loud enough for it to be heard but not so loud that the Nashes would think their house was on fire. It would be jarring enough to have someone at your front door this early.

The outside light came alive and then the deadbolt was being unlocked. At least they secured their house, unlike so many in rural towns who didn't bother. Honestly, it was a miracle there weren't more murders and home invasions in the country.

The door was cracked opened and a thirty-something man, presumably Lorraine's husband, poked his head out. "Yeah?"

"Prince William County PD," Amanda said and pulled her badge. "Are you Mr. Nash?"

"Yes," he said, wary. "Ben."

"Hi, Ben, we're Detectives Steele and Stenson with Homicide."

Ben opened the door all the way. He was dressed in blue jeans and a sweater.

She added, "We're sorry for the early hour, but we need to speak with your wife, Lorraine."

"Lorraine? Why?"

"We'd like to discuss *that* with your wife."

Ben let his gaze dance over them and eventually gestured for them to come inside. "I'll get her."

Amanda and Trent stayed in the entry, and Amanda soaked in her surroundings. Modest, plain, but well-loved and well-lived-in. There was a family portrait of a man, woman, baby, and a child of about six on the wall next to a coatrack and a pair of children's shoes on a mat. A pang of heartbreak gripped her as she was reminded yet again of all she'd lost.

A woman in blue plaid pajamas walked toward them, her slippered feet scuffing along the floor. She squinted at the entry light. "You want to speak with me?"

"We do," Amanda answered. She introduced herself and Trent to Lorraine. "Do you have someplace we could sit?" She glanced at the living room off to her and Trent's right.

Ben flicked a light switch on the wall inside the doorway, as if reading Amanda's mind. The Nashes sat on a couch while Amanda and Trent took up in a couple of chairs.

Amanda leaned forward just slightly, establishing a conversational but not overbearing posture. "A man was found dead in one of the rooms at Denver's Motel last night… well, close to midnight."

Ben took Lorraine's hand and squeezed. Beyond that, neither spouse showed any obvious emotion, not even shock. Then again, Denver's didn't exactly cater to high-caliber customers.

Amanda went on. "His name was Chad Palmer and he was in room ten. Perhaps you remember him?"

Amanda turned to Trent, hoping that he was prepared with a photograph of Palmer, because she'd dropped the ball. "Do you have a picture of him, Detective?" she prompted Trent.

"I can get one." Trent pulled a small tablet from the breast pocket of his jacket. She saw the screen and could tell he was going to the DMV database. Palmer's license had been revoked, but his picture would still be on record.

"Here," Trent said and swung the tablet for Lorraine Nash to see.

"Do you recognize him?" Amanda asked her.

Lorraine paled and nodded.

"Do you remember anything about him?" Amanda said. "If he had any visitors at the motel."

Lorraine tapped her husband's hand and mouthed, I'm fine, to him. She withdrew her hand from his, crossed her legs, and bobbed the top one quickly up and down. She was clearly uncomfortable, and while the topic of suspicious death could make even the brave timid, Amanda wondered if there wasn't something more substantive that was upsetting Mrs. Nash.

"That man was there alone, far as I know. Not like I really had much chitchat with the guy, but yesterday afternoon, he called the front desk—me—and reported a problem with his TV. I sent Bill to check it out."

"And who is Bill?" Trent chimed in.

Lorraine looked at Trent and answered, "The maintenance guy for the motel."

"Last name?" Trent had his pen posed over his notepad.

"Hannigan."

Bill Hannigan must have fixed the problem then, because the TV had been working fine when they'd arrived on scene. "What time was this on Sunday?"

"Say early afternoon."

Amanda nodded. "What shifts does Bill normally work?"

"Think most days starting at seven in the morning."

"Did Mr. Palmer have any visitors?" Amanda asked.

Lorraine rubbed her arms like she was fending off a chill. "Not that I saw."

Amanda got this feeling that Mrs. Nash was afraid of something or someone she'd seen, but if she felt the risk could touch her home, Amanda could hardly fault her for keeping quiet. And maybe if Palmer was anyone else, she would have pushed Lorraine harder, but she said, "Are you sure about that?"

"Yeah, I'm sure."

"And no girlfriends stopping by?" Amanda was thinking of Ms. Ruby Red Lipstick.

"Not that I saw," Lorraine affirmed.

"Huh. I would have sworn you might be able to tell us something." She sighed. "A man's dead and we're just trying to figure out what happened to him." Often an appeal for empathy could work wonders. Lorraine's face hardened.

"I wish I could help." Her tone of voice belied the claim.

"Okay, fair enough." Amanda held up a hand. "Did you happen to see if Mr. Palmer left his room on Sunday?"

Lorraine's eyes darted to her husband, then flicked to Amanda. She nodded slowly, hesitantly.

Amanda wasn't sure why Lorraine seemed concerned with her husband, and asked, "What time was that?"

"Not long before my shift ended. Say five thirty or five forty-five."

"Do you know where he went?" Trent intercepted.

"I have no way of knowing."

"Which direction did he go—east or west of the motel?" Amanda asked, retaking the interview's reins.

Again, Lorraine's gaze went to Ben.

"I was going to let this go," Amanda started, "but why do you keep looking at your husband?" She allowed time for Lorraine to answer, but she didn't seem inclined. "We're just trying to find out what took place and fill in the final hours of this man's life. You could be one of the last to have seen him alive."

Lorraine rubbed her neck. When she removed her hand, her neck was all blotchy.

"I'm not sure entirely what's going on here, but if you're afraid of someone I can help." As Amanda heard herself fighting to gleam nuggets of insight, hypocrisy burrowed into her marrow. After all, did she truly care if Palmer had been murdered and whether his killer was brought to justice, or was her motive more selfish and all about closing a horrid chapter in her life, fulfilling her word, and moving on?

Ben popped up from the couch. "I think my wife's told you all she knows."

"They went west," Lorraine said, and her husband dropped beside her again.

"They? He was with someone?" If this person was the basis for Lorraine's fear, that would imply she also knew who Palmer had been with.

Lorraine nodded. "A guy. I'm sorry but I really can't say any more." She stopped bouncing her leg.

"If this man scares you and poses some sort of a threat to you, your family, we can—"

"Please just leave it alone," Lorraine ground out.

"Will you describe him for us?" She tried to pry just a little more.

Lorraine chewed her bottom lip and shook her head.

"All right; that's fine." Amanda might not be able to whittle a physical description of the mystery guy but there was another tact she could try that might eventually get them where they needed to be.

"Could you describe the vehicle? I assume they left in one?" Amanda held her next breath, curious if Lorraine would answer.

Lorraine nodded. "A four-door sedan, powder-blue."

Not a common color these days. "An older car?"

"Yeah."

Her next question would certainly be a reach, but she had to ask. "Did you catch the plate number?"

"No."

"Just one more thing and we'll be on our way," Amanda began. "Did you happen to notice if Mr. Palmer had a duffel bag with him at any time?"

Lorraine bit her bottom lip and shook her head. "Not that I remember."

"Okay, thank—"

A baby's cry arrested Amanda's words, injecting anguish through her system. She clutched her abdomen and could hear her doctor's words replay in her head: *"I'm truly sorry to inform you, but due to the injuries you sustained, you won't be able to have any more children. Please know we did all we could."*

"I should—" Lorraine pointed toward the doorway, the implication being she had to check on the baby.

Amanda gestured for her to go ahead, and Lorraine jumped up and left the room.

Ben stood, as did Amanda and Trent. She pulled her card and handed it to Ben. "Please let your wife know that we appreciated her cooperation today and to please call should she think of anything else that she wants to share with us. My cell number's on there."

Ben grunted something incoherent and tossed the card onto the coffee table. "I'll show you out."

And he did just that. The second both Amanda and Trent cleared the front door, it was closed heavily behind them. They loaded into the department car, Trent claiming the driver's seat again. Amanda was more than fine with that. He was actually a good driver and hadn't made her reach for the dash yet.

She did up her belt, her mind a million miles away. She hadn't anticipated hearing the baby cry and it had picked an emotional scab. She'd never told anyone that the accident had also stolen her unborn baby. She hadn't even known she was pregnant. Now, she'd never know whether her baby was going to be a boy or another girl. She'd never hear their laugh or tend to their cries; she'd never hear him or her call her "Mommy" or be able to watch them grow up.

"Amanda?" Trent's voice pulled her from her thoughts.

She looked over at him.

"You all right?"

"I'm fine." She stiffened and refocused on the case. "I want to know who this guy is with a powder-blue sedan that has Lorraine Nash terrified into silence."

"It has to be someone with street creds," Trent replied. "I'm guessing our next stop is David Morgan's?"

"Uh-huh," she said coolly. "We talked about our stops before leaving Central."

Trent put his gaze out the windshield. "Yeah, sorry." He set the car in the direction of Morgan's residence.

She faced out the passenger window, not in any mood to talk. Really, why the hell did she care about Palmer at all? Damn the investigation. But as she was ready to shut her involvement down, she thought of the little coffin, the little grave, her sweetheart Lindsey's little face. Her daughter might not be here anymore but, if she were, Amanda would want to set an example, be a role model, show Lindsey that keeping one's word in easy situations was not as strong a testament to character as it was when adhered to during the tough times.

Trent brought the car to a standstill for a stop sign, and she caught him looking at her.

"What?" she spat.

"Nothing." He quickly looked away.

"Do you have any idea all that I've lost?" The question was out before she could reel it back. After all, it wasn't like she wanted to talk about her husband, daughter, and unborn child. And she certainly didn't want special treatment from Trent, so what was her aim?

He turned to her and kept them sitting at the sign.

"You can go." She flailed a hand at the road.

He pressed the gas.

She shut her eyes; opened them. She could feel the bitterness inside of her taking on a life of its own, and it sought an audience, to be seen, heard, and acknowledged—as if by receiving such her feelings would be validated.

"My guess is you know Palmer wiped out my family because he was a selfish bastard who drank and got behind the wheel. Yet you haven't offered any condolences or expressed any sympathy. You haven't touched on it—at all."

"I didn't think that—"

"No, you know what? It's fine. I shouldn't have…" The bite had completely left her tone, but she couldn't bring herself to continue. She felt ashamed for crossing the line. She had no right to expect anything from Trent, and she didn't need a new friend. He was her partner—temporary partner, if she had her way. It would be best to remain detached. Do the job, call it a day, start over.

"I didn't say anything about the accident because—"

"It's fine. Really. I shouldn't have brought it up. We have a job to do together, and that's what we'll do."

Even if it kills me, she thought. Then again, she didn't give a shit if it killed her because she was already dead inside.

CHAPTER ELEVEN

Trent hadn't said anything else to Amanda the rest of the way to David Morgan's apartment. It was located across town from the Nashes' place. It might not have been a long drive, but it was tense. Maybe he didn't know how to execute a conversation after her mini breakdown, and she still wasn't doing so well. So much for keeping all drama out of the investigation. At least for the most part she'd bottled it up inside. She could even blame it on having been awake for hours on end. She'd kill for a coffee.

Trent pulled them into the driveway of the apartment building, parked in a visitor spot, and said, "From what I could find out about Morgan, he lives here alone. Apartment one-ten."

She simply nodded, then got out of the car and led the way inside the building. She was the one to knock on David's door and he answered in jogging pants and a T-shirt. He was in his late twenties and his hair was mussed and sticking up at the front. He rubbed his face, and said, "Yeah?"

"Detectives Steele and Stenson with PWCPD." Amanda held up her badge. "Are you David Morgan?"

"That's me, but—" He narrowed his eyes. "I'm not sure what you want with me."

"Let us in and we'll tell you."

David danced his gaze over her, Trent, then back to her. "Sure, why not?" He stepped back and opened the door wide.

The apartment was compact, likely a one-bedroom unit, and the furnishings were the bare minimum. Right across from the door was the living room, which was a plain couch, a TV stand with a flatscreen sitting on it, and a sole coffee table. The place was tidy, but the air was stale.

"We're with the Homicide unit," she said, and David's eyes snapped to hers. Now she had his attention. "A man was found dead at Denver's about an hour before midnight."

"Really? Oh, wow." David blinked a few times, part shock, part his not being awake yet.

"His name was Chad Palmer, room ten," she put out and watched him for a reaction.

David's forehead pressed in thought, then smoothed out. "I know the guy… Well, I don't *know* him, but I brought towels to his room during my shift on Saturday."

"You did? The front desk is basically housekeeping too?" Amanda asked.

David smiled. "You've seen the place, right? My job is to tend to our customers' needs as best as I can."

"Okay," she said. "What time did Palmer call you?"

"I dunno, say five or so."

"And what do you remember about him?"

"You said you're with Homicide—" He paused there to glance over at Trent. "The guy was murdered… in the motel?"

"It's an open investigation," Trent interjected the diplomatic answer.

"Mr. Morgan, what do you remember about Mr. Palmer? How did he seem to you? Did you see him with anyone?"

"Nice guy, you could say. He thanked me for the towels, said 'please' when he called the front desk for them."

"So he called for towels because he didn't have any in his room, or needed more…?" Amanda asked.

"He was looking for a couple of extras."

"How many are provided in the room?"

"Two bath towels, two hand towels, two facecloths."

"And they're changed out every day?"

"Yeah."

Palmer had enough for himself, so what had prompted the request for more? It would seem there was only one logical explanation. "Did he have company?"

David's mouth opened, shut. He winced.

"You're not going to tell us." Her voice was more snarl than genial. She was tiring of the Denver's Motel employees' code of silence and was curious if their employee handbook directed employees not to speak with cops.

"It's not personal."

"I never assumed it was." She crossed her arms and tilted her head. "But it's because we're cops."

David chewed his bottom lip and didn't say anything, but he didn't have to. His body language confirmed she'd reached the right conclusion.

His failure to communicate was telling her more than he realized though. It would seem that David had seen someone in his room, but he just wasn't going to talk about it. She'd push a little harder. "Was it a guy or a girl?"

David avoided eye contact, and eventually said, "I'm sorry, but I need to respect our customers' privacy."

"At a place like Denver's?" she volleyed back.

"We have some standards."

"Uh-huh." She uncrossed her arms. "Did you happen to notice if there was a duffel bag or anything in the room when you delivered the towels?"

"A duffel bag?" His tone was incredulous, as if he was trying to understand what that could possibly have to do with a dead guy.

And it might not have any bearing on the case, but then again, it could. "Follow the money" was an adage for a reason.

"Yes," she said.

"I didn't go in the room, but yeah, I saw one inside the door."

If what David was telling them was the truth, then the duffel bag—and presumably the money—was stolen, went missing, or was given to someone between Saturday and Sunday. Possibly even to his mysterious Saturday visitor. "What did the bag look like?"

David's gaze flicked to Trent. "Blue with a gray stripe through it like a wave."

Trent scribbled in his notepad.

"I'm going to give this one more go, and I'd like to remind you that a man is dead," Amanda started. "Did you see anyone in his room? Notice any vehicles in the lot outside his room?"

David rubbed his jaw.

"A powder-blue sedan, perhaps?" she fed him.

His eyes met hers, and, again, he didn't need to say a word.

She handed him her business card. "If you ever feel like talking, call me."

She led the way back to the department car and once inside, Trent behind the wheel again, she said, "Morgan saw the powder-blue sedan, I'm positive. I can only assume it's the same one Lorraine Nash saw. So who does it belong to and does that person have something to do with the missing money? Whatever the case, we need to find out where it went. It seemed to have left Palmer's possession between Saturday and Sunday evening."

"Unless Palmer just left the bag in the room while he went out on Sunday." Trent looked over at her.

That possibility opened up theft, but why would anyone leave twenty-five thousand unattended—in a cheap motel no less?

"Yeah, I don't think so. Either Lorraine Nash is lying about not seeing a bag or Palmer no longer had it by Sunday afternoon when he went out."

Trent nodded.

"Regardless, we've got more questions than answers. Now, Lorraine said that the maintenance guy, Bill Hannigan, was sent to Palmer's room Sunday afternoon. Maybe he'll be able to clarify some things for us."

CHAPTER TWELVE

Lorraine Nash had told Amanda and Trent that Bill Hannigan started work at seven, and it was twenty minutes after that when Trent was parking once more in the lot of Denver's Motel. There were two cars already there, and one was a PWCPD police cruiser. Amanda didn't recognize the officer behind the wheel. Becky would have been sent home, as well as Officer Deacon.

"I'll catch up with you in a minute," she told Trent and went to talk to the officer while Trent headed toward the motel office.

The officer got out of his car as she approached, his posture straight, his chin slightly jutted out, his eyes steely. He was assessing her and trying to gauge whether she was a threat. She'd save him any more trouble. She held up her badge.

"PWCPD. Detective Steele."

His shoulders relaxed. "Officer Cooper."

"What's going on here? It's looking rather quiet."

"Everyone rushed to check out, apparently. I got an earful from the motel manager about it." Cooper shook his head. "Guy gets under your skin."

She wasn't going to argue and looked toward the office, where she could see Flynn waving his arms like mad. Case in point. "Anyone go near the room?" She nodded toward number ten.

"Absolutely not. I wouldn't have allowed it."

Trent was walking toward them, his cheeks flushed, and his nostrils flared. "Hannigan's not here. Flynn canceled everyone's shifts today and is just about to head home. The guy's fit to be tied. He's bitching that he has a quota he's to reach and it's our fault he lost all his customers."

She jacked a thumb toward Cooper. "Just heard a rendition of that. Curious though."

"About?" Cooper asked.

She glanced at him but looked at Trent when she spoke. "He's choosing to shut down the motel for the day—why? We've only cordoned off one room. He could rent the others." She flicked a finger toward Cooper. "It just proves that Denver's clientele aren't fans of cops."

"Pardon me," Cooper interjected, "but most people aren't."

She could conjure hundreds of headlines to that effect, but what would be the point? As much as people griped about the police, the world needed them—the good ones anyway. The ones that abused and soiled the badge were worse than the criminals on the street.

"All right, well, let's go to Hannigan's house." She dipped her head at Cooper to bid him goodbye, and she and Trent loaded back into the department car.

Trent logged into the onboard laptop, clicked in a search, and retrieved Hannigan's address. "What do you know? He's in town too. Just a couple of blocks over."

There was no answer at Bill Hannigan's front door, but Amanda heard clanking and banging coming from around the side of the house. She followed the sounds to a detached garage. Its door was open, and a person was bent under the hood of a classic car.

"Hello," Amanda called out.

The person, a man in his fifties, straightened out with a grunt and a hand to his lower back. "Can I help you?"

"You can if you're Mr. Bill Hannigan," she replied.

"That's me." He squinted.

Amanda held up her badge. "Detective Steele, and this is Detective Stenson."

"What can I do for ya?" He grabbed a soiled rag hanging over a side mirror.

Amanda walked around to see the top of the hood. "A '69 Camaro, and the first year Chevy offered the super scoop that was designed to enhance the power of the high-performance V8 engine. I'm going to guess this is either the SS or the Z/28 model."

"The SS. You know your cars."

"My brother had a bit of an obsession. I picked up on some of the knowledge over the years."

Bill smiled. "Good for you. A woman can do whatever she puts her mind to, just like a man."

Amanda was certain his words were well intentioned, but they still made her bristle. Probably more because the man felt the need to say them. "I'm sure you've heard by now that a man was found dead in room ten at Denver's Motel."

"I heard about it." He twisted the rag and tucked it into a back pocket of his jean coveralls. "Manager's none too happy about it. I assume you know that?"

"We do," Amanda said. "We heard you got the day off. Hence the house call."

"Lucky me, I tell ya. I was already up so I figured I've just got more time to restore this beauty." Bill paused and looked upon his car with pride.

For good reason, Amanda thought. Kyle would have killed for this car when he was younger. "We understand that you were sent to room ten on Sunday afternoon. Is that right?"

"I might need a little more information…?"

"Apparently his television was having issues," she said.

"Ah, yes." Bill rubbed the back of his neck and nodded. "It was just a couple of cables that came loose. Nothing he probably couldn't have figured out for himself if the world wasn't so damn lazy and amped up. Especially considering he said he was just wanting to pass some time."

Amped up and passing time. It would seem Palmer'd had immediate plans. "Did anyone come to his room while you were there?"

"Nope."

"Was he drinking?" Amanda asked.

"Not that I figure, and probably a good thing. He got in his car and went somewhere not long after I got into the room."

"His car?" She squeezed the question out.

"An old Caprice."

The skin tightened on the back of her neck. "The color?"

"Light blue."

"And he was driving?" All sorts of emotions were whirling through her and she couldn't pin any down except for anger.

"Yeah."

She'd somewhat come to grips with the fact that Palmer had returned to the bottle so quickly after prison—that's if he hadn't been force-fed the stuff—but it took some brass balls and demonstrated a careless and unrepentant attitude for him to drive. After all, Palmer's license had been revoked. But she tamped down her anger and focused on the case. Hannigan's insight also raised the questions of where had Palmer gotten the car and where was it now? And did the car's existence explain where the money might have gone? But then an old Caprice wouldn't have cost twenty-five grand.

Trent cleared his throat, and she glanced at him. He held his pen poised over his notepad and asked Bill, "Did you catch the license plate on the car?"

"I wish I had." Bill met Amanda's eyes, and his were soft. "What did you say the man's name was again?"

She hadn't said, but she did now. "Chad Palmer."

"I see."

She didn't care for the way he said that or for the way he was watching her like she was fragile. "Did you happen to notice if he had much in the way of luggage?"

"Kind of a strange question, isn't it? I mean considering the guy just got out of prison recently." Bill peered into her eyes.

"How did you know that?" She could barely find her voice.

"Something he said."

Amanda's heart pounded. She had a sinking feeling there was a lot more to Bill's knowledge than his intuition stitching together verbal clues. "You know who I am."

"I might, yeah."

She forced a smile. "Come on, Mr. Hannigan, be honest with me."

"I know you're the former police chief's daughter. I recognized your name when you introduced yourself. And Palmer... I know what he did to your family. Real sorry about that." He frowned. "I'm sorry I can't be more help, and had I realized then who that scumbag was, I never would have let him drive."

"You've actually given us a lot to go on." She held his gaze for a few seconds, then said, "Good day, Mr. Hannigan," and headed back down his driveway, Trent at her side.

"Good day," he called out behind her.

She should have known better than to think she could investigate Palmer's death without someone recognizing her at some point, but it certainly hadn't taken long.

CHAPTER THIRTEEN

With the interviews completed with Denver's Motel employees, Trent and Amanda's next stop would be Jerrod Rhodes, who lived in Woodbridge. She'd sit back and enjoy the ride—she could get used to being chauffeured around—but she was feeling sick after her encounter with Bill Hannigan. Sweet man, but he could destroy her career by going to the press if he were inclined. Hopefully, the bond she'd made over classic Camaros would be enough that he'd keep his realizations to himself.

Her phone pinged with a text message. It was from Rideout. She read it to herself and then shared the update with Trent. "Palmer's autopsy is happening this morning at eleven." That wasn't much notice but still gave them a couple of hours and plenty of time to speak to Rhodes.

"Are you wanting to attend?"

"Why wouldn't I?" Her darkest thoughts were focused on seeing the man dissected as a catalogue of parts—he deserved no less—but she also judged herself for thinking that way.

"Yeah, of course."

She stared at Trent's profile, just wishing for him to question her decision. *Fight with me*, she thought. If he did, maybe she could convince Malone to let her work this case solo, but that was probably foolish thinking.

Trent parked in front of a rundown duplex that was split down the middle.

"Palmer's old place is the unit on the right," he told her. "Rhodes is actually living where Palmer used to."

"Good to know. All right, let's do this." She was the first out of the car and down the walk. The advantage to tracking leads in Woodbridge was that fewer people would know her.

A sixty-something man answered the door in a cotton robe and slippers, holding a steaming cup of aromatic coffee. If her brother would have killed for a classic Camaro, she'd have done pretty much anything for a coffee at this point.

"Can I help you?" the man asked.

"You Jerrod Rhodes?" she asked, holding up her badge.

"Yeah," he dragged out.

"I'm Detective Steele"—she gestured to Trent—"and this is Detective Stenson."

"Steele, you say?" The older man peered into her eyes. "The former police chief's daughter?"

Maybe she was wrong to assume he wouldn't know her. Just as long as he didn't know her past connection with Palmer. "I am."

"Your father was a good chief. Best one the department's ever had in my opinion."

"Thanks."

Hearing this man's admiration for her father burrowed deep. He had retired not long after her accident, and though she was still talking with her family then, she'd never had the courage or emotional fortitude to ask her dad why he'd left his post. She figured she was aware of the answer—loss of motivation due to grief—and just couldn't bring herself to extend platitudes and words of comfort when she was hurting so badly herself. She probably should have stayed in the car and let Trent handle this call, but it was too late to turn back now.

"We need to ask about a former tenant, if you have a minute," she said, her words coming back to her ears as if she was presenting his talking to them as an option.

"For a Steele, I always have the time." He slurped some coffee and moved back, giving them room to enter the home. He took them to the kitchen table and sat at the one end. "Make yourself comfortable."

Amanda and Trent each took a chair, across from each other and bookending Jerrod.

Jerrod hugged his cup. "So, I'm going to guess the tenant's Chad Palmer. Am I right?"

He had to know her history. After all, he seemed up on her father's life. "Yeah, how did you—"

"Last person I rented it to before moving in myself five years ago. He went to prison and left owing three months in back rent. Don't suppose you know where I can reach him?"

How did a person in possession of twenty-five grand owe back rent? The only answer she could think of was it hadn't been Palmer's to touch.

"We're actually here because Mr. Palmer was found dead this morning," she pushed out.

"Oh." Jerrod looked up toward the ceiling and took another slurp of coffee. "The Lord works in mysterious ways."

She recoiled at the mention of the Lord. And mysterious ways? If there was a greater being, they were distant and aloof, uncaring and doing nothing to rectify the suffering of humankind.

"We're here because we're trying to piece together a bit of Mr. Palmer's life before prison. Maybe you know of someone he was close with. A girlfriend perhaps?"

Jerrod mumbled something indiscernible. "He lived with some blond tart. She wore far too much makeup if you ask me."

Including Ruby Red lipstick?

Jerrod went on. "They'd get into some doozies of arguments. He'd be drinking and fly off the handle. Not that I ever think he struck the girl—that I know of. I would have wrung his dang neck for that, but I think they threw stuff at each other."

"And how do you know all this?" Trent asked.

"I was living in the house next to this one at the time," Jerrod said. "The lady in the neighboring unit would come get me and I would come hustling over straightaway. I wasn't having them damaging my property."

"Understandable, but probably not too wise." Domestic disturbances were often the most dangerous—and unpredictable—calls a cop responded to.

"Ah, maybe not, but nothing went awry, and I never did find any damage."

"That's good at least," she said. "And the people who rented the neighboring unit?"

"Long gone now. Moved on."

She nodded. "What happened to Mr. Palmer's girlfriend after he went to jail?" It twisted her gut to demote his action to simply that when her heart continued to cry out for justice.

"I gave her the boot. Right away. I'm not anyone's banker. I'd reached my limit. Tried going after her in small claims court but got nowhere." Jerrod was getting red in the face. "And can you believe that she tried to strong-arm me into letting her stay because she claimed she was pregnant?"

Amanda gulped. It seemed so incredibly unfair to think Palmer may have had a child out there while her beautiful daughter was six feet under, and her other child would never know life outside of the womb. "With Mr. Palmer's kid?" she forced out.

"I don't know. Who knows? She probably didn't."

"Do you remember her name?" Amanda asked.

"Courtney Barrett."

"Do you know where we could reach her now?"

"Don't. Sorry."

"No, you've been a big help," she assured him.

"Anything I can do to help Chief Steele's daughter," Jerrod said as she got up.

She stopped at that, cringing. She considered her next words. "Thank you for your time, help, and discretion," she said, and she and Trent saw themselves out.

Back in the car, she stared at Jerrod's front door. Go back five-and-a-half years and Palmer had lived right there. He would have stood on that porch, walked through that door, made memories and lived a life there. She clenched her fists. He could have made a child there.

Trent looked over at her in the passenger seat. "If Palmer owed Mr. Rhodes three months' back rent, why was he carrying around twenty-five K?"

"Thought the same thing. I think it's safe to conclude that the money wasn't really Palmer's. Maybe his girlfriend can help us figure out who it really belonged to."

CHAPTER FOURTEEN

The address on file for Courtney Barrett was in Dumfries and, after a few knocks, either no one was home or no one was answering. "We'll have to try again later," Amanda said.

"And now what? We still have a little time to pass before the autopsy."

The clock read just after nine AM. It would take place thirty minutes away at the Office of the Chief Medical Examiner in Manassas. They could go back to the station and dig into the cold cases, but she was fiercely craving a coffee after spending the last twenty minutes or so smelling Jerrod Rhodes's. "Let's head toward Manassas. Better early than late, and we can get a coffee, something to eat."

"A Jabba. And I was thinking you'd never say it." He smiled.

"A Jabba?" She hooked a brow.

He laughed. "Coffee. Blame my little sister."

"I didn't know you had siblings."

Trent smiled. "It's not like you asked."

"Okay, I deserved that." She managed a small laugh, but like any expression of mirth these days, it felt shallow and void of true emotion.

"Not that you'd have a reason to ask or know. But, yeah, I have two sisters. One younger, one older. I'm the middle child."

"As I put together from 'one younger, one older.' But how did Jabba become your term for coffee?"

"Wendy was seven, and I was fourteen when I started drinking coffee."

There was quite a gap between the siblings. There was a fourteen-year span between all her siblings, but the largest existed between her and her older brother Kyle, who was four years older. "You started drinking coffee at fourteen? And I thought I had an addiction."

"I think all cops are coffee addicts."

She bobbed her head. "I can get behind that. Go on."

"She was seven, as I said, but already a movie lover with an affinity for sci-fi. She loved the old *Star Wars* movies and watched them repeatedly—back to back."

"Ah, Jabba the Hut, and sorry to hear that… about the back-to-back thing." It was bad enough that Kevin had insisted they watch the original three movies once a year at Christmas.

Trent smirked. "It's not that they're bad movies, and they have quite a following, but over and over? Anyway, one day Wendy tattled on me to our parents and said, 'Trent drinks Jabba.'" He laughed. "My parents figured out what she meant was *java*, not Jabba, and grounded my butt for a week."

"Sounds like you have strict parents. And you could have done a lot worse than drink coffee." She wasn't going to dredge up all the things she'd done behind her parents' backs. Sneaking out of the house to meet up with a boy, drinking in the woods, tipping cows in farmers' fields—not an urban legend but also not the nicest thing to do upon reflection—and those acts of tomfoolery and defiance just scraped the surface.

"It didn't feel like it at the time." He turned serious and glanced over at her as he slowed at a yellow light. "Seeing that disappointment in their faces destroyed me."

"Obviously that effect wasn't long-lasting," she said.

He smiled and shook his head. "Well, I still can't drink the stuff without thinking of Jabba the Hutt."

She narrowed her eyes. "You're a strange one, Detective Stenson."

"Thanks. I'll wear that compliment with pride. It certainly beats normal."

"What the heck is normal anyway?" she countered.

"Precisely."

"All righty then, let's go get a Jabba."

He started them down the road toward Manassas.

What her new partner didn't know was their light, jovial conversation had riddled her with pain—not just at the memory of an annual ritual with Kevin—but she was stabbed with the recollection of how close she'd been previously to her five siblings. The six of them had been more than blood; they'd been the best of friends. But now, because of what Palmer had done, the toll he'd taken on her soul, she'd created a chasm between herself and all of them. Each of them had tried reaching out to her several times after she'd worked to withdraw herself, but after she continuously shuffled them to voicemail or sloughed off their invitations, they had given up. She couldn't blame them, but she also had to stop blaming herself. If only it was as easy as simply deciding how to feel about something and *poof* that's how it was.

CHAPTER FIFTEEN

There was always something about seeing a body on a metal slab that made death seem more final, not that Amanda could define why. Regardless, she had mixed feelings as to how she'd feel upon seeing Palmer's body draped with a white sheet. It had her breathing shallow and her skin clammy.

"I wasn't sure if you were going to turn up for the autopsy or not." Rideout was all chipper for standing in a smock readying to perform what was essentially a dissection of a once-living, breathing, human being.

"Oh…" She put her hand over her back pocket where her phone was. "Sorry, I should have texted to let you know." She normally did but she was starting to realize nothing was "normal" about this case. It had her feeling more scatterbrained than was her usual since the accident. She kept thinking about Hannigan and Rhodes and how they'd known who she was and the connection between her and Palmer, the victim. She could be on borrowed time with this case.

"Trent, is this your first time attending an autopsy?" Rideout asked.

Trent nodded.

"Really?" Amanda asked, surprised. He was new to being a detective, not to being a cop.

He pressed his lips together and shrugged.

"Huh," was all she said, but maybe if she were him, she wouldn't have told her either for fear of being berated or judged. She was surprised, though, that he'd made it to detective without attending one.

"Well, a lot of people can't stomach this," Rideout chimed in, "but it's part of the circle of life—at least for those less fortunate. I won't get into when an autopsy is necessary and when one isn't." He grinned and waved a hand. "Maybe when I have some time though."

No one could say Rideout was rigid and all business. He obviously loved his job and took pride in sharing his knowledge. "I'm pretty sure Trent knows what necessitates an autopsy…" She glanced at Trent.

"I do," he said.

"Swell then." Rideout rubbed his hands together. "Now, I'd already conducted a preliminary investigation of the body before you got here, and I have found some things of interest." Rideout snapped on gloves and pulled back the sheet to Palmer's waist, exposing his naked torso.

She was staring into the face that had haunted her nightmares, her waking thoughts, her memories and now it stalked her present reality. In her mind it had always been a face of destruction, of evil. Here in death it was more a reflection of calm, peace, and serenity. Similar to how she'd felt at the motel when she first saw him, Palmer appeared vulnerable, more man than monster, but looks could be deceiving.

"Detective?" Rideout prompted.

"Ah, yes?" Amanda looked up to meet Rideout's eyes.

"You all right?"

"I'm fine."

Rideout didn't say anything for a few beats and Trent was so still beside her she wondered if he was breathing.

"Sorry, go ahead," she said with a limp smile.

"As I was about to show you…" Rideout pointed to some light discoloration at the base of Palmer's throat. "I didn't notice this at the scene. In fact, I didn't see them in any pictures that were taken, but in cases where tissue is damaged closer to the time of death, contusions can surface afterward."

Amanda angled her head, focusing on Palmer's neck, trying to tell herself the entire time it was someone else's body. "Someone strangled him?"

"Restrained him with force at least. Then there's this." Rideout lifted Palmer's left hand and traced a bruise that circled his wrist. "Both wrists are like this, as are his ankles."

"He was bound," Trent said, barely above a whisper. "But with what?" Trent leaned in closer to the cadaver, showing he had no issue with being around the dead.

"Your guess would be as good as mine. The markings are not distinguishing enough to make a firm conclusion, but I'd hypothesize it was something narrow and rigid."

"Zip-ties?" Trent suggested. "They're easy to come by from any hardware store."

"Kidnap/murder kit one-o-one," Amanda said drily. She noted her internal conflict.

Rideout proceeded to turn Palmer onto his side. "As you can see, livor mortis is present in his shoulder blades, lower back, and it continues down to his buttocks."

In layman's terms, livor mortis was the process of blood settling in the lowest parts of the body upon death. It could tell a lot about the position in which a person had died and disclose whether they had been moved some time after death.

"He died in that bed, or lying down anyhow," Trent said, impressing both her and the ME.

"Bravo. But look at this." Rideout pointed to faint vertical bruises on Palmer's back. "I had CSI Donnelly return to Denver's and check the spacing between the spindles on the chairs in the room. Based on her measurements, I feel confident in saying that he was probably bound to one of them."

A small dining table with two spindle-back chairs, both tucked in like they were never used…

Rideout added, "Everything in that room was staged—Palmer, the bottles, the open curtains, the TV being on—to make it look like he just accidently drank himself to death."

Amanda shivered, suddenly colder than she ever remembered being in her life. "So alcohol overdose was the cause of death?"

"More precisely, aspiration caused by ethanol poisoning, as I said on scene. Only I think someone forced the alcohol on him. And that means you're looking for a determined, yet controlled and patient killer." He paused and leveled a meaningful eye on her. "It could be someone affected by his drinking to choose this method to kill too."

The coffee she'd drunk before going there rushed up her throat, and she clamped a hand over her mouth and swallowed roughly. "I've gotta— I've gotta go."

"Wait," Rideout called out. "Aren't you staying for the autopsy?"

She waved a hand over her head. "I've got all I need for now."

"Amanda," Trent called out behind her as his footsteps slapped the linoleum floor. "You all right?"

She kept hustling. She wasn't all right by a long shot. Palmer's death was starting to feel very personal.

CHAPTER SIXTEEN

Amanda's body was dragging but her mind was still sharp. As a cop you either adapted to long hours without sleep or you found another career. She had to get her alibi in order, and she had to get it now. Palmer had destroyed her life five and a half years ago and it seemed he was back to stomp out any embers. She waited by the passenger door of the department car for Trent to unlock the doors. He didn't say anything to her as he got in and silence spanned between them for several minutes before Trent spoke.

"Guess we know it was murder now," he said, likely believing that he was treading on neutral ground.

"Right, but you heard the murder method?" She turned on him, her entire body quaking. Somehow having the MO confirmed out loud by the medical examiner had stamped it further home.

"I did… Not sure—"

"Let me lay it out for you. After the accident, all I wanted was Palmer dead. I fantasized about taking him out." She paused there and scanned Trent's eyes for disgust, judgment, shock, but none of those emotions were present. She shot out, "I thought of doing exactly what happened to him."

"You're obviously not the only one," Trent volleyed back.

Not the only one… His words jarred a memory loose. "When I was healing from the accident, my father and I dug up whatever dirt we could on Palmer. You know, to supply to the prosecution to establish his character and typical conduct. My dad tracked someone down whose son had been friends with Palmer as a teenager. They were both sixteen when the car his son was driving lost control and veered off the road. His son became a quadriplegic. Palmer walked away with barely a scratch. But the father of this boy told my dad he was quite certain that Palmer had been driving, despite evidence to the contrary. He said he never liked his son hanging around Palmer."

"Maybe we should pay him a visit."

"Sounds like a good idea, but there's something I'd like to take care of first."

"Name it."

"My alibi."

"But you didn't kill him," Trent said gingerly.

"Of course I didn't— if that was a question."

"It wasn't. Besides, I can't imagine anyone thinking you killed Palmer. You're a good person—a cop at that."

"I don't know about that." If only her rookie partner had any idea of the hedonistic murder methods that she had fantasized about closer to the time of the accident and after Palmer's lame sentence hit. Her mind skipped to the Xanax in her coat pocket. Why hadn't she taken one yet? Hadn't she already done the worst of it just by scoring them from a drug dealer and thereby putting her career in jeopardy? She was busy with the case, sure, but she was also procrastinating, rethinking whether she really wanted to get hooked. Because once she was back on them, she wasn't sure she'd have the willpower to stop again.

"So tell me where I'm taking us."

"Us?"

"I'm your partner and I want to help."

"Fine." She went on to tell him about picking up Motel Guy at a bar.

"Okay, we'll pop by the bar. Which one is it?"

"Tipsy Moose Ale House in Woodbridge. Thinking I'll just go in and flash my badge."

"Sure, because we've seen firsthand how it gets people to open up."

"Mr. Sarcastic." She found herself smiling. "Okay, then, how would you suggest I handle things?"

He put the car into gear and said, "I'll tell you on the way."

If the Tipsy Moose Ale House was a sad-looking sight at night with its dim lighting, beer-soaked tables, and peanut-shell-covered floors, then during the day it was downright pitiful. Diffused sunlight came through the slimy windows and sparkled off floating dust particles in the air.

Amanda glanced around. No sign of the waitress from last night. Amanda went straight to the bar where a male tender was wiping out the inside of a glass with a towel. She'd never seen this man before, but she didn't make a habit of coming in during the daylight hours.

"Good day, darlin'," he said.

"Hi." She smiled at him and coyly tucked a strand of hair behind an ear. Act flirtatious but give the impression she was just out of reach. She'd become the mystery a man wanted to solve, but as Trent pointed out, men also wanted to help a damsel in distress. She'd be working to take advantage of that psychology—even though she despised playing the role.

He grinned, flashing a couple of dimples, put down the glass and braced both of his hands on the counter. "What can I get ya?"

"I was actually hoping you could help me with something." She started to sit on a stool but bounced back up. "Actually, ah, you know what? I should go. It would be too much to ask of you."

"No—" He reached out to stop her. "Why don't you try me? You can talk to Bud."

"And you're Bud?" She flashed another smile.

"I'm Bud," he affirmed.

"This is probably dumb…"

"Talk to me."

"I was in here last night with my boyfriend."

"Were ya now?" A flicker of disappointment crested over his face.

"Uh-huh. He's the rugged type, calloused hands, strong, blond." As she rattled off Motel Guy's attributes, she became turned on again. No wonder she'd succumbed to the guy's charms.

"That could describe a lot of us." Bud stood taller and laid a hand on his chest. He was a good-looking man, but too cocky and arrogant for her liking.

"Yes, but now don't take this wrong way, he is younger."

Bud covered his heart with both hands. But he quickly recovered from any feigned insult and smirked. "Just more experienced in the ways of pleasuring a—"

"I'm sure, but I need to find this guy…"

"Your boyfriend?"

"Yeah, my boyfriend." She'd messed up but hopefully recovered fast enough.

"I see."

"I haven't been able to reach him and it's real important that I do." Amanda put a hand on her stomach, and with the motion, the fabrication she was spinning made her physically ill. She recalled Lindsey moving inside of her and how it had felt like the fluttering of a butterfly's wings. When Trent had suggested that she act as if Motel Guy had been a boyfriend she couldn't reach and that she was knocked up, her mind had strictly been on securing her alibi. A means to an end.

"Oh… *Ooooh*." Bud stood up and crossed his arms. "Well, I'm not sure how I can get a hold of him."

"I think he— I mean, he likes to come here and have a beer or two." That latter part was the truth; she'd seen Motel Guy here on a few occasions. Last night they'd just advanced from their winks and smiles from across the room.

"Huh. I'd like to help but…" He rubbed his chin and looked around the bar.

"You can." She perked up. "Just if you see him, could you call me?"

"Sure. Give me your number and I can have him call you." He bobbed his eyebrows.

"You're a devil. You're just eager to get my number."

"Not gonna lie."

"I have a bun in the oven." She made a sulky face, but what was wrong with this guy hitting on a pregnant woman? "It would mean a lot to me if you could call me if you see him. Then I'll come back here."

"I might need a little more description."

Amanda pried her memories and inhaled deeply. "He smells like a campfire." *He knows how to trace his hands over—*

"A campfire? Do you expect me to sniff him?"

She giggled. "Yeah, I guess that's nuts."

"Just a little."

"He often wears this black leather jacket that's seen better days. It's a little worn around the hem and cuffs."

"Oh, yeah, I think I know who you're talking about."

She waited him out, hoping he'd say a name, but he didn't. "Good," she eventually said.

"He likes his draft beer."

"Sounds like we're talking about the same guy. That's good that you know him." She couldn't exactly ask his name given her shtick, but if only his first name slipped out then she could cross-reference it with black Dodge Ram pickups in the area.

"Well, I don't *know* him, but I've seen him. But go ahead, write your name and number down and I'll call you next time I see him." Bud plucked a square napkin from behind the counter and placed it in front of her with a pen.

"Great. You're a lifesaver." She scribbled down her first name and number, realizing she was breaking the primary rule of one-night stands, but she had no choice.

CHAPTER SEVENTEEN

Amanda returned to the car where Trent was tapping on the wheel to some song on the radio. She could hear it filtering out into the parking lot. She couldn't pin down the tune, but if she had to guess, she'd say it was country music. He turned it off as she got into the passenger seat.

"He's going to call," she said, lacking all enthusiasm and hope that her little ruse would actually pay off.

"So the damsel-in-distress routine worked?" Trent smiled at her. He either didn't pick up on her pessimism or didn't want to poke it and get into an argument.

"Like a charm." This time she tried to infuse her voice with optimism, but she'd love nothing better than to pop one of the Xanax in her pocket. She hadn't been feeling good ever since she'd first laid her hand on her stomach and the memories of being pregnant had come hurtling back—and dragged the memories of her sweet little Lindsey's face along with them.

"Men usually can't resist coming to the rescue."

"Yeah, base creatures," she plugged, hardly believing the bartender had continued to hit on her once he'd thought she was pregnant. What a creep.

"We consider ourselves wise creatures."

Kevin had certainly loved giving advice, even when she didn't want to hear it. Sometimes a person just needed to vent. "Uh-huh. Well, wise creature, we should try Courtney Barrett again."

"Oh, yes, we should, but you'd like to know, while you were in the bar, I got Palmer's visitor list from the prison and the list of items he was booked with. I forwarded the emails to you, so you have a copy of each."

She pulled out her phone and brought up her email app and watched as they filtered into her inbox. She first opened the attachment with the item list.

Duffel bag—Blue, gray stripe

Cash—25K

Wallet—leather with ID and misc. papers cards and such, $30 in bills and change

Jacket—Jean, Men's Large

Belt—Leather

Keyring—two keys for house and one for vehicle (Honda HR-V)

Bracelet—Silver chain

She looked over at Trent. "Did the investigators recover a bracelet?"

"I don't think so."

She pulled out her phone and called the forensics lab and was patched through.

"Emma Blair here."

Amanda cringed at the sound of the investigator's voice. Apparently, it had been too much to hope CSI Donnelly would have answered. "This is Detective Steele." She paused expecting that the CSI would interject with some expression of recognition, but nada. Amanda continued. "I was at the Palmer crime scene this morning."

"I know who you are. What can I do for you, Detective?"

Chilly. Amanda pushed on. "Did you or CSI Donnelly happen to recover a silver bracelet from the victim's possessions?"

"No."

"You're certain? You don't want to go check—"

"I assure you that I am well aware of all the personal effects that were collected from the motel room, and there wasn't a bracelet among them."

"Okay then."

The line went dead.

Amanda was left holding her phone, a little in shock. "She's such a sweetheart."

Trent laughed. "Let me guess: you spoke to the senior CSI from the scene."

"What gave it away?"

Trent pointed to her phone. "She hung up on you?"

"She's a charmer," Amanda lamented. "But she did confirm—or at least seemed confident—that there was no silver bracelet recovered from the scene."

"That's interesting," Trent said. "There's no sign of the bag or the cash, and now the bracelet is missing. Was it of value too?"

"A regular silver bracelet, probably not too much, maybe a couple of hundred dollars." She had to admit, though, it was "interesting" just as Trent had said.

She returned to her email app to glance over the visitor list. It was organized in reverse chronological order and the oldest visits on record had her full attention. "Courtney Barrett and Jackson Webb."

"Yep. I noticed. Barrett about a week after sentencing and Webb a couple of days afterward, one day before his murder."

"And when were you going to tell me?"

"I thought that you'd— I figured you'd see it yourself, and you did," he added at a softer volume. He cleared his throat and added, "Courtney Barrett also returned to visit Palmer a couple of weeks ago."

"And that's all? Just the two visits?"

"All I could see running down."

"Huh. Doesn't sound like a warm relationship to me. Makes me wonder though if she showed up at the start of Palmer's sentence looking for the money. Webb, too, possibly if his and Palmer's murders are connected."

"Thought the same. To Courtney?"

"Yep." It was certainly too late to talk to Webb…

CHAPTER EIGHTEEN

Courtney Barrett's house still looked dark and asleep and it was going on mid-afternoon. Amanda knocked for the third time, stubbornly refusing to accept no one was home. Perseverance paid off and footsteps padded toward the door, and shortly thereafter it was swung open.

"What is it?" a woman barked. All wild eyes, wild hair, wild energy.

Amanda held up her badge. "Prince William County Police Department." She added, "We're looking to speak with Courtney Barrett," though she was quite sure she was looking right at her, and she was the woman with Palmer in that photo from his wallet.

Courtney sighed. "That's me, but I don't have time for this right now. I—"

"Mom!" A young boy of about five came running toward the door—the image of Palmer. Same nose, lips, shape of face.

Amanda's legs buckled. Trent reached out to her, but she waved him off.

"Get your shoes on. Now!" Courtney barked at her kid.

"I don't wanna go." The boy dropped to the entry floor and crossed his arms and sulked.

Amanda had a hard time taking her eyes off the kid. Hurt was swelling in her chest. The unfairness of it all that Palmer had a living, breathing child while hers were—

"This really isn't a good time." Courtney started to run a hand through her hair but stopped at the crown and dropped her hand. Just a guess but it was probably too full of knots to get her fingers through.

"Ah," Trent started, and Amanda saw him glancing at her in her peripheral. "We won't take much of your time," Trent eventually pushed out.

Courtney scowled. "What's this about?"

"We have something important to tell you," Trent said. "Could we come in?"

Courtney eyeballed him, appearing somber for the first time since she'd answered the door. "I don't have long, but if you keep it quick." She shooed the boy, and he inched across the floor.

"You'll have to excuse him," Courtney said. "He's not good with company."

Amanda could say the same thing about Courtney, but her issue was probably more with cops on her doorstep than people in general.

"Justin, go play in your room. For now. But then we've got to go."

The boy glared at his mother but relinquished his spot on the floor and ran off down a hallway, yelling, "Yay!"

"Is there somewhere we can sit?" Trent asked.

Courtney showed them to a living area that was part war zone; children's toys were scattered everywhere.

Amanda moved a plastic solider off a couch cushion and sat down. She felt like she was observing from a distance and not really there. Her mind was preoccupied with that little boy—Palmer's little boy.

Trent sat next to Amanda and looked at her as if asking whether she wanted him to handle the notification.

She jumped in. "I'm here to tell you that Chad Palmer was found dead this morning in a room at Denver's Motel here in Dumfries."

Courtney dropped into a chair. "He was— You're kidding right?" She glanced at Trent, back to Amanda.

"I'm sorry, but no." Amanda pressed her lips together and crossed her legs. Normally she'd deliver such news with more finesse and feeling, but in this situation, she had none to offer.

"Well... uh... what happened to him?" Courtney's voice cracked, but no tears sprang to her eyes.

"He was murdered," Amanda deadpanned.

"Someone killed him," Courtney mumbled; she seemed about as devoid of emotion as Amanda was. Could be shock, could be something else. She also didn't give Amanda the impression the news came as a real surprise.

"Was he shot?" Courtney asked stiffly.

Amanda shook her head and studied the other woman. "Why would you think he was shot?" she asked, though she had an inkling as to the reason she'd leaped there.

Courtney's eyes flicked to hers. "You really don't know? His former business partner was shot, murdered, around the time Chad went to prison. I don't think police ever figured out who killed him. You could look up his file, I'm sure."

"Yes, we know Mr. Webb." Amanda watched Courtney as she worried her lip and bounced her legs. "Do *you* have an idea who killed him?"

"Doubt any of my suspicions matter, Detective."

"Try us, and we'll determine whether they do."

Courtney shook her head.

"Mr. Webb's murder was connected to a woman killed in Georgia." Amanda watched Courtney for any tells. Nada. "We believe she originated from Dumfries or Prince William County. Her name was Casey-Anne Ritter. Did you know her?"

"Never heard of her." Courtney's answer was quick, but she met Amanda's eyes. It would seem she was telling the truth, but Amanda still had to push.

"We're trying to figure out what happened to Chad, and anything you can tell us would be of help." A guilt trip often worked to get people tapping into their humanity and opening up, and maybe if Amanda put emphasis on someone more personal to Courtney, she'd be more compelled to talk.

"I don't owe him anything," Courtney hissed.

"Not even as the father of your child?" Amanda slapped back, and it had Courtney narrowing her eyes.

"Are you sure you don't have any names that come to mind?" Trent interjected, pulling out his notepad and pen. "People who might have wanted to harm Mr. Webb and/or Mr. Palmer?"

Courtney bit her bottom lip and shook her head. "I'm not snitching to cops."

Amanda glanced at Trent; she was going to try another tack. "Chad had twenty-five grand on his person when he was arrested."

Courtney's eyes flicked to hers.

Amanda went on. "Do you know why he had all that money?"

Courtney sat up straighter, but her body language was rigid. She had knowledge of the cash.

"Why did he have all that money?" Amanda prompted. "I'm quite sure you know."

"It's none of your business."

"It may be quite pertinent to the case, and it's missing," Amanda punched out.

Courtney visibly swallowed. "It's—it's…"

"Yep. Any idea where it might have gone?"

Courtney tugged on the hem of her shirt. "He owed it to someone, but that's all I'm gonna say."

"Was it this someone who came looking for it and ended up murdering Jackson Webb when he didn't have it?" Amanda asked.

"Your guess would be as good as mine." Courtney jutted out her chin, but her voice wavered.

"You're afraid of whoever he owed the money to," Amanda concluded, not a question in her mind.

"I just need to move on with my life."

"We know that you visited Chad a week after he was sentenced," Amanda began. "Did you visit him to follow up on the money?"

Courtney remained silent.

Her non-answer was enough of an answer for Amanda. "When did you see him last?" She was aware of the visit from a couple of weeks ago but was curious what would surface.

"Two weeks ago, give or take."

"Were you still interested in the money?" Trent interjected and warranted Courtney's gaze.

Slowly Courtney looked at Amanda. "He told me he'd take care of things when he got out."

"And did he?" Amanda asked.

"You can't find the money and I'm still alive, so, yeah, I guess he did."

Amanda studied Courtney. She obviously assessed Palmer's creditor to be dangerous—even life-threatening—and she wasn't giving them a name. She'd try to play it from another angle. "Aren't you worried this person Chad owed money to might come after your son?"

Courtney looked away and rubbed her arms.

Amanda stared blankly at Courtney, hoping the silence and eye contact would be enough to get her to speak.

"I'm pretty sure everything is fine now."

Amanda lifted her shoulders. "Sounding more confident than a second ago. Did Chad tell you he paid off whoever it was he owed?" She hated not having a name to work with.

"No."

"So you haven't been in contact since his release? I find that hard to believe given that Justin's his son."

"Nah, you don't get to come here with that. And you have no right to bring up Justin again. Chad didn't even know about him.

I kept it from him. What good would it do anyway? Not like he was around to be a dad."

"Still, Chad never came over after getting out last Friday?" Amanda was skeptical the lovers wouldn't have reunited, but, then again, it's not like she'd visited him a lot in prison. There was also the request Palmer had made for additional towels niggling at the edge of her mind.

"He doesn't know where I live now. Or, I guess, *didn't* know. I just can't believe he's gone."

Amanda wasn't about to let herself get waylaid or dragged down with empathy for this woman; she couldn't find the emotion in her to tap into regardless. "And you never met up with him at Denver's Motel?"

"What part of what I'm saying don't you understand? Last time I saw him was two weeks ago."

"I'm pretty sure that you have your reasons for not telling us who you suspect of Jackson's and Chad's murders," Amanda began, "but if Chad was mixed up in something, and we're looking at the same killer here, what's to say they won't come for you next? Talk to us, and we can help you," Amanda appealed.

Courtney pinched her eyes shut for a moment, opened them, sighed. "Fine. Jackson and Chad fenced stolen goods through their pawnshop. You happy now?"

"Who did he fence for?" Amanda ignored Courtney's snide remark, not surprised by what she'd just told them. Pawnshops made great fronts for criminal activity. Stolen goods were turned in and bought at a fraction of what they were worth and turned around and sold at a hefty profit. Inventory sometimes hit the books, sometimes it didn't.

"I told the cops back when Jackson was murdered that I had nothing to say." Tears brimmed in her eyes. "And it kept Justin and me safe. It also protected Chad. I didn't want to make his situation any worse."

Amanda clenched her fists. She had no idea what a "bad situation" was by comparison to what Amanda had lost. "Who did they fence the goods for?" Amanda said through gritted teeth.

Courtney's gaze dashed to Trent, then back to Amanda. "Some guy who goes by Freddy."

"Freddy," the name scratched her throat upon exit.

"Yeah."

Freddy, the drug dealer and apparently a thief. Freddy, who knew she was a cop and had her personal license plate and make and model of her car. Freddy, who could destroy the rest of what she had left to lose. That same Freddy could be behind the murders of Webb, Palmer, and that girl in Georgia. Bile shot up Amanda's throat almost faster than she could swallow it back down.

CHAPTER NINETEEN

"Unlock the car," she barked at Trent and she heard the distinct clicks in the department car's handles. She got behind the wheel and said to him, "Hurry up, and get in." She just needed him close by with the keys and the ignition would turn.

"Everything all right?" Trent spaced out his words slowly and methodically.

Everything was far from all right, but she couldn't tell him that. She had to deal with this on her own, like she'd dealt with all the crap that had come her way in the last five and a half years.

"If you know this Freddy character," Trent began, "we could bring him up in the system and show his picture to Lorraine. Maybe he's who she saw Palmer with on Sunday night? Just a possibility."

"Freddy's a no-good lowlife. He has a record for drug dealing, though I doubt that comprises his entire criminal portfolio. Now we have Courtney Barrett telling us he's involved with stolen goods. You should also know that Freddy's friend, Rat, was questioned during the course of a homicide investigation years ago. But as a witness not a suspect."

"Still confirms the world this Freddy guy's a part of, and with that sort of knowledge on the street, it could explain why the Denver's Motel employees aren't talking. They're afraid. And we know from Courtney that Palmer could have very well owed that cash to Freddy. She seemed fearful."

"Yeah, but the fact that Palmer planned on hanging around for at least a month—given how long he rented his room at the motel—tells me he settled his debt with Freddy. That's probably what happened to the twenty-five K. But if Palmer paid Freddy, where's his motivation to kill him, and if Freddy also killed Webb and Casey-Anne—we know the same gun was used—what would be his motive there?"

There was a passage of silence.

Amanda's thoughts were skipping from the recent slip that had brought her to Freddy's door to the possible repercussions, but she was also thinking about a connection. The pawnshops for the partners, but Casey-Anne… Then it struck. "You said you couldn't find any Casey-Anne Ritters in the area."

Trent nodded.

"Maybe that's because she didn't want to be found. And, if that was the case, what would that tell you?"

"That she might have been on the run and hiding from someone," he suggested, but the lack of enthusiasm in his voice told her he hadn't stitched together the full impact of that conclusion. "Freddy?"

"Not so sure, but… and this is just a theory. But Webb and Palmer ran a pawnshop, and what does anyone on the run need?"

"Money."

"Right. So let's assume for a second this Casey-Anne didn't have any. What would she do?"

Trent's forehead pressed in thought. "She could have pawned something for money."

"Right, and maybe whatever that was hadn't been hers to turn over and the real owner wanted his property back."

"Freddy's, though?"

"Guess there's only one way to find out."

Trent looked from her to the steering wheel, back to her. "Are we going to go pay him a visit?"

"Actually…" She wasn't ready to show up at Freddy's door, and depending on how things panned out with him, she might never need to. She could delegate that while she explored another avenue. "Why don't you go talk to Freddy, feel him out, and I'll go talk to the father of that boy. We'll cover more ground that way." She might not be able to put off questioning Freddy forever, but she would delay it for as long as she could.

Trent's brow bunched down for a second. "Ah, sure, no problem. I could also swing by the Nashes and see if Lorraine can ID Freddy from a picture. She might be able to say if he was the one with Palmer."

"Good luck on that one, but, yeah, not a bad idea. When you're talking to Freddy, make sure to bring up Casey-Anne and gauge his reaction to her."

"Will do."

"Also, when you're at his house, question his friend, Rat, real name Damien Rodriguez." She just put the car into gear when her phone rang. She put it back in park. Caller ID told her it was Malone. She answered reluctantly.

"Detective Steele," she answered.

"Formal. I like it, but you had to know it was me. I just heard from the ME's office that Palmer's death was a murder."

"Yeah."

"I assume you have your alibi?"

She cringed. She knew it had been a bad idea to answer her phone. "I'm working on it."

A few seconds of silence, then Malone said, "I need more than 'working on it.'"

"That's all I got right now."

"Where are you?" Malone's question on the surface was a redirect, but he had asked for a reason.

"Headed back to the station." Once there, she and Trent would sign out a second department car and go their separate ways.

"Good. I'd like to talk face to face."

A warm flush shot through her and she glanced over at Trent who was watching her. "Sounds omin—"

"Don't give it too much thought. Just come straight to my office. Alone."

"Okay."

Malone was gone before she could say, "Goodbye."

"That Sergeant Malone?" Trent asked.

"Yep. You clairvoyant now?"

"That's my older sister," he deadpanned.

She faced him. "Are you being serious?"

He smiled and bobbed his head side to side. "She likes to think she is anyway. Me? I don't really buy into all of that."

"Huh." She regarded him a little longer. Trent was interesting and a bit of an enigma.

"Lieutenant Hill's pleased you've finally been paired with a partner. How's it going anyhow?" Malone sat back in his chair and it creaked beneath him. Amanda was seated across from him in a single visitor chair in his office at Central District. It was a small, yet adequate space. He had a steel and laminate manager's desk and a long filing cabinet that ran along the one wall and did double duties as a credenza. On top were a few framed photographs—one of him and his wife; one of their two boys; and one of the family on a trip down south. Hawaii, if Amanda remembered right. The walls were painted a rich, deep blue—somewhere between blueberry and midnight navy, and a window across from his desk looked over the woods at the back of the station. His entire office was organized, and everything had its spot.

She should have known that it was Hill who'd insisted she have a partner. "Does she know—"

"That you're working the Palmer investigation in any capacity?" Malone cut her off. "Not as long as I can help it."

"She'd probably take pleasure in knowing that I'm reporting to a rookie." The statement came out with a little more zing than she'd intended.

"That can be rectified," he snapped back.

"I'm sorry."

"I should say so." Malone clasped his hands in his lap. "So the word just came in from the medical examiner's office. Palmer was force-fed alcohol and killed as a result."

"That's what I was told."

He peered into her eyes. "You know how this might look?"

"I know how it could be construed."

"And I'm pretty sure you know what I need... Just so we're in front of this."

Amanda gripped the arms of the chair. "My alibi. As you said on the phone."

"Bingo."

"There are a couple of leads Trent and I intend to follow. One is a man whose son was in a car accident with Palmer as a teen."

Malone leaned forward, put elbows on desk. "Ah, yes, I remember. The father's name was Albert Ferguson if I remember right."

No one could claim Malone had a poor memory. "That's him, and did you happen to know that Palmer's business partner was murdered... not long after Palmer's arrest?"

"I did." He squinted as if not sure where she was headed.

"What about Casey-Anne Ritter from Georgia?"

"Yeah. It was connected to Webb's." He angled his head and studied her eyes. "You think the same killer is back?"

She shrugged. "Why not? It's a possibility we haven't ruled out."

"Yeah, you have to exhaust every angle."

A fact she was very aware of, but she wasn't going to point that out to Malone and risk offending him.

Malone continued. "I've spoken to the forensics lab and have asked that everything related to this case is rushed through. You should also be getting a list of items deemed evidence before the end of the day. Obviously any DNA evidence may take longer to process, but you should have a good springboard to start with."

"Thank you. We've also become aware that Palmer was in possession of a large amount of cash at the time of the accident—"

Malone shuffled and sat up straighter, but his gaze drifted to the top of his desk. "Always follow the money."

"Intend to. If we can find it."

"It's missing?"

"Seems to be. Can't be accounted for anyhow." This would be the perfect time to name Freddy, but she couldn't bring herself to come out with it. Somehow verbalizing him to her sergeant made the nightmare and her regrettable decision that much more real.

"We were told by Palmer's old girlfriend that Palmer and his partner fenced stolen goods at their pawnshop."

"Huh." Malone studied her face. "This missing money could have been owed to someone then."

She nodded. "What we're thinking." She glanced away; looking at him in the eye and withholding from him was torturing her conscience.

"This money could have gotten Palmer's partner killed and Palmer."

"That's if Palmer didn't pay off his debt. It seemed he intended to stick around."

"Do you think Palmer's murder is connected to both cold cases? Truly?"

"I think it's far too soon to dismiss the possibility."

Malone leaned back in his chair again, a flicker of angst dancing across his face. "This could get out of control fast. I can't stress enough how important it is that you get out in front of this. Just in case his murder doesn't link to the cold cases beyond his previous relationship with Webb."

"I know."

"Certainly not settling my stomach. And lots of people could have wanted Palmer dead because of his drinking."

She could barely bring herself to nod and hated that the conversation had circled back to this point.

"I don't have to tell you what small towns are like and how they like to talk."

"Just about as bad as police departments." She tossed that in, in an attempt at lightening the air, but it didn't come close to working.

"Keeping your name and connection with Palmer out of the news is going to be an uphill battle." He sighed. "You are being careful?"

"Yeah." She lowered in her chair, if only slightly. She'd already been recognized by a couple of people as she and Trent had made their rounds, but she sure as hell wasn't confessing that much to Malone.

Whether Malone missed her subtle body language or chose to ignore it, he said, "Regardless of what way this case turns—isolated incident or number three in a string of murders—I won't be able to keep Lieutenant Hill out of this forever. You know what she's like."

"How she likes to put her nose into everything. Yep, I know."

"Especially when it comes to you."

Amanda's hunch that the lieutenant held a vendetta against her was confirmed yet again. "Joy. She's always been more concerned about her public image than the department's."

"Yeah, well, if this blows up, it will be both images that suffer and I know you care about that. The latter one anyhow."

She tried to muster the zeal to protect the department she represented, but ever since the accident, her enthusiasm just wasn't there anymore. She was more going through the motions than she was any crusader for justice.

"You do?" he stressed.

"Yeah."

"I'll accept that, but a tad more enthusiasm would be nice." He paused as if he expected her to intercept but she remained silent. He went on. "Okay, then. May I suggest—for your own good—get that alibi yesterday and follow the money as I said, but I also think talking to Ferguson would be wise."

"He's my next stop."

"*Your* next stop?"

It was too late to retreat from her slip that she'd be on her own. She opened her mouth to defend herself, then shut it.

"You can't be doing solo interviews, Amanda. What if someone recognizes you? Tell me you haven't branched out on your own."

She could argue that with Trent by her side she had been recognized, but that wouldn't help her cause.

Malone narrowed his eyes. "Where's Trent?"

"Following a lead."

"Oh Lord." Malone massaged his left temple. "I feel a headache coming on."

"He'll be fine, trust me."

Malone opened a desk drawer and withdrew a bottle of ibuprofen. He popped a couple into his mouth and swallowed them dry. "This whole thing could turn into a real nightmare quick. Have you at least called your family yet?"

She tilted her head. "When was I supposed to do that?"

"Make the time."

"You're so chummy with Dad, you do it." She snapped her mouth shut, regretting her words and tone instantly. She hated putting that scowl on Malone's face when all he was trying to do was help. "Sorry."

"I can only imagine how hard this is for you, but you remember what I said? No drama."

"Yeah," she mumbled. "I'll keep my shit together." After all, a Steele keeps their word.

"Or get it together." Malone winked at her. "But, yes, I'd be much obliged if you did."

She'd never want to let Malone down. He had been there for her after the accident, supportive and understanding. "I'll firm up my alibi." A promise that was spoken with far more confidence than she had any right to convey.

"And you'll—" Malone rolled his hand, prompting her to finish his sentence.

"Call my parents."

Malone grabbed papers from a tray on his desk and set it in front of himself. "All a sergeant can ask. See ya."

She let herself out of Malone's office. She'd thought her life had turned to shit from the moment of the accident, but more clouds were moving in. She had reason to want the victim dead, an alibi she couldn't pin down, her drug dealer was a murder suspect—and her boss was telling her to call her parents. Could this day get any worse? Getting hit by a bus might be a blessing.

CHAPTER TWENTY

Albert Ferguson lived in an apartment complex in Woodbridge above a convenience store with bars on its windows. A discarded mattress leaned against the side of the building and kept company with a well-worn sofa chair and a picnic table. It wasn't exactly a classy neighborhood. Amanda parked the department car along a side street. She should have called Trent back and gone with him to question Freddy, but if that angle never panned out at least she wouldn't have wasted her time—or, more importantly, put her career in further jeopardy.

She slipped her hand into her jacket pocket and wrapped it around the baggie of pills. If only she'd allow herself to swallow one and slip away. But that would require getting past her panging conscience and having the time to rest and possibly sleep. Even if she could overcome the first block, crawling into bed felt like a luxury she wasn't sure she'd be graced with again. Or at least it felt that way. She'd been up for over thirty hours at this point, though it felt far longer with all the stops and interviews they'd made already. That was the problem with catching a case at midnight—the day felt like it would never end. She had crossed over the threshold from walking-zombie exhaustion to becoming a touch wired. After she spoke with Ferguson, she'd grab another Jabba and suck back on it until it infused her with some spark. Then again, asking a drink for motivation was probably a little unreasonable.

Jabba. Now she was thinking like Trent, Lord help her. But she was starting to find that her initial resistance to him was wearing down—just a little. He was so passive. Did that trait just come naturally to him or had he been told to be accommodating by Malone? The latter would be worse, as if she needed Malone handling the situation to the nth degree. It was possible Trent was one of those hold-it-in-and-explode types too. The kind who did well enrolled in anger-management classes. How had he survived to reach detective rank otherwise? The fellas would have eaten him alive, along with most of the women. Law enforcement might still mostly be a man's world but the women who did the job weren't ones you wanted to mess with. She'd met enough, besides herself, to know.

She found the doorway marked 144. There was a black mailbox mounted crooked next to it.

She rang the doorbell. She couldn't hear the chime, but footsteps pounded down stairs and the door swung open.

A man in his fifties stood there, unshaven with gray stubble on his face and a thick mane of gray hair that came to his shoulders. He looked like a hippie. He was wearing blue jeans and a T-shirt with pit stains. He stank of stale cigarettes and had a mouth full of yellow teeth, when he pulled his lips back and said, "Yeah?"

Amanda held up her badge and introduced herself. "Are you Albert Ferguson?"

"Uh-huh." He looked beyond her toward the sidewalk.

"I'd like to ask you a few questions about your whereabouts Sunday night," Amanda said, re-earning his gaze.

"Why?" he snarled.

"Chad Palmer was found murdered."

Albert swayed and reached for the door for support, but his judgment of the distance was flawed, and Amanda helped him.

"Do you have somewhere we could sit down?" She eyed the coat on the hook just inside the door. "Maybe someplace outside? I noticed a picnic table around the side."

He grabbed his coat and regained enough composure to walk unaided to the table. He sat down, and Amanda found herself breathing easier when the thing didn't crumble to sawdust. She sat across from him.

"You knew Chad Palmer," she started.

"He destroyed my son's life." Albert ground his teeth and tears filled his eyes.

"How?"

Albert met her eyes. "I think you must have some idea, as you're at my door." He shifted his jaw side to side.

"There was an accident years ago, when your son and Chad were teenagers," she said. "The report said your son was behind the wheel."

"Utter bullshit. Taylor, my son, and Chad were headed home from a party they never should have been at in the first damn place. Boys being what they are, they were drinkin' but, instead of calling for a ride, they drove—more accurately, Chad drove," he spat. "Paramedics and police say they pulled my son from behind the wheel, but I say that Chad had been driving. It was his car and there's no way he would have let Taylor drive it. He dragged my son from the passenger seat and put him in the driver's seat to save his own selfish self."

The last bit was shoved out with disgust and bitter rage. It made the skin tighten on the back of Amanda's neck. There was definite motive here for Albert Ferguson, and despite the passage of years, the wound still seemed fresh. She could relate, but she hadn't killed Palmer so maybe she shouldn't rush into thinking Ferguson had.

"What makes you think that Chad moved him?"

His eyes snapped to hers. "I don't think it; I know it. Doctors told me that Taylor could have survived the accident unscathed had he stayed still and waited for the ambulance. I asked Taylor many times over the years if Chad had been driving. See I really think Chad moved him, but Taylor was insistent that he was driving. After all, he'd been the one found behind the wheel. But when paramedics arrived, Taylor was unconscious, and I think he'd blacked out on impact, and Chad took advantage of that and moved him. Though how do you prove that? I know he ruined my boy's life, but no one was taking the case. Chad got away with it. And now my sweet Taylor is dead."

She bristled at the past tense. "He died?"

"From that day if you ask me. His life was never the same. He was a quadriplegic for the rest of his life." Albert rubbed his hands and blew into them. There was a little nip to the air, but at least they were somewhat sheltered by the side of the building. Albert continued. "He died a few months ago."

"I'm sorry for your loss." Had Taylor's death been the final trigger for Albert?

He reached into his coat pocket and she tensed, preparing herself instinctually for him to pull a gun or weapon. He held up his other hand. "Just want to show you something."

She relaxed but watched the man closely.

He withdrew a leather wallet and pulled out a photograph and handed it to her across the table. The photo's edges were frayed and whitened; it had been in and out of his wallet many times over the years.

Albert pointed to the picture. "That was taken a few years ago. Not long after Trixie left."

"Trixie?"

"My wife."

Amanda nodded. She studied the photograph, which showed Taylor in a specialized wheelchair—it would have cost a fortune. Albert had lost more than his son. He'd lost his wife and his money, judging by his current living arrangements. Taylor's care wouldn't have come cheap. But Amanda noted that Taylor's face was familiar. She'd check when she left here, but she was quite sure Taylor had been one of the two boys with Palmer in that photo he'd carried around. But why had Palmer held on to it? To remind himself of what he'd done, to remember the good times, to punish himself? And who was the other boy?

"He was a handsome kid," she said, handing the photo back to Albert.

"He took after his mom."

Amanda saw quite a bit of Albert in Taylor, but it would be awkward to say as much and flatter a potential murderer. After all, motive was stacking against him. "It must have been tough, caring for him by yourself," she said.

"It could have been worse. Thankfully, I've got myself a good family to fall back on, but yeah, it drained my finances." He jacked a thumb toward the building. "Why I live here now. All I can afford. And I'm laid off from work right now, which isn't helping either."

Her heart pinched at his mention of having a good family. She'd had one of those, but instead of letting their efforts to console her do just that, she viewed them as suffocating and as a brutal reminder of what had happened to Kevin and Lindsey. At least money had never been an issue for her; Kevin's insurance policy had seen to that, but she kept most of it squirreled away in case she ever did act on the urge to run far away and start fresh. She'd only pulled from it for their funerals and for the family plot. Otherwise, every time she thought about touching the money, she was inundated with flashbacks to that horrid night and guilt that she should somehow profit by what had happened.

"I have to ask this…" She wished she could backpedal her words, make herself sound more authoritative, but the truth was a part of her wouldn't blame the man for killing Palmer. But she had her word to see through. "Where were you Sunday night from six until midnight?"

"I was out with my girlfriend. I stayed at her house. I could get you her number." Albert's reaction to the question was calm and collected.

If he was guilty, he was a cold, hardened psychopath. Just the kind who would hang around for hours to see the job through. "I'll need to call her."

"Name's Karen Smith." He pulled out his phone from a pocket in his jeans. "Can never remember her number."

"That's why we have contact lists." She smiled at him and he returned it.

"Here it is." He rattled it off and she keyed it into her phone. She'd call Karen after she left there.

"Actually, while I have my phone out, I'd like to show you something. You might be able to help me with it." She brought up the picture taken from Palmer's wallet of the three boys with their bikes. "I'm pretty sure that's Taylor—" She pointed to the boy in a striped shirt and camo shorts.

"That's him, all right. The kid insisted on dressing himself, but he had horrible taste. Couldn't coordinate his wardrobe."

She recalled the day Lindsey had announced she was a big girl and could dress herself. She had one outfit she kept returning to—a pink princess gown, which had originally been a Halloween costume. She and Kevin had taken her out to restaurants and to the park in it on many occasions—though not nearly enough. She took a deep breath, composed herself again and pointed to the third boy. "Do you happen to know who that kid is?"

"Yeah. Ricky… Can't remember his last name. He was Chad's cousin."

Chad's cousin, Ricky… Could this be the Rick Jensen who Trent had told her was Palmer's only living relative?

Albert continued. "Those cousins were thick as thieves. I know because Taylor would go on about how lucky he was they paid him any attention. Think he really felt like he'd been admitted to a club." The tail end of Albert's sentence was riddled with sadness.

It was certainly a club Albert had wished his son had never joined.

She got up from the table and said, "Thank you for your time and cooperation."

"Sure."

His short response had Amanda looking at him.

Albert went on. "I can understand why I'd look guilty. I'd have motive, and Lord knows I thought about taking my own revenge over the years. The only thing holding me back—besides my family—is knowing that Taylor never would have approved. He didn't want me carrying hate in my heart, and I'd be lying to say it's all gone, but I'm taking things one day at a time."

Amanda dipped her head and briefly shut her eyes. "I appreciate your honesty."

With that, she headed back to the department car, her heart heavy with feeling for a man who'd lost his son, but she was also fired up. She would honor her daughter's memory by sticking to her word, doing the right thing, and see Palmer's case through.

CHAPTER TWENTY-ONE

A quick call to Karen Smith was all it took to firm up Albert Ferguson's alibi. Amanda was jealous that hers wasn't so easy. She drove back to Central District where she figured that she and Trent would catch each other up, but Trent hadn't returned yet.

It was sort of like the good ole days before she'd been saddled with a partner. So quiet, no one to loop in or bring up to speed. Trent was okay as a person, but she didn't need a partner, and the second this investigation was over she would be tossing Trent back at Malone so fast his head would spin.

She took the necessary steps to get a be-on-lookout bulletin issued for the powder-blue Caprice. They didn't have a plate, but they had a description and that would have to be enough. Two people had now confirmed Palmer's connection to the car so finding it might lead them somewhere worthwhile in the investigation.

She was just finishing up when Cud walked past her to his cubicle. She followed and rapped her knuckles on the partition. He slowly looked at her, as if she'd interrupted something he was working on.

"Yeah?" He was chomping on gum in his usual fashion and arched an eyebrow.

She perched on the edge of his desk. "Why didn't you mention that Palmer's business partner was murdered?"

"What are you talking about?"

The fact he hadn't said anything at the crime scene had niggled at her enough, but now he was playing stupid. "Jackson Webb. You were the lead detective on the case five and a half years ago. Apparently, a messy murder scene."

"What about it?" Cud tapped his pen against his other palm and swiveled so he was more face-on.

"You didn't think it was worth mentioning?"

"Why would I?" He enlarged his eyes and regarded her as if she were crazy.

"I dunno. Two business partners murdered…"

"Didn't know Palmer was murdered," he said, flippant. "I'm guessing that was confirmed."

"It was."

"A gunshot?"

"Ah, so you do remember the Jackson Webb case."

"Sure. Never denied remembering. I just don't see the connection."

She studied him.

"Listen, I would have said something if I figured it mattered."

"Would you?" she shoved out.

His eyes narrowed and he scowled. "I need to get back to work, so if you'd kindly get out of here."

She held his gaze.

"Bye-bye." He finger-waved and she rolled her eyes and left. Cud was acting strange, even for him.

She settled herself at her desk after grabbing a coffee from the cafeteria. She was curious about Webb's murder case but found herself more caught up in the enigma of Casey-Anne Ritter's.

She brought up Casey-Anne's case file on the computer. The lead investigating detective in Atlanta, Georgia, was a Detective Montgomery Banks. She could spend time reading or she could reach out to the detective for his take. Sure, a lot of years had passed, but he might still have something to offer that wasn't on record, or something he felt was worth more attention than it had received. She called his number and got voicemail. She left a rather vague message but hinted that a recent murder in Dumfries, Virginia, might be connected with his cold case. Hopefully, that would be enough to prompt a callback.

Next, she opened her email. She was going to look at Palmer's visitor list, but a new message with an attachment filtered in above it from CSI Emma Blair. It was probably the evidence list that Malone had mentioned. All the subject said was *Palmer Investigation.*

She opened the email, expecting some pleasantries in the body, but it simply read *See attached.*

She clicked on the spreadsheet, which was a list of the potential evidence from room ten and its surroundings at Denver's Motel. She scanned the document and stopped on line sixty-six. A receipt from a Dumfries bar by the name of Happy Time. According to what was noted, the receipt had been found in garbage outside the motel office. It could have belonged to anyone, but she wasn't that big of a believer in coincidence.

Her insides went cold. That had been Palmer's watering hole the night of the accident.

*

"Mommy, Mommy," Lindsey chortles in the back seat as I snap her seat belt into place.

"You have fun?"

"Loved it." Lindsey grins and the moonlight picks up something on my daughter's chin. I wipe it and find sugary syrup that I must have missed before getting her ready to leave. "Love ice cream cake!"

*

Amanda blinked away the tears that had sprung into her eyes. That had happened just minutes before the accident, as she was getting Lindsey situated in the back seat. They were leaving from Amanda's sister Kristen's house. It had been an afternoon and evening of birthday fun as her niece Ava had just turned seven.

Lindsey had been so excited to be a part of the celebration. She'd been to other parties for her friends and cousins, but she hadn't been old enough to truly appreciate them. Lindsey had just been coming alive when—

No, she couldn't go down that path. Nothing good would come from that right now.

But Happy Time. She knew that bar—and not for the good. Technically, bartenders and the establishments they work in are legally liable if they overserve a patron who proceeds to get behind the wheel and wind up in an accident. But Happy Time—the business and its employees—had escaped any charges. For being a dive bar, it turned out they had deep-enough pockets to afford a small team of defense lawyers. The fact no one affiliated with Happy Time had paid any fines or served any time was just another miscarriage of justice on top of Palmer's ridiculous sentence.

She called Trent's cell to get an ETA on his return to the station. His line rang several times and went to voicemail.

She returned the handset to the cradle. Maybe she should be worried about him, but she was sure he could handle his own. He was probably in the middle of questioning Freddy or Rat. It would be nice to hear something from him though. But she also had to give him some space to be his own detective.

She signed out a department car again and was heading toward Dumfries when her phone rang from a blocked caller. She answered, thinking it could be Trent as she hadn't exactly had time to program his number into her phone, and cops' numbers never came up announcing them as police. There was nothing but breathing on the other end of the line. "Hello? Can you hear me?"

Click.

It was probably just Trent trying to call her back or a wrong number, but goose bumps stood on her arms, telling her otherwise. Trent could be in trouble. She flattened her foot on the gas pedal, intent on going direct to Freddy's house, and then her phone rang again.

"It's Trent," her caller said.

She took a few deep breaths. There had been a part of her that for a few moments had feared she might not hear his voice again. She really needed some sleep before paranoia crept in and took full hold.

"Detective Steele?" he prompted.

"Yeah. How are you making out?"

"Still having a chat here with Freddy and Rat."

"It's going all right?" She measured her tone, trying not to make it too obvious that she had been concerned with his safety.

"It's going. You all right?"

"Good." Now she knew he was fine, she said, "I'm going to follow another lead that came in, but I'll catch up with you in a bit at the station."

"Sure."

"You didn't just happen to try calling me a minute ago, did you?"

"No. Why?"

"No reason." She ended the call, dread pricking her flesh. It must have been a wrong number. No sense getting all worked up over nothing.

She rolled the sedan into the parking lot for Happy Time in record time, mainly because she drove a good stretch at fifteen to twenty over the speed limit.

This bar would certainly attract the same clientele as Denver's Motel. It was a much sadder sight than the Tipsy Moose in Woodbridge, day or night. In fact, Happy Time was in an old, rundown building and gave the impression its happy times were all in the past. It was nearing six thirty, and there were a few cars in the lot.

Inside, country music was playing over the speakers and three drunken patrons were seated on stools at the bar. One of the men ogled her with red-rimmed eyes and lifted his glass with a couple fingers' full of amber liquid to her in a toast gesture.

She ignored him, approached the bar, and pulled her badge when the tender came toward her.

He was broad and tall, easily over six feet, but at the sight of her badge, his shoulders dipped, and he swept a hand through his hair. "We're legal here. Have our license."

"Do you think I'm here to cite you for health-code violations? Although, putting your hands in your hair isn't exactly hygienic. I'm Detective Steele with Homicide, Prince William County PD, and you are?"

"Not interested."

"Yeah, see, it doesn't work that way. Your bar served a man last night and that man's now dead."

The drunks within earshot lowered their drinks. One stopped with his glass to his lips. The oldest of the three had soft-blue eyes but the weathered face of a man who'd had a hard life.

The bartender waved a hand, dismissing the hinted-at correlation between a man's death and the bar. His customers didn't seem to need much encouragement and returned to draining their drinks.

Amanda brought up a picture of Palmer, from the crime scene, on her phone.

"Ah, Jes—" He stopped midway through the blasphemy under her glare.

"Do you recognize him?" She showed him Palmer's DMV photo.

"Sure."

"Anything else you'd like to add? For example, was he alone or with someone? Was he in a good mood? A bad mood? Celebrating or wallowing?"

"I didn't chat him up, but he was alone."

"When did he show up here?"

"Not his keeper."

"Just give me a rough time."

"Six."

"In the evening?"

"It certainly wasn't in the morning."

So if Palmer had been with someone just before Lorraine's shift ended at six, as Lorraine had told them, what had happened to Freddy—if it had indeed been him? "You keep giving me attitude, I just might turn you over to the health board." She didn't need much encouragement when it came to this place.

He put up his hands.

"And I still haven't gotten your name."

"Because I haven't given it to you."

She stared him down.

"Charlie Brown," he eventually pushed out.

"You're shit— You're serious?"

"Unfortunately."

"Like the cartoon? The kid with a beagle who sleeps on the roof of his doghouse." She smirked, enjoying the irony that such a formidable man had such a comedic name. "Someone's parents had a bad sense of humor."

His jaw tensed. "You think?"

"Listen, Mr. Brown, I'm just trying to fill in this man's last few hours alive."

"What happened to him?"

"Ah, no, not at liberty to say," she told him, "but you have a chance to possibly be a hero."

"Never been an aspiration of mine."

"Hey, Charlie, another!" one of the drinkers called out and held up his empty glass.

"You'll have to excuse me." Charlie fulfilled the order and returned.

"What was he drinking?"

"Him?" Charlie jacked a thumb at the drunk.

"The guy who died."

"Vodka on the rocks."

Vodka. Not only had Palmer returned to the same bar he'd frequented the night of the accident, he had drunk the same thing. The world really was a better place without him in it. An opinion she'd keep to herself. And she couldn't forget the promise she'd made at Lindsey's grave. She took a deep breath and asked, "When did he leave?"

"See ya, Charlie." Blue Eyes got off his barstool and headed out.

"See ya, George," the tender said back.

What was this place—Cheers?

"Time. He left," Amanda prompted, trying to wrangle Charlie's attention back to her.

"Say, ten."

"Early night. Was he drunk when he left?"

"Guy couldn't walk straight, so yeah."

"So you called him a cab?"

"Not my job."

It took recollection of Malone's stern reminder to keep drama out of the investigation for her not to climb over the bar and throttle Charlie where he stood. She could introduce her fist to his nose. She could have lectured him about the responsibilities that go with his job. She could have reported him to the liquor board. But none of those things would keep him talking. "So he was driving," she accused.

"No idea. Not like I'm outside watching everyone as they come and go."

"One more question. Any of the customers in here now that were around last night when he was here?"

Charlie picked up a cloth and wiped the bar. "Ah, yeah, George, but you just missed him."

She shot to her feet and seethed, "You do realize that you have a legal responsibility for the people you serve." She rushed out the door.

In the fresh air, she inhaled deeply a few times, trying to rein in her racing heart. It was so disgusting how everyone had moved on with their lives—everyone but her and her sweet family. She balled her fists and searched for George, but there was no one in sight. She headed back to her car swearing to herself that she'd missed a potential good lead. George could have seen if Palmer had arrived with someone, left with someone, confirmed the car, maybe even a license plate. She had her hand on the driver's-side handle when she spotted George against a fence at the back of the lot, one leg bent and cocked against it. She headed his way but kept her movements slow to avoid startling him. George didn't seem affected by her approach at all. He casually lowered his leg, lost his balance a bit, but kept himself upright.

"George?" she said.

"That's me."

She hadn't caught his odor in the bar, but whoa, this guy reeked of whiskey. She'd take short, shallow breaths for this conversation. "Detective Steele with Homicide. I understand you were here last night."

"I'm here a lot. I heard you asking Charlie about some guy who died."

"He was murdered, but yes, that's right."

George didn't flinch. "I heard Charlie say the guy was drinking back vodka last night." He burped and spittle bubbled in one corner of his mouth; he wiped the drool away with a flick of his wrist. "I'm pretty sure I know who you're here asking about. I don't know his name, but I did see him."

"Did you see if he came alone or left alone?"

"Like Charlie said, he was alone… until someone came up on him when he was working to get in his car."

George had seen the car, but she was stuck on the other part of his sentence and felt a sense of excitement. She could be on the verge of hearing their first solid lead. "Someone came up on him? Attacked him you mean?"

"Yep, exactly what I'm saying." George scratched at his scraggly chin whiskers and hiccupped. "Think he struck the guy with a gun. He stumbled back like he'd been hit real hard."

A gun. She squirreled away this fact to consider later. "Did you try to intervene?"

"Wasn't in any shape for that. And I haven't stayed alive all these years by playing hero."

That caused her to smirk. George smiled back, a twinkle in his otherwise dull blues.

"It was smart of you to stay out of it," she assured him. "No sense getting yourself shot."

"That's what I thought." His mind seemed to drift, carried on booze to somewhere far away.

"So this guy with the gun," she prompted, "what did he look like?"

"I didn't get a real good look at 'im, but he was wearing a black hoodie."

She nodded. "You're certain it was a man?"

"From what I could tell."

Not exactly solid assurance, but she'd run with it. Especially considering this hooded assailant could be connected to the past cold cases. Factor in, too, that Freddy was a suspect and male.

George went on. "When the guy with the gun first approached Vodka Drinker—sorry I don't know his name—he turned and tried to talk himself out of the situation."

"Drunks always think they're invincible." The words birthed of their own accord and she wondered if that's what Palmer had thought of himself the night he'd got behind the wheel and killed her family.

"We are, darlin'." George smiled again, this time showing a hint of charm still lived in the older man.

"I'm sure. So do you think they knew each other?"

"Not sure, but whatever was said didn't work, because the next thing I know the guy butted him in the head with the gun."

"Did you see where?"

"Right here." The drinker put a fingertip to his right temple.

The unexplained gash in Palmer's forehead... "Then what happened?"

"The gunman forced the guy to get into the front passenger seat." George's eyelids started sagging like he was going to drop into a pile and fall asleep right there in the parking lot.

"Then," she prompted. She just needed this guy to stay awake a little longer.

"The gunman took the guy's keys, got in the driver's seat, and drove away."

"And did you report this to the police?"

"No. Should have, I know, but I typically like to mind my own business. Figure it's worked so far."

She wasn't about to reprimand an older man, and it wouldn't get them anywhere. She was no one's caretaker and no one life's coach.

"Besides, I don't see any cop believing me, ya know. I was drinking. Drunk." The last word came out tethered to a lot of shame.

"Well, I believe you."

"That I was drunk?" George winked, picking up on what she really meant. He added, "Thank you."

"You're welcome. And thank you. You've been a lot of help."

George grinned. "Happy to be of service." He saluted, making Amanda wonder if he was former military.

She winked at him. "Ah, just a couple more things..."

"Whatever you want, darlin'."

"Did you happen to see where the gunman came from?"

He shook his head. "Sorry, can't help you there. I just came out of the bar."

"Okay." She gave him a tight smile. "And what's your full name, you know for the record?"

"Oh, I don't know if I want to become entangled that way. Just think of me as George, the curious monkey."

One of her daughter's favorite stories had included the escapades of the adventure-loving monkey. She held eye contact with him for a few moments. There was something secreted in this man's past he didn't want to come out and she of all people could respect his desire to keep his history to himself. "Okay, well, if I have more questions—"

"You can usually find me here."

"All right. Thank you."

George dipped his head and retreated down a back alley. She watched him disappear and put her gaze to the bar's roofline. At the back corner there was a small black globe secured beneath the eave. A security camera.

She tromped back into the bar and didn't let Charlie's grimace dissuade her. "Does the camera in the lot work?"

"Far as I know."

"I need the footage for last night."

"Then I'll need to see a warrant." Charlie poured a drink and slid it down to one of the drunks who was still perched on his stool.

"Be assured I'll get one."

"Until then, princess…" Charlie fake-smiled at her and the guy who'd just got a refill laughed.

She walked out of the bar again, not preoccupied with securing a warrant. She was quite sure that would be easy, but she was thinking about Palmer drinking vodka. If someone had taken out Palmer because of his drinking, surely they would have poisoned him with his drink of choice so it would look more like an accident—or would that appear too obvious a connection? But Palmer had been found with empty bottles of *whiskey*. Was that intentional or an oversight on the killer's behalf?

She was well aware that alcoholics had a favorite drink. Her own father had battled with alcohol addiction when she was younger. It had almost broken up her parents, but when she was young her dad had started working through the twelve steps with Alcoholics Anonymous. She couldn't remember what his preference had been, probably because of her age at the time or the passing years.

But she had to seriously consider why the killer would have chosen the murder method they had. Was it to throw off the investigation? To make it look like an accident instead of homicide. Was it really that simple? Or were there more layers to its purpose?

And returning to what Charlie had said: Palmer had been drinking alone. So if he had left Denver's Motel with Freddy in the afternoon, what had happened to Freddy? Had Palmer dropped him off somewhere? And if so, where and why? Was it a simple matter of business being concluded between the two of them?

Her phone rang. Blocked caller ID again. "Detective Steele," she said firmly.

"I'm back at the station." It was Trent. "And there's something you need to know."

"Just spit it out. I'm not one for surprises."

"I brought Freddy in for questioning."

Her stomach turned into acid. "I'll be right there."

CHAPTER TWENTY-TWO

"I stopped by to see Lorraine Nash again before going to Freddy's," Trent told her. "She wouldn't say as much, but her eyes lit up when I showed her Freddy's picture. She recognized him, no doubt, and I'd say it was Freddy who Palmer left the motel with on Sunday afternoon."

"Did you ask Freddy about this?"

Trent's eyes narrowed, the tiniest tell that her lack of confidence in him had pissed him off. *About time*, she thought.

"And," she prompted. She'd finally detected a pulse and felt like ratcheting it.

"Freddy's real name is Hank Cohen," he said, speaking slowly, likely trying to piss her off. She was finally getting a reaction.

She rolled her hand as if bored and impatient with his detour. "I know all that. Catch me up on why he's next door in an interview room."

"He confirmed that he got together with Palmer yesterday afternoon and that they left Denver's in Palmer's Caprice."

"Okay, and where did they go? What did they do?"

"He said that if I wanted that information, he'd demand a lawyer."

Trent must have been deliberately trying to piss her off by dragging things out. "Sure, and…?"

"I told him that if he wants his little operation to be left alone," Trent said, "then he best consider being more cooperative. He still didn't want to talk, so I threatened to drag him down here."

"And then you did. So we still don't know what they were doing together Sunday afternoon?"

Trent deflated. "All he gave me was that they took care of some business."

"Did you get what sort of business out of him?"

"Not exactly, but I have a feeling it was something illegal."

"No shit."

"I was thinking maybe if you had a go at him…" Trent met her gaze briefly.

Her heart picked up speed. She'd had a bad feeling it would come down to this when Trent had told her that he'd dragged Freddy in, but she wanted more intel before she saw Freddy again. Anything that would give her the upper hand in the interaction. "How did he react to Palmer's murder?"

"No real reaction, but he wasn't surprised."

"Because he killed him or had him killed perhaps?" she tossed out.

"Maybe? Not sure. That's why I thought it best you have a go at him. But he did say something to the effect of Palmer wasn't exactly an angel."

"Go on." She didn't want to dwell on that because it would just lead her into the darkness.

"He confessed that he and Palmer had a business disagreement before Palmer went to jail, but things were all good now."

"So should we assume Palmer owed him the twenty-five grand and paid him back? Though Palmer would have had to dip into it to pay for his stay at Denver's Motel. Freddy was okay with being short-changed?"

"I thought of that too and asked about it. All he'd say was they were good."

If the money was paid back, she had to wonder what Freddy's motive might be for killing Palmer, but there were other ways Palmer could have burned Freddy. "Short-changed, but 'they were good.' Hmm. Sounds to me like Freddy might have gotten something else of value from Palmer. Maybe he had him doing a job for him."

"All I know is Freddy said he had no reason to want Palmer dead. He asked me when the murder happened and said during that time he was shooting pool at Corner Pocket Billiards with Rat."

"And you questioned him too, like I asked?"

"I did, but he didn't set off any alarms."

"Okay. We'll need to verify the alibi."

"Yeah, still haven't had a chance, but it'll be easy enough to make a call."

"Do that now, before I go in."

She looked through the one-way mirror at Freddy. Just watching him made her skin feel slimy. She was still wearing her jacket with the pills in the pocket and was doing all she could to put that out of her mind. "I'm still not entirely sure what made you drag him down here."

Trent huffed out a breath but didn't say anything until he had his phone to his ear and the person on the other end had picked up. She listened as he asked about Freddy's presence at the pool hall. "Okay, thanks." He hung up. "He was there."

"Wow, so we're here for what reason?" To say she was a little disappointed in Trent's rash decision to drag Freddy in would have been an understatement.

"I hadn't… hadn't expected the alibi to stand." His cheeks flushed but he met her gaze. "What's the deal with you and this Freddy guy anyway?"

"What do you mean?"

"He obviously gets under your skin. I figure you must have a history there."

"What are you suggesting? That he's my drug dealer on speed dial?"

"I never said any such thing, nor would I suggest—"

"Good."

Trent kept his gaze on her, and she regretted making any deal about Freddy. From the second his name had come up she would have been better off pretending to know nothing about him. But her emotions had become involved and dissolved her logic.

"There's something else that's missing here, besides the money and the bracelet. Palmer's car. Did you ask Freddy anything about it?"

"Yeah, he claimed not to have a clue where Palmer obtained it or how."

"Huh. I see." She thought about what Courtney had told them about Freddy's arrangement with Palmer and Webb and wondered if the business he'd referred to was robbery and subsequent fencing of the stolen goods, but it wasn't like Palmer still had a pawnshop or legit business front to make him valuable to Freddy. However, if Palmer had been forced to hand over the rest of the twenty-five K to Freddy, that would have left him with zilch to live on. Maybe Palmer was going to become a part of Freddy's team and start stealing. She'd press Freddy on that when she got in there. But if Palmer had stolen from the wrong person or made off with goods he was supposed to liquify, that could spell motive for murder. But that wouldn't gel with the MO. That type of motivation would likely lead to a bullet to the head.

In the interrogation room, Freddy got up and took off his coat. He set it on the back of the chair, but it was what she saw on his wrist that had her on the move.

"Amanda?" Trent called out to her. "Wait. Should we talk a bit more before you go in there? His alibi did check out."

She stopped and spun around. "Freddy could have that billiard hall in his pocket, but—look at his right wrist." She watched him follow her direction.

"A silver bracelet," he said.

"Did you ask him about that?"

"Never saw it."

"Uh-huh, and what do you bet the chances are that used to be Palmer's?"

"Okay, but—"

"No, I'm going in there and you're going to dig up whatever else you can on Freddy. I want to know all his movements from the time that Palmer got out of prison. And did he or any of his pals ever visit Palmer in prison? Did you ask him about Casey-Anne Ritter?"

"I did, and he claimed not to have heard of her."

"Not surprising. Go—look at Freddy's activities."

"Where should I start?" Trent's cheeks were burning crimson.

"We assume that the Caprice might have been taken by the killer—"

"We do?"

She realized she'd been so flustered by Freddy's presence that she hadn't filled Trent in on her trip to Happy Time. She did that quickly now.

"So do you think Freddy or one of his cohorts could have done that, killed Palmer, taken off in the car after?" Trent said, brainstorming out loud.

"If that's the case, something went wrong during their business arrangement." She put finger quotes around business arrangement. "Do a search for all of Prince William County for any robberies or break-ins since Palmer was released on Friday afternoon."

Trent was still standing there, but she needed him to leave. When she went in to talk to Freddy, she needed to be alone with him.

"Go. Do that while I'm in there." She flicked a hand toward the interview room.

"Okay. On it."

Trent left and she took a deep breath.

She made sure that whatever conversation she had in there with Freddy wouldn't be recorded and headed next door.

CHAPTER TWENTY-THREE

Amanda opened the door to the interrogation room, and Freddy grinned wide.

"Civic six four six. How lucky I am to see you." He slouched in his chair and draped an arm over the back. "What can I do for you today? Back for more?" He bobbed his eyebrows at her.

Inside she was quaking. She'd rushed in here on impulse, without really thinking things through. She pointed to the silver bracelet on Freddy's wrist. "Nice bling. Why don't you tell me about that?"

"Not feeling too chatty, but I could start talking if you don't get me outta here."

Shadows danced across his features. For her own good, she should cut him loose, but she had her damn word to keep.

"I'm pretty sure you know what I'd be saying."

"You're not going to intimidate me, Hank."

"Oh yeah. All I need to do is have a little talk with your boss."

"Really? And why the hell would he believe you over me?" She was shaking but doing her best so Freddy wouldn't see through her. She'd seen careers destroyed by rumor.

"Whatever."

"Now that's out of the way…" She leaned forward and placed both elbows on the table. "Your friend, Chad Palmer."

"Whoa, hold up. No one said the guy's my friend."

"Well, you were in business with him," she volleyed back. "That's what Detective Stenson told me you said. Was he wrong?"

"Sure, fine. But he wasn't my friend."

"You and your crew would steal stuff and fence it through his pawnshop," she said, matter-of-fact.

Freddy's gaze flicked to hers.

She smirked. "You're not denying it so we're off to a good start."

He snarled and for an instant she feared for Courtney's safety.

"Then maybe you don't need to tell me anything. I have ways of finding things out. Just like how I'm going to find out what the deal was between you and Chad on Sunday and where his car went."

Freddy swallowed roughly and rubbed his throat.

Amanda was following a feeling in her gut. "The fact the car's missing mean something to you?"

"Ah, nah." Freddy traced a fingertip on the table, his fidgety movements belying his verbal claim.

His body language was sending off strong signals that his ass was on the line with the car gone. But why and did it have anything to do with Palmer's murder? Was Freddy a killer as well as a drug dealer and thief? She was failing to see clear motive, but Freddy had a connection to Webb, and he was one of the last people to see Palmer alive. She'd strive to fill in more of Palmer's last hours.

"After you and Chad left Denver's Motel, where did you go?"

"I went to shoot pool with Rat. I don't know what he did."

She couldn't just sit there and let him steer the direction of this interview, no matter how uncomfortable and compromised she felt by his presence. It was time to claim her power. "You know that I can hold you for twenty-four hours without laying charges. Can you imagine what your crew might think you're doing with the cops for that long?" She hitched her shoulders. "Then again, that's not my problem."

"You better watch your back, cop bitch!"

She launched her upper body across the table and was in his face in a second, her nose mere inches from his. "Try me. Call me cop bitch one more time," she snarled and it took all her willpower not to grab him by the scruff of his neck, but it was the reflection in his eyes that had her shrinking inside. It was an image of herself she didn't like.

She dropped back into her chair. "Listen, you and I have a lot of talking to do and until I say we're done—"

"I'll just lawyer up."

"Nah, I don't think you'll do that."

"No? And why not?"

"Because something was in that Caprice Chad had and you need it back. Why draw attention to that?"

Freddy rubbed his jaw, the bracelet dangling from his wrist. "I ain't never said I need that dumb car."

"But your body language did. What's in the car, Freddy?"

"Nope. Not talking."

"Fine, then you're spending the night. I'll make sure the word spreads on the street you're giving up your guys."

He bunched up his face in an ugly, massive scowl.

"Nuh-uh." She wagged her finger. "Don't say what you're thinking." The words "cop bitch" were rolling in his eyes like ticker tape.

He spat on the floor like he was some sort of mad camel.

"Okay, you don't want to talk about the car, that's fine. We'll find it ourselves and figure out what's so special about it. Tell me where Chad got the car."

Freddy slouched in his chair. "How would I know?"

"Quite sure you're the one who hooked him up with it." She was just following a gut feeling but wanted to see it through. "Maybe you're indebted to that person and they're not going to be too happy to hear it's missing."

"Not talking." He crossed his arms.

It was interesting how Freddy thought by keeping his mouth shut he wasn't communicating, because she was picking up the words not being said out loud. His body language was shut to this topic, which told her he had been involved with getting Chad the car and was trying to protect whomever he'd gotten it from and himself from them. Given the age of the vehicle, she'd wager that it wasn't stolen but rather obtained from another lowlife who ran in Freddy's world.

Her gaze dipped to the bracelet, but she had another question to ask before she returned to the jewelry on his arm. "Did you go to the Happy Time bar last night, say around ten?"

"No, man, I was with my guys at the pool hall until early morning. I told the pretend cop all that. And I'm pretty sure you knew where I was around four…"

She cringed at the reminder, but she wasn't going to let it derail her. "That 'pretend cop' dragged your ass down here, and I assure you he also has the authority to lock it up." The words were out before she processed them; she'd just defended Trent?

"Whatever."

"Fine, you don't want to tell me. We're going to get their video and when we see your face on there—"

"I wasn't at that crappy bar. I have nothing to hide."

She set her mouth in a straight line and angled her head. "I think we both know that's taking things a little too far."

"If one of us has something to hide… You should be afraid of me," he hissed.

She refused to let him steer the conversation. "Listen, I've got a dead body and it's my job to find out what happened."

"Yeah, your job, not mine."

"Jackson Webb," she tossed out.

"Who?" He scrunched up his face.

"Chad's former business partner."

"Okay," he dragged out.

"He was murdered five and a half years ago. Did you kill him?"

"What?" he spat. "No, why would I?"

"Chad owed you a lot of cash," she said, running on the assumption the large sum Palmer'd had was, in fact, to pay off Freddy. "You could have come after Jackson for it."

"No, I didn't. Not how I operate."

"Sure about that?"

"Hell yeah."

There'd be no point in asking him where he was the night of Jackson's murder as he'd probably counter with how could he remember as it had been five and a half years ago. She made a mental note to see if Freddy had ever been questioned about the murder, but if Courtney hadn't opened up to the police, as she'd told Amanda and Trent, the investigation probably never took them to his door. "What about Casey-Anne Ritter?"

"The little detective asked about her. I don't know who she is."

"She was murdered a few days before Jackson."

"I'd send flowers, but…" He laughed and the expression of mirth chilled her; it was understandable why people feared him. But some bullies got off more on psychological games than inflicting physical brutality.

She nodded toward his wrist. "Where did you get that?" She may have been reaching here, as this particular bracelet might not have anything to do with Palmer. Then again it could be the connection between Webb, Palmer, and Ritter. Webb had visited Palmer not long after he'd gone to jail. She and Trent had assumed it was about the money, but what if it wasn't? What if it had something to do with—

"This? Take it." He tossed the bracelet across the table. "Damn thing's giving me a rash anyway."

She examined it where it came to rest on the table. She wouldn't be touching it without gloves. "Did Chad give it to you?"

Freddy's jaw was clenched, and he was looking at the table. She'd take his silence as a yes.

Maybe it wasn't silver but rather a worthless imitation? Some people were allergic to fake jewelry; some were allergic to the real thing.

"Hey." Freddy snapped his fingers. "Can I go now?"

She got up from the table, weighing the options. Freddy could have been involved in Palmer's murder and the two cold cases, but she didn't have the evidence to support that and he did have an alibi. Sure, he'd been involved with Palmer and up to something illegal, but until she could figure out what and get the proof to back up her hunch, it was in her best interests to let him go. She slipped her hands into her jacket pocket. "You can go. For now. But stay close."

Freddy jumped up and beelined for the door, but he stopped before letting himself out. "I'd just watch your back if I were you." He smirked and let himself out.

She could charge him for threatening an officer, but going that route could mess up her life, and he knew it, the smug son of a bitch. Now, to get her hands on a pair of gloves to transport this bracelet…

CHAPTER TWENTY-FOUR

Amanda carted the bracelet back to her desk in the palm of a gloved hand, holding it like a piece of valuable china, and dropped into her chair.

"You really think that was Palmer's bracelet?" Trent eyed her skeptically from the doorway of her cubicle.

"We talked about Casey-Anne being connected to Webb through the pawnshop," she started.

"We speculated she might have turned something in for cash, but that doesn't look like much." He gestured to the bracelet.

She looked down at the bracelet in her hand, her mind spinning. Trent was right that it didn't look like much, but she'd wager, based on its weight, that it was real silver. But how did the bracelet factor into Palmer's murder—if it did at all? And was his murder actually linked to the Ritter and Webb cold cases? They had been shot, while Palmer had been force-fed alcohol. The MO couldn't be more different. But she couldn't ignore the connection that Freddy had with Palmer and Webb. Ritter was the piece that didn't quite fit.

"Amanda?" Trent prompted.

"Yeah, I was just thinking about everything, whether maybe we're making a leap to think the three murders—Ritter, Webb, and Palmer—are linked." That's what she said, but there was a niggling in her gut that didn't find the possibility too far-fetched.

She looked up from the bracelet and met Trent's gaze. "Freddy handed this over rather easily, so we can assume it means nothing to him. Heck, we don't even know if it really means anything, period. But the car… it was a definite connection between Freddy and Palmer on the day he was murdered, and I'm confident Freddy's hiding something about it. I think he's on the hook with it missing. How that factors into Palmer's murder though… I don't know yet if it does."

"Well, you had me look up recent robberies." He walked back to his desk.

"I'm well aware."

"There was a home invasion at the Stewarts' residence in Woodbridge last week. Jewelry was stolen, with a combined value of over fifty thousand dollars."

"Fifty, as in five-o?" She wasn't sure if she'd heard him correctly.

"Yep."

"So if the car was taken by Palmer's killer and maybe the stolen items along with it… That could explain why Freddy's upset that it's missing."

"Couldn't it," he agreed.

"Maybe Palmer was going to fence the items, somewhere, somehow. He probably made some 'friends' while he was in prison."

"Leopards don't change their spots, as they say."

"Something like that."

"Well, we find the car and we might get more answers. Maybe Palmer had done something with the goods, someone wasn't happy and killed him."

"I don't know." She saw it as a possibility. Trent's words "we find the car" reminded her she'd missed filling him in. "I forgot to tell you I already had a be-on-the-lookout issued for a powder-blue Caprice."

"Okay."

"We'll also need to get a warrant for the surveillance camera from the Happy Time bar. Do you think you could manage the paperwork on that?"

"Of course."

She set the bracelet on her desk and stared at it as if she could just zap it for its history and value. She really needed some sleep! The first twenty-four hours of a case could be killer at the best of times. She glanced at the clock on the wall. It was after nine thirty at night.

She'd lost track of how long she'd been up, and she was pretty sure the last time she'd eaten had been just before the autopsy that morning.

She tinkered with the bracelet, flipping it over in her hands.

What are your secrets? Do you have any?

She ran her fingertips over the links and stopped at the clasp. Took a closer look.

What the—

She held it up and twisted it in the light to confirm her eyes weren't playing a trick on her, but there was something tucked into the clasp. It was silver in color, but it wasn't an actual part of the bracelet. She put her fingertip on top of it and applied just the smallest bit of pressure. Out popped the teeniest data chip she'd ever seen.

"Trent!" She held up the chip pinched between two gloved fingers.

He looked at her over the partition. "What is that?"

"I think we might have just found out what's so valuable about this bracelet." She smirked, feeling validated for following her instincts. Her dad had always told her instinct and intuition helped make the cop.

She shot to her feet, Trent trailing her.

"Where are you going?"

"I'm going to get this to Digital Forensics, and you, well… get the paperwork for the warrant started and go home, get some rest, and we'll catch up in the morning."

For the first time in this case, she really felt like they were getting somewhere.

CHAPTER TWENTY-FIVE

The department that handled tech, such as phones and computers, was the Digital Forensics unit under the Property Crimes Bureau. They were housed in the Eastern Police District Station, a two-story redbrick building, also in Woodbridge, and located on the curve of a residential street.

The place closed to civilians off the street at five, but she had the number for a detective she'd worked with numerous times in the past. He'd been assigned the evening shift and told her to show up and call him again once she got there and he'd let her in. She was at the front doors and just put her phone to her ear when he stuck his head out.

"Detective Steele."

She smiled and headed over to him. "Do I have something for you."

"Fun, fun." Detective Jacob Briggs loved his job just about as much as Rideout loved his. Jacob was a middle-aged man with a slight paunch and a full head of brown hair. His most arresting feature by far was his contagious smile.

He led her through the hallways to his office and turned to her. "What do you have?"

She extended the bracelet to him, which was inside an evidence bag. "I'm really hoping you can tell me."

"Well…" He stepped back, angled his head this way and that. "Looks like a bracelet to me."

"Very funny."

"Okay, hand it over, let me have a look." He snapped on a pair of gloves.

She did as he requested, and he withdrew the bracelet and set it on the bag.

"All right, when you called you said there was a data chip?" He looked at her, brows pinched.

"Look in the clasp." She'd put it back there for safekeeping.

"All righty." Jacob worked the bracelet. "*Aaaah*. Here we go." He grinned at her, then proceeded to hold the chip to the light. "Tiny little thing."

"Yeah, I'm hoping you have something that you can stick it in to find out what's on it."

"You've always had such a way with words. But, yeah, I have something I can stick it in."

He dropped into his chair and pulled out a laptop. He pointed to a small port on the side. "It should fit in there nicely." He powered up the computer and put the chip into the port he'd indicated. "We should know in just a— Oh."

"What?" She moved around to get a better view of the laptop screen. A pop-up window asked for the administrator password. "That can't be good."

"Whatever's on there, someone took great lengths to protect it. I've seen this before, and sometimes I can hack in, but—" He paused and winced. "I hate to say it, but you're going to have to leave this with me."

"Can you just give it a go with me here? I'm not in a hurry." Her curiosity trumped her exhaustion as her mind played over the possibilities. Maybe it contained a tracking and inventory of stolen goods.

"I can, but I can't make any promises."

She put a hand on his shoulder. "If anyone can crack this thing, it's you."

"I appreciate your confidence, but I suggest you get comfortable. Maybe even get yourself a coffee. I might be a—"

Her phone rang. "Sorry, just one second," she said to Jacob. Her caller ID read, *Tipsy Moose*. "I have to get this."

"Take your time. I'm going to be a while likely." Jacob pulled a book out of a drawer and flipped its pages as she answered her phone.

"This is Amanda."

"Hey. Your boyfriend just showed up."

Her heartbeat tapped a little faster at the thought of seeing Motel Guy again. It would have been far easier if she didn't have to. After all, that would mean no complications, entanglements, or explanations.

"You there?" her caller prompted.

"I am. Ah, thanks."

"Uh-huh. You coming?"

She looked at Jacob who was now chewing on a pencil, tapping his foot, and clicking on the keyboard, lines of code on the screen.

"I'll be right there." She hung up. "I've got to go somewhere," she told Jacob, who carried on being Jacob.

Amanda spotted Motel Guy's black Dodge Ram in the Tipsy Moose's parking lot and parked a few slots away.

She undid her seat belt and it caught on her badge.

Can't be taking you in there with me, she thought, and unclipped it and put it in the glove box, along with her Glock and holster.

Inside, she spotted the bartender from earlier in the day. He pointed across the room, and she followed the direction of his finger. Motel Guy was in a booth, drinking alone.

Thanks, she mouthed to the tender. She smoothed a hand over her hair and headed over.

She slipped in across from Motel Guy. Suddenly she found her heart was pounding and she felt self-conscious. Her face would be a mess of freckles thanks to her Scottish lineage, but it wasn't like she'd had time to refresh her makeup before coming here. Besides, she wasn't here to pick the guy up again—she just needed him to provide a little statement to her boss.

Motel Guy looked up, eyes wide, mouth slightly agape. Shock followed by a flash of irritation. "What are you doing here?" He turned his rocks glass in his hand.

She gestured toward his drink. "No beer tonight?"

"Are you stalking me?"

She glanced over at the bartender. He was watching them and smiled at her. Had he told Motel Guy about their arrangement?

"I'm not stalking you," she hissed, "but I do need to talk to you."

"Didn't think you wanted to talk at all. One night, that's all you wanted. No names, no strings." He swept a hand across the table and almost upset his glass. He covered by lifting it for a drink.

"I've changed my mind." She was prepared to say anything if it got her alibi. As she took in his features, her heart and stomach lurched like she had crested a hill on a roller coaster. A rogue strand of his blond hair fell in front of his left eye. She had to fight the urge not to tuck it out of the way. "What's going on with you tonight?"

"None. Of. Your. Business." Every word slurred. Business sounding like it was spelled with Zs. "'Sides," he went on, "women like you don't want anything more. You told me so yourself." He slurped his drink.

She stiffened. The man who had been so confident last night was crumbling before her eyes, but she didn't have time for his wounded ego to take center stage. "Fine, maybe I haven't changed my mind." She wasn't sure where *maybe* came from but continued. "But something's come up and I need your help."

"Mighty convenient. You know I came here even though I thought I might run into you. I told myself that would be okay. I mean, so what if we slept together."

His voice rose and projected, and she sank in the booth.

"What? You're embarrassed of me now?"

He got this little indent in his brow that she wanted to dip a fingertip in. Whatever was weighing on his mind, it likely had nothing to do with her or their night together. He was facing his own demons.

"Not embarrassed at all," she said calmly. "But if you would just let me talk to—"

"No. We had an arrangement. You set up the terms and I only live by them. Just like every other woman on the planet has their rules."

So he was drinking because of some woman…

He pulled out his phone and tapped away at the screen. A few seconds later, he pocketed it and exchanged it for his glass, which he raised in a toast gesture then shot back. "Night." He got up and stumbled toward the door.

"Where are you going? You've been drinking." She hurried behind him. For a drunk guy he could move.

"Just ordered a cab. Bye-bye." He swung the bar's door open and stepped outside.

She couldn't force him to stay and talk to her or even be civil for that matter. But if she didn't get her alibi ironed out then she was screwed.

The door started to close, and she slapped it with so much force it flew back at her. "Ugh. Can't we just talk like adults?" she called out to him.

He turned. "Not feeling much like talkin', but if you're interested in something else."

"I'll pass."

"Not what you said last night."

She'd only been with him for one night, and she didn't really know him, but she liked to think she was a better judge of character than this. "Listen, I don't know what the hell your problem is, but I need you to shut up and hear what I have to say."

He stepped toward her; she stepped back. Still, his towering height of six-foot-something was overwhelming to her five-nine frame.

"Fine. Go ahead," he told her.

"I need you to testify that we were together last night."

"No need to deny it. It was good." He winked at her. "But it was a one-night special."

"Let this sink in," she said slowly. "I need you as my alibi."

"Alibi?" The corner of his lips curved. "Someone's been a naughty girl."

"Oh, please stop. You're not as charming as you think you are," she snapped. "You're actually a real ass when you're drunk."

His eyes met hers and she felt a twinge of regret for speaking her mind.

"And I haven't done anything wrong," she said. "That's why I need you to come forward and confirm that we were together last night."

"How much detail is needed?"

"You're impossible to talk to right now."

"Let's not talk then. Nighty-night— Oh, looks like my cab's here anyway. Saved by the cab." He laughed at his own joke and walked toward the yellow taxi that had pulled into the lot.

"Unbelievable!" she said to the night air, and apparently a couple headed into the bar, as both looked at her. "Never mind. Just the boyfriend's driving me mad," she told them.

They barely acknowledged her, but Amanda could have sworn she saw the woman roll her eyes as she nestled closer to her date.

Amanda stood there with her arms crossed. This ridiculous interaction had driven home why she only had one-night stands.

It meant she didn't have to deal with impossible man-babies who carted around their own emotional baggage.

Malone would just have to accept she couldn't pin down her alibi. No matter what she'd face at his hands, it couldn't be as bad as what had just transpired here. And maybe she'd get removed from the case and have a way out of keeping her word. It had been what she'd wanted anyway, right? At least before the investigation got interesting with the bracelet and the data chip…

She stomped back to her car, chastising herself the entire way. She'd blown any chance of securing her alibi. She doubted Motel Guy would be returning to the Tipsy Moose anytime soon, especially if he viewed her as some crazy who couldn't let go of their night together.

She stopped walking. She was right next to the bumper of Motel Guy's Dodge Ram pickup.

She pulled out her phone, brought up the notepad app, and keyed in the license plate. "Got you, you son of a—" Her phone rang. It was Jacob.

"You got something?"

"Oh, yeah, and it's not pretty."

"What's on it?"

"Spreadsheets, photos, tracking of bank-transfer confirmations." Jacob sounded like he was chewing on bile. "Whoever this bracelet belonged to, Amanda, was or still is involved in sex trafficking. There's hundreds of them, Mandy, and some of them are just babies—as young as six and seven."

She put a hand on her stomach. "We've got to get Sex Crimes in the loop." Amanda typically did her best to curtail her involvement in sex-related crimes; she preferred grisly murder scenes instead.

"They'll be my next call."

"Okay, keep me posted. But when could I take a look at what's on there?" It was a path she felt necessary, though she wasn't looking forward to it by any means.

"If you want to... I'm having nightmares tonight. But I'll do my best to get everything loaded onto the mainframe tonight. Should be there come morning. I'll text you once it is."

"Thanks. Oh, and Jacob..." She went on to explain a bit about the history of the bracelet and how it had come into her hands, then said, "I realize the chain of evidence may be a little broken—"

"A little."

"Yeah, well, I still want someone from Forensics to see if they can get any epithelial, possible DNA. We won't be able to use any results to confirm ownership of the bracelet in court, but it could point us in the right direction to evidence we can use."

"We? You keep saying we. Sort of stuck on that. Aren't you a lone wolf?"

She sighed. "Don't get me started. Bye."

There was little more she could do tonight. She highly doubted Freddy was aware of the bracelet's chip and contents or he never would have handed it over so easily. Really the same went for Palmer, it occurred to her now. If he was involved in the ring, he wouldn't have given the bracelet to Freddy.

She massaged her temple. This case was proving to be physically and mentally exhausting. She glanced back at the bar. She'd grab a couple of sliders to go and head home.

She scarfed the mini burgers as she drove and cracked her car's windows, hoping the cold night air would wake her up and backed it by blaring some rock station out of Washington. But as exhausted as her body was, her mind was awake. At least she had something to help with that. She slipped her hand into her jacket pocket, as if to simply assure herself the baggie of pills was still there.

Her phone rang over the speaker, cutting out the music, and it jolted her and caused her to swerve slightly. Maybe she shouldn't be driving, but it was too late to worry about that now. Besides, she'd be home soon.

She took a steadying breath, regained control, and looked at the display screen. Caller ID was blocked. Again, it could be Trent; it wasn't like she'd had any time to add his number to her contacts yet.

She accepted the call. "Hello."

Silence and deep breathing.

"Who are you?" The skin pricked on the back of her neck and she had this feeling she was being watched, even though she was barreling down the highway.

Silence.

Could it be Freddy or one of his crew harassing her, trying to scare her or intimidate her? The thought came and went. It wouldn't make sense for it to be him. She'd had one of these calls before he'd been brought in and what would he have to gain from harassing her? Amusement? It could land his ass in jail.

"I'm a police detective," she ground out. All her patience was gone, and with the latest revelation, she wasn't in the mood to waste any time playing games. "Talk or stop call—"

Headlights were getting bigger in her rearview mirror as a vehicle quickly closed in on her bumper. Her heart hammered. Maybe someone had been watching her, the thought raising hairs all over her body.

The caller clicked off and her music came back on, but her focus was on the aggressive driver behind her. Was it her caller?

"Who are you, you son of a bitch?" she hissed, more bravado than true courage. She tapped the brake pedal—a potentially stupid and risky move.

In response, the vehicle swerved out and around her. The driver honked their horn as they passed.

"Jerk!" she yelled and looked at her speedometer. No wonder the drive was taking so long; she was barely putting along.

She pulled to the side of the road and collected her breath. What the hell was up with this person calling and doing nothing but breathing? Were they trying to freak her out? If so, it was working. Maybe it had nothing to do with Freddy, but maybe the owner of the bracelet somehow knew that she had it. Shivers ran through her. She really needed rest before her paranoia ran her off the road.

CHAPTER TWENTY-SIX

The next day Amanda was up before her alarm. She flung her legs over the side of the mattress with more purpose than she'd had in a long time. Just thinking how those poor girls needed her was enough to spurn her forward, and she had the day's itinerary all mapped out in her head. Jacob would likely have the information from the bracelet's data chip ready for her this morning; she'd always found him to be a man of his word. She and Trent would bring in Freddy and Courtney and drill them about the bracelet, see if they could get any further there. With any luck, they'd make some headway toward bringing down the sex-trafficking ring.

"Time for Mommy to keep her word, baby girl," she said to the walls, to the spirit of her dead daughter. Who truly knew what happened to us when we died? What she couldn't deny though were the nights she could have sworn she'd felt Kevin moving on his side of the bed. Whenever she'd reached out or looked—nothing, no one. It was likely just her carrying his ghost around in her mind.

She headed down the hall and went through her morning routine. On her way out of the house, she grabbed her keys from the bowl by the front door and shoved them into her jacket pocket. Her fingers brushed against the baggie of pills and she pulled it out. She'd be able to concentrate much better without worrying about them being discovered on her person.

She looked down at them in her palm. There were still six pills. Despite her intention, she hadn't taken a Xanax last night. She'd just had a sleeping pill, crawled into bed, and left the day behind. She had more willpower than she realized, but she'd keep them for a moment of weakness. She took the pills and Freddy's card to her bedroom and put them in the top drawer of her nightstand, then exited her house to hit the road.

First stop would be Hannah's Diner for a coffee.

The door chimed when she entered the shop. May Byrd, who owned the diner and had named it after her first daughter, was behind the counter and offered her a gigawatt smile. May was easily in her early sixties and always lit up when she saw Amanda. May had told her once that she reminded her of Hannah, even though she was several years older than Amanda. She was a big-shot defense attorney in Washington.

"Good morning, May."

"How are you, sweetheart?"

"I'm fine." Amanda's gaze drifted to the pots on the counter behind May. "I'd love a coffee."

"Of course ya would." May grabbed an extra-large to-go cup and filled it to the brim, then snapped on a lid.

"You know just the way I like it." Her dad had always said don't trust a cop who doesn't drink their coffee black.

"Hey, hold up a minute." May hustled along the counter to where there was a confection display cabinet, slid the doors open at the back, and pulled out a blueberry muffin. She put it into a bag and extended it to Amanda. "Here, take this. Baked fresh this morning."

In all the years Amanda had been coming here, May had given her only two freebies. The first was when her fraternal grandmother had died, back when she was in the police academy; the second was after the accident. The pattern wasn't one that was encouraging, but nothing bad had happened— Oh, unless word had already got around about Palmer's death. But was that bad news per se?

"What's this for?" Amanda indicated the muffin.

"You certainly haven't had it easy, dear, but at least your luck is changing. That horrible man is dead."

She let out the breath she'd been holding, almost as if she'd expected that May was going to say something else. But it made sense that Palmer's death would get back to May. She was the heartbeat of the small community and every morsel of gossip passed through the walls of the diner. And anything May might miss there, she would hear from her book club, which convened once a month to discuss their latest paperback but weekly to shoot scuttlebutt.

"Okay, well, thank you for the muffin and the coffee." She dropped two dollars on the counter and left.

She'd just bit into the muffin when her phone rang. Chew, chew, chew... She swallowed a large chunk and fished her phone out of her pocket. Caller ID told her it was Malone. "Hey."

"Where are you?"

"Just about to head in."

"Good. Come to my office straightaway." With that he clicked off.

Something had Malone worked up, and that, combined with the strange way May had been with her, gave Amanda the niggling feeling something wasn't right.

She drove to the station, breaking a few speeding laws, but when she walked through the building, she found her legs weren't moving fast. She made her way through the cubicle maze belonging to the Homicide Unit, passing Cud, who looked up at her but turned away just as quickly.

"Come on—get in here." Malone was waving her down the hallway like a marshal corralling an airplane into a parking spot.

She went inside, him behind her, and he shut the door.

"We don't have long," he said.

"What happened?" She had a sick feeling crawling over her skin, and it tamped down the urgency of filling him in on the bracelet and data chip.

"First, please tell me you have that alibi."

"You're freaking me out a bit."

"Never mind that… Your alibi?"

She hadn't done anything with Motel Guy's plate last night, but she had a link to hunt him down. "Working on it."

"Working on it. Oy vey." He started pacing his small office. Stopped. Put his hands on his hips. "What seems to be the issue?"

"It's a little complicated, and I'd been up for over thirty hours and needed sleep."

"Just don't tell me you don't really have one because I'll wind up with a hernia."

"Oh, I have one."

"Okay, good, good." He looked at her as if expecting her to hand it over, despite the fact she'd just said she was working on it.

She shrank. "As soon as I have it, I'll—"

There was a knock on the door.

"There's the shit hitting the fan," Malone mumbled. "I didn't even get a chance to warn you."

"Wha—"

Malone got the door. "Lieutenant Hill, how nice to—"

"Save it, Malone." Lieutenant Sherry Hill strode into the room wearing a navy-blue pencil skirt with matching jacket, a cream silk blouse spilling over the neckline—a string bean on stilettos holding on to a black leather attaché case.

The lieutenant looked around the room and pursed her lips, which were painted a bright red in stark contrast to her otherwise fair features. "Small little office, isn't it? We should have moved this meeting to mine, but it's best we get down to business." She leaned against the filing credenza and reached into her attaché.

Amanda glanced at Malone, who closed his eyes and shook his head. Whatever was coming out of that thing was not good news. Malone was a shade of green or, as Lindsey would have said, "he had gills." It was how she described it when she wasn't feeling well.

"You could sit in my seat if you'd like," Malone offered Hill, likely more a delay tactic than out of any real concern for her comfort.

"I'm fine. Thank you."

Hill withdrew a folded newspaper from her bag, handed it to Amanda, and set her bag on the cabinet next to her. "Not sure if you've had a chance to read the latest?"

Amanda glanced at the copy of the *Prince William Times* in her hand. "What am I looking at?"

"Right on the cover." Hill pointed with a manicured fingertip. "By all means, go ahead and read. We'll wait." Hill pasted on a tight-lipped smile for her and let it carry to Malone. "Go ahead," she reiterated.

Lead sank in Amanda's gut, a premonition setting in that everything was about to come crumbling down on top of her. She'd rather Hill scream and shout, but that wasn't how the woman operated. She toyed with her subordinates through the subtleties of misleading displays of compassion and understanding. Like a psychopath, she batted her opponents with her paws, claws retracted until the final moment when she was going in for the kill. Amanda could feel her demise breathing down the back of her neck.

She set her coffee on the edge of Malone's desk and slowly flipped and unfolded the paper. In large bold letters were the words *PWCPD Playing Favorites and Murder Victim to Pay the Price*. The article had been written by Fraser Reyes and, as Amanda read, her stomach twisted and balled, and her chest grew tighter. Reyes had painted the PWCPD as a bunch of cops more loyal to a former police chief than to finding justice. It alleged that by letting Detective Steele, the former police chief's daughter, work an investigation into the murder of the man involved in the accident that had claimed her family's life, the PWCPD was hosting a faux investigation, intent on sweeping Chad Palmer's murder under the rug. Reyes also reported that Detective Amanda Steele had been so ardent in questioning Palmer's girlfriend—who preferred to remain unnamed—that she was considering suing the department for harassment.

Amanda gripped the paper, the newsprint crinkling under her fingers. She wanted to hurl the thing across the room.

"All of this came as a shock to me," Hill said, drawing Amanda's gaze. "The fact that you'd be working this case in any capacity at all… Abhorrent thought, really." Hill's words were concise and prim, laced and dripping with acid.

Sure, Amanda had messed up, but it was the damn small community of slack jaws that had truly bitten her in the ass! If only she'd sent Trent solo to Courtney Barrett. And to think that she hadn't the decency to acknowledge that she knew who Amanda was to her face. She glanced at Malone.

"He can't save you from this mess, and there's a lot to be cleaned up, Detective. All because you put your nose in where it didn't belong." She smoothed out her skirt. "Now, I'm sorry for what happened to your family—" She paused; she must have witnessed the rage in Amanda's eyes.

Amanda wanted to lash back that she highly doubted the lieutenant was sorry at all. She'd wager Hill may have even reveled in her tragedy.

"As I was saying," Hill continued, "I'm sorry for what happened to your family, but I can't have the community thinking that Prince William County PD turns a blind eye to justice, to conflict of interest. I'm sure you understand."

Amanda clenched her teeth so hard, a pain shot through her jaw. All those girls caught up in the sex-trafficking ring. Was she just supposed to turn her back on them?

"Sergeant Malone has explained to me that this reporter, a Mr.…" Hill nudged her chin toward the paper still in Amanda's hands.

"Fraser Reyes," Amanda said coolly. Hill knew exactly what his name was but just wanted to exert her power. More batting of her paws.

"Yes, well, Sergeant Malone has assured me that Mr. Reyes has exaggerated his facts, but just the hint of scandal, that we as PWCPD are willing to sacrifice our service to the community, well, it's to be taken seriously indeed."

Hill stopped talking and crossed her legs at the ankles. All a play at dramatics to relax her prey, when her softened posture just meant the claws were about to come out. "Malone did confirm that you had made some inquiries early in the case, but that you've taken a back seat in the investigation itself. Is that correct?" She arched her brows and managed to look down on Amanda, who was standing, from her seated position.

"Detective?" Hill prompted.

"That's correct," Amanda forced out.

"From what I understand from Malone, the actual lead on the case is Detective Stenson." Hill leveled her gaze at her, expecting a response.

"Correct," Amanda confirmed.

"So you both expect me to believe that you've been reporting to a rookie?" She scoffed laughter, looking from Amanda to Malone and back again. "Excuse me, but I'm calling complete and utter bullshit on that." A splash of red filled her cheeks. "But it's a good thing for you that I'm a reasonable woman and a team player." She shot a threatening look at Malone. "And if those who report to me tell me something, I like to believe them, I endeavor to believe them, but I really should suspend you both."

Hill let the threat sit in the air, and the room went silent except for breathing and the ticking clock on the wall. Eventually, Hill spoke again. "But I'm not going to—officially anyhow. At least not yet. However, let me make this perfectly clear, Detective. You are not to touch this case again."

A ball knotted in Amanda's chest. Just when she had started to feel a spark of purpose again, this witch had stomped it out. Well, screw it! She wasn't the only cop who could save those girls and bring the sick bastards involved to justice. She'd fill in Trent, and someone from Sex Crimes was probably already on it.

"You know what?" Amanda unclipped her badge from her waist. "Take it!"

Hill's eyes enlarged, but a smirk toyed at the corners of her mouth. Malone was shaking his head.

Amanda proceeded to remove her holster and firearm. "Take it all." She shoved the items toward Hill, but the lieutenant wouldn't take them. Amanda dropped them on the cabinet next to her.

"Are you quitting?" Hill asked, sounding too pleased by the prospect.

"I'm doing what you don't have the guts to do; I'm suspending myself."

"You can't—"

"I just did," Amanda shoved out.

"All right then…" Hill hoisted herself off the cabinet and grabbed her attaché case. "Suit yourself. Take some time off, get a massage or something. You do seem rather tense, Detective."

At the door, Hill looked over a shoulder and flashed her a smug, self-satisfied smile that Amanda would have happily smacked off her face.

Malone was quick to get the door and shut Amanda inside with him. "What the hell are you doing?"

"I'm not living with a threat hanging over my head. She tells us 'oh, I'm not officially suspending you, at least not right now'? It's a manipulation tactic and I'm not anyone's damn puppet, least of all Hill's!"

Malone put his hands on his hips and let out a puff of air. "I admit that I expected a lot worse."

"She's just saving it up for a time in the future. People like her work the favor system."

"I'm not going to dispute that, but"—Malone glanced at her items on the cabinet—"I just don't want you to throw everything you've worked for away."

In this moment she wasn't so sure what she had was worth fighting for. She hadn't been the same since the accident; she'd lost purpose and direction. Her motivation gone. Any dreams of an amazing future gone. She wasn't cut out for this job anymore. She'd been a pretender, a fake, for the last five and a half years.

"I know you've experienced horrible loss," Malone said softly, inching toward the cabinet. "And I can't begin to imagine how much you're still hurting. And maybe"—he shrugged—"some time off would do you good. Maybe get out of town, take a real vacation somewhere outside the county. But don't leave this behind because you let Hill get under your skin." He took her badge, holster, and gun and extended it to her. When she didn't reach for it right away, he nudged it toward her. "Don't make Hill happy by leaving the force. Then she'll win."

Amanda looked down at the items that had defined her entire adult life. She should have felt a draw to take them from Malone, but she stepped back and shook her head. "I'm taking—" She was going to say *a break* when her phone rang. One quick glance at the caller ID and her breath froze. *Dad.* Of all the times!

She squeezed her phone. All she wanted to do was slam it to the floor, stomp it to pieces. Anything so it would stop ringing.

"Your dad?" Malone wagered a guess, his voice respectful and tentative.

She clenched her jaw and nodded as the ringing continued. She expected Malone to give her some lecture about how she should pick it up, that her father wouldn't want her to throw her career away, that her father was attempting to traverse the chasm between them and mend things. But did all of them think it had been an easy decision to stop talking to her family and back away? She'd just done what she needed to do in order to survive. She shook off the guilt that was worming its way through her, but her entire body was pulsating.

The ringing stopped—her father would have been shuffled to voicemail—and the room somehow became quieter than before.

Malone was still holding out her badge, holster, and gun. Again, he nudged it toward her.

"I've gotta go." She brushed past him and hurried out the door. Self-doubt rattled through her mind, crippling her, hindering her steps, but she was making the right decision for her. She couldn't cling to her job just because it was familiar or because victims depended on her. Other cops would rise. It was time for her to be brave enough to face a new world of her own making. Get out of town as Malone had suggested. Just maybe she wouldn't come back. After all, the sobering truth was that Hill's claws hadn't come out at all. No, Amanda was quite sure the lieutenant wasn't finished batting her—or Malone—around yet, but she didn't have to sit around and take it.

CHAPTER TWENTY-SEVEN

The tape icon in the top-left-hand corner of Amanda's phone screen burned a hole in the heart. Just knowing that on the other side it would be her father's voice, a voice from her past, from before life had been flipped on its head… Yes, it was time to get out of the county. Maybe never look back again.

She pulled into her driveway. She'd just slip into her house for a quick moment, pack a couple of bags, and hit the road. Who knew where it would take her and when she'd stop?

She was partway up the front walk when her phone rang again. She stopped and took it out of her pocket. It was probably going to be Malone appealing for her return or Trent checking on her whereabouts, but she wasn't in the mood for either conversation. She also wasn't in the mood for some idiot trying to scare her. "Unbelievable," she called out at seeing the caller ID was blocked. She slid the call to voicemail and hurried to her door.

She put the key in the lock and twisted. But it was already unlocked. Her hand moved to her holster—only to be reminded it wasn't there. For the trace of a second, she regretted her brash decision to leave her badge and weapon behind.

She slowly opened the door and stepped inside. At a quick glance, everything looked the way she'd left it. She relaxed her shoulders and took a deep breath. She'd probably just forgotten to lock the door on the way out that morning. She spun to latch the deadbolt, but mid-turn she heard footsteps behind her. She knew what she had to do: unlock the door and run outside. But her body wasn't listening to her; fear had frozen her in place.

"Turn around, nice and slow. Make one move for your gun and I'll blow you away."

A man's voice. She noted he assumed she was armed; he knew she was police. Likely this was the one who'd been prank calling her, but what was his motivation?

She proceeded to turn, hands in the air, and stood still as he approached to frisk her. He was easily six-foot-four, with a muscular build. From the look of him, he could bench-press her. He was also armed with a handgun.

"I'm not carrying," she said. If she could get to her bedroom and her dresser, in one of its drawers she had a Beretta in a gun case, but the distance seemed unpassable with this mammoth and his weapon in her way. Maybe she should just surrender and accept this could be the end for her. After all, she was on borrowed time anyhow; she should have died with her family five and a half years ago.

Satisfied that she was unarmed, the man moved suddenly, kicking her legs out from under her. Amanda slammed to the floor; the back of her head smacked against the laminate. She scrambled to get up, fighting instinct taking over regardless of her earlier thoughts.

He circled around in front of her and held the gun in her face. She wanted to ask him who he was but feared that would anger him more, as if he'd expect her to know the answer already. It would be better if she just kept quiet.

His dark eyes met hers, but he said nothing.

"Are you the one who called me?"

Still he remained quiet. The silence was more disturbing than his outbursts of anger. At least then she knew what emotion was taking the lead. "What do you want?"

"What do I—" He bared his teeth, bent down, and slapped her across the face with force. Her neck torqued to the right and she heard her bones crack. Pain crackled down her spine and she sucked in air through clenched teeth. But before she could catch her breath, he struck her again and her vision became a wall of exploding white fireworks. She clambered to get off the floor. He grabbed her hair and yanked so hard she felt her scalp rise from bone, and he dragged her down the hall toward her bedroom.

She spat blood, her tongue coated with the coppery taste. She kicked her feet, bucking against him with all her strength, but it was like a kitten taking on a mountain lion. And the more she resisted, the more pain fired through her. She clawed at his hand, sinking her nails into his flesh until finally he let her go. Built-up momentum caused her to lose her balance and she fell to the floor; this time her head didn't hit.

She snarled and asked again, "What do you want?"

He was occupied staring at the blood that stained the back of his hand as if it were unexpected. He didn't look at her when he spoke. "You should have died."

His words didn't refer to right now, and his gaze was distant, as if he were raptured in the past. Then she saw it, in just the slight contortion of his lips, in the arch of his brow, in the spacing between the eyes. The man before her had been in the photo with Palmer as a boy. "You're Chad's cousin. Rick Jensen."

He flared his nostrils and came at her with murderous rage, though she didn't know why. She closed her eyes, expecting the next thing she'd feel would be the cold blanket of death. But he twisted her hair around his hand again as he positioned himself behind her—then he started dragging her down the hall.

She screamed—the physical pain was blinding—but she hoped and even prayed that a neighbor would hear and call for help. She stopped fighting him though. If he was taking her to the bedroom, he was getting her closer to the gun in her dresser.

Once in her room, he set her next to the end of the bed on the floor and clambered over her. Her brain was stuck on one fact: there was no way she was going to let this shit rape her. She slapped at him and bit his upper arm, sinking her teeth through his shirt, tasting the coppery flavor of blood again.

But her assault didn't stop him or slow his actions. He pawed around until he found her handcuffs around the back of her waistband—it figured they were the one thing she'd forgotten to hand in—and slapped one on her right wrist. He then adjusted her so that she was sitting against the leg of the bedframe and wrapped his arms around her, taking her right and left wrist and snapping them together behind the leg.

She bucked, but there was no place for her to go without taking the bed with her.

He stood up and stared down on her. Mirrored in his eyes she saw the hatred she felt toward Palmer and for this man right now. Her head was pounding, and with every breath the pain intensified.

"You have no right to investigate Chad's death," he spat.

Now all the pieces aligned, and it was clear that his love for Palmer had driven him to this point. "That's what this is about?"

"Shut up!"

"I'm off the case!"

"Liar!" he bellowed.

"No! Please! I have no badge and no gun." She blinked heavily, grateful again that she'd had the courage and tenacity to leave them behind. Maybe, if she convinced him, it could be what saved her life.

"Courtney called me. Said you were looking into Chad's murder." He scrunched up his face in a knotted ball. "You have no right," he seethed.

"You're… you're right, I don't, and I'm not. I'm off the case."

"You're probably happy he's dead," he kicked back, as if her words hadn't even hit his ears. "But you don't know what kind of a man he really was. The childhood he had." Tears buffeted his cheeks as a torrential downpour.

She moved, trying to figure out her range of motion. It wasn't much. Nothing she could really work with. Her legs were free, but she'd have to time any defensive kicks with precision. Really, her best chance of living another day was getting him to talk and open up, and then relate with him. "Tell me about him," she requested, the words rubbing against the grain of her being. She didn't see Palmer as human—he was the monster, the boogieman who had taken her family.

"And I had to find out about… about…" Rick knotted up his face and his chin quivered as the tears continued to fall. "I found out about his murder from Courtney. I hate that bitch." His gaze steeled over.

"You're right. You should have been notified."

"By you," he barked. "What a joke! You probably celebrated when you found out he was dead." Rick sobbed into his hands.

She had to find a way to get the hell out of here. The situation was breaking down quickly. Rick's heightened state of emotion was more volatile than outright displays of aggression. If she didn't muster some genuine empathy—at least some that Rick would buy—she'd have no hope of walking away. But from where would she pull the strength?

CHAPTER TWENTY-EIGHT

"You're right," Amanda repeated. "I should have told you. For that I apologize."

"Huh, for that, but not for my loss. You hated Chad; you probably believe he deserved to die. You have no right investigating his death." He was talking in circles like a madman and trained his gun on her.

Her entire body thrummed with rage and disgust. "He murdered my family!"

"How dare you." He smacked her so lightning quick, she didn't have time to defend herself and kick.

With this assault something sharp bit into her cheek. The pain tearing through her was so visceral it brought a high of its own. This was the most she'd felt in years; he'd penetrated the layers of numbness to where she could experience emotion. She sniffed, swallowing snot and blood.

"You're going to listen to me, and you're not going to interrupt." Rick shook the hand he'd struck her with, and she saw a ring; it must have been what cut her. "I said you're going to listen." He glared at her, daring her to speak.

She clamped her mouth shut. The pain had her head swooning anyway.

"Chad was my"—he ran his arm under his nose—"best friend. More than family."

She flashed back to the photo of the boys with the bicycles. It had looked like a happy summer day that would have brought good memories.

Rick went on. "We were more like brothers, not cousins. We were all we had in this world." A fresh batch of tears fell.

Rage was causing her skin to pulsate; she could anticipate the direction of this conversation. Rick was going to paint Palmer as some saint who'd made one slip and she was going to be forced to listen. He'd not only killed her family, but he might have been involved with the sex trafficking of young girls. But how could she bring up the topic without enraging Rick and getting her head blown off?

Rick continued. "Our dads were never in the picture, and our moms didn't care about us. They were too busy hooking up with men and getting drunk off their asses." He paced in a wide loop but never took his eye from her. Not that she could have done anything to free herself anyhow— Though she then recalled she had the key for the cuffs still. He hadn't taken it. But the key was in the right front pocket of her jeans and with Rick watching her there was no way she could maneuver the amount she needed to reach the pocket.

Rick stopped, looked at her. "Chad had a hard life."

She wanted to scream, *"And my fucking family had to pay the price for that?"*

Rick tapped his gun against his thigh. "He deserves justice, and I want justice for him, but you're not going to get that for him."

"I told you I'm not working the case any—"

He raised the gun. "No talking."

She ground her teeth.

"That's why I have no choice but to—" He sniffled loudly and steadied his gun. "Give me one reason why I shouldn't shoot you."

She looked to the wall where a portrait used to hang of her, Kevin, and Lindsey. It had been taken on Lindsey's third birthday.

She recalled the photo as clear as if it were there right now and remembered how hard it had been to get a three-year-old to sit still. They'd had to bribe her with the promise of vanilla ice cream topped with colored sprinkles.

"One reason," he repeated. "Why should I trust that you'll find justice for Chad?" His eyes were glazed over, his facial features dark and hardened. She could see that, although compromised and hurting, Rick Jensen didn't really want to pull the trigger—but that didn't mean he wouldn't.

She considered his question, a variation of the same one she'd asked herself several times throughout the investigation. Every time the same answer kicked back. "I gave my word," she pushed out.

Rick studied her eyes, palmed his cheeks. He seemed surprised by her response, maybe skeptical.

"I always keep my word." Hot tears filled her eyes at the recollection of her daughter's small coffin lowering into the ground. She met Rick's gaze.

"That's not enough," Rick said. "People lie all the time." He clenched his jaw and ground out, "Give me a real reason why I shouldn't pull this trigger." His voice rose with each word and the volume pounded in her head as booms of thunder.

"I took an oath," she hissed as a shot of pain tore through her. He was watching her; he seemed to be encouraging her to continue. With his focus on her, it nailed in that she'd given her word a long time ago—further back than this case. She'd taken the oath to serve and protect. It just seemed like so very long ago that she'd graduated the police academy, her entire family cheering her on from the audience. But she had been a different person; the tragedy had changed her—but had it? If she concentrated hard enough, she could still feel a subtle stirring within her. Maybe more like the flickering of a flame. Before the article and Hill's intervention, she'd tasted what it used to feel like to be a cop, driven to get justice.

She stuck out her jaw and made sure to cement eye contact with Jensen. "I'd be lying if I said I'll ever forgive your cousin for what happened that night."

He steadied the gun on her, and she shut her eyes, certain she'd be dead soon. But he didn't fire, and she opened her eyes.

"But I will find justice for him." He didn't need to know her desire to do so was more rooted in living up to the expectations she'd set for herself, for her daughter, and those girls on the data chip who needed her. Her motivation had nothing to do with any empathy for Palmer.

"That's what I'm here to do," she added. The words zapped her of strength and her eyes felt as heavy as her limbs. "I always keep my word," she mumbled.

"I'd like to believe you." He still held firm on the gun.

"My life's in your hands." She blinked slowly, her mind, her body, her spirit wanting rest.

She remained still as he lowered the weapon and gripped her jaw. He put his face mere inches from hers and stared into her eyes for what felt like forever. Eventually, he got up and tucked his gun into the waistband of his jeans. "I'll let you live."

All she could do was blink *thank you.*

"But if you don't keep to your oath…" He pulled a photo from his shirt pocket and tossed it toward Amanda. It came to rest face-up. It was a picture of her parents' house, her father in the driveway standing next to a gray four-door sedan. "Just know that I can get to your dear old daddy at any time."

She shivered, suddenly freezing as she looked at her father. Despite the passing of the years, he hadn't changed too much; he just had more gray around the temples. She nearly drowned in the rush of emotion that washed over her with the tenacity of a flash flood. It was as if all the time and distance between them had been amplified and she felt so incredibly heartbroken. "You stay the hell away from him!"

"Just keep your word or POP!" Rick mimicked a gunshot to the head. "But if his life isn't enough motivation, there's always this too." He held up the baggie of pills and took Freddy's card out of his front pocket. "I'm pretty sure the drugstore doesn't package them this way, and I'm guessing this F guy is your dealer?"

"I don't know what you're talking about." She couldn't meet his eyes or speak above a whisper.

"I'm quite sure you do." He let that sit, then added, "If you don't find justice for Chad, I'll also report your little drug habit, maybe even find a way to plant some in your desk and have your boss find them. Just the hint of suspicion will be enough to get you benched and investigated."

Yesterday she had come to realize Freddy only held relative power—a case of he said/she said—but after her run-in with Hill and her storming out of the station, she couldn't take the sort of hit Rick promised. He was capable of destroying everything.

He left the room, and not long after she heard the front door close behind him.

She sobbed until the tears ran dry and she passed out.

CHAPTER TWENTY-NINE

Amanda's eyelids fluttered open and it took her a while to orientate as to where she was while she assessed her surroundings and tried to make sense of them. But it was dark, and everything was in shadow. She strained to see and made out a nightstand, a lamp. She went to move her arms, but they were restricted behind her back. And there was thrumming in her skull that pulsed in a staccato rhythm. Then the recollection came to her and her eyes widened. She must have passed out.

Rick Jensen. Her house. Her bedroom.

Her heart sped up as she recalled she was bound at the wrists with her handcuffs around the leg of her bedframe. She could hardly feel her arms, and her shoulders and neck were tight and full of kinks.

But it had been daytime when she was restrained, and it was obviously now after sunset. She looked at the clock on her nightstand—*7:03 PM.* The same day? The next?

She had a vague memory that her cuff key was in her right front pocket. She spun on her ass and maneuvered her arms as far as she could, but she still couldn't get anywhere close to reaching the pocket with the bed in the way. But she had to keep trying—she was on her own. Maybe if she could lift the bedframe and slip the chain of the cuffs under the leg and out… It was a Houdini move but what other choice did she have?

She angled herself so her legs, up to the knees, were under the bed. Now she just had to lift the bedframe.

She counted to three in her head and gave it a go. It turned out it was far easier to pull off in her head. She tried again and again, getting more frustrated with each failed attempt and in more pain. But she became more resolved to break free.

One more go.

Finally! She mustered enough strength to lift the frame the amount she needed and squirmed free. She was still cuffed behind her back, but she could handle that.

She sat and rolled back on her hips, tucked her legs up, and wriggled and wormed until she was able to pull her arms around them and through to the front.

"Gah!" she screamed as a ripple of pain fired up her back to the top of her skull. She took a few heaving breaths and contemplated her next act.

Her arms were still cuffed but now in front of her. She swung her arms to her right hip and worked her hand into the pocket, grasped the handcuff key, and silently coached herself that she had this, but, as her fingers came free of the pocket, they released, and the key tumbled out and across the floor.

Shit!

She traced the sound of the clattering in her head. It had traveled across a few laminate planks under the bed.

She flattened out on the floor and held her arms overhead and reached out. Her fingers danced over the key. She shimmied under the frame a little more and got a hold of her prize then inched back out. She held tightly to the key and worked her wrists until she found an angle that worked to insert it into the lock.

The click of the first cuff releasing might as well have been angels singing. She quickly freed her other wrist and alternated rubbing both. They throbbed, along with her entire body, but no wonder.

Amanda pulled out her phone. She unlocked it and confirmed the day was still the twelfth. It also showed six missed calls—two from blocked numbers, one from Malone, a couple from Trent, one from Becky—and a text message from Jacob.

Jacob's text was straightforward and concise. Just that the files from the data chip were on the mainframe server of PWCPD and he'd left a message for Patricia Glover in Sex Crimes.

She keyed back a quick *Thanks* then turned her attention to the voicemail icon in the top-left-hand corner. She knew at least one message was from her father.

She looked at the photo that Rick had left of her father, picked it up, and ran her fingertip over her father's face. She'd have to warn him about Rick. Might as well listen to his message. She dialed into her voicemail and played her messages.

"Sweetie, it's Dad."

He sounded so tired and sad.

"It's all over now. You can come home if you want to. You know we're here for you. We'd love to see you."

A pocket of silence, followed by, *"End of message. To—"*

She hit the button to save the message and hung up without listening to the others. She didn't know what she had expected at hearing her dad's voice. Overwhelming emotions, sure, but not in this magnitude. For the last five years she'd lived numb, hardly feeling or feeling too much but doing her best to drown her emotions out whatever way she could. But upon hearing him, his loving plea… She heaved with deep sobs and the tears fell in a rapid torrent.

He'd sounded so broken, so destroyed, so destitute. And the guilt rolled over her, threatening to bury her alive. The accident wasn't his fault, or her mother's, or her family's, but she'd cut them off. Again, not for anything they had done but because she was protecting herself. It hurt so much to see them, but there was more to it. She'd lost the love of her life and her sweet little girl, and the baby she'd never know. If she could distance herself from other people, barricade herself behind iron, cloak herself in chain mail, she'd never be able to be dealt such a lethal blow again. She'd acted preemptively and cut the emotional connection because as long as humans were mortal, death was inevitable.

But she had an obligation and her word to keep—to her daughter, to Rick Jensen, and to the oath she'd taken. She willed herself off the floor. As much as the thought of coming face to face with her parents hurt, she had to warn her father about Rick Jensen, and she had to get back to the Palmer investigation—even if it was off the books.

First, she'd need to get herself cleaned up.

She staggered to the bathroom and turned on the light. She cried out at the brightness and flipped the switch again, taking a few moments to prepare herself for the onslaught of two one-hundred-watt-equivalency LEDs.

She opened her eyes in increments, letting her vision adjust in stages. When she saw the reflection of herself in the mirror she gasped. Her eyes were puffy, and her lip and cheek were cut and marked by dried blood. The latter was also encrusted around her mouth. But the blood could be washed down the drain; it was the bruising that gave her a ghoulish appearance.

She wet a cloth with warm water and dabbed it to her face, slowly and gingerly, wincing with each contact and being reminded that she could have died today. That before today she thought she'd welcome the chance, but now there was something in her that had changed, if only a fraction.

She took her time cleaning her wounds and opened her cosmetic tray. She had a foundation brush in hand when she heard a noise.

She stalled all movement.

The front door. It had moaned when it reached about two-thirds open.

Footsteps.

He was back!

She quietly tiptoed to her room and grabbed her Beretta. She held it at the ready and crept to the side of her door and tucked against the wall. From this vantage point, she could see down the hall and get the upper hand on her intruder.

A glimpse of a shadow and her body tensed. She slinked back and shouted, "Stop right there!"

Arms shot up in the air in surrender. "Whoa! It's Trent."

She lowered her gun. "What the hell, rookie? Announce yourself."

"Sorry, sorry, sorry. Yeah, I should have." He wiped his forehead.

"I could have shot you!" She brushed past him toward the bathroom.

"I was worried about you. I haven't heard anything from you and then I get here, and your front door was ajar. Are you—"

"I'm fine." She stood in the bathroom doorway, but enough light must have spilled into the hallway to show the bruising and cuts on her face. Trent's mouth gaped open.

"What happened to you? Are you okay?"

"I'm fine." She went into the bathroom and closed the door. "I'll be out in a minute," she added, feeling a little bad for shutting him out when he'd just been worried about her.

"Ah, sure. I'll just be… *ah*, in your living room."

"That's fine." She finished caking on foundation, then added some more, followed by powder, and winced with every stroke of the brush. It was a relief when she'd finished.

She found Trent sitting on her couch. He jumped to his feet when she entered the room as if a pin had been pulled on a grenade and he needed to move.

She started to smile but the expression hurt. "One second." She held up a finger to Trent and returned to the bathroom, grabbed a couple of ibuprofens, and downed them with a glass of water in the kitchen. She slowly lowered herself onto a chair that faced the couch and gestured for him to return to his seat. "What are you doing here?"

"I told you. I was worried about you."

She studied him, looking for any sign that he was pissed she'd just left him without a word, but she didn't see any anger. He was either one of the most forgiving people she'd ever encountered, or he was a good actor. "How did you know you'd find me at my house?"

"I thought there was a good chance."

"Huh. So none of my neighbors called anything in? No complaints of yelling or shouting?"

He glanced over at her. "Not that I'm aware of."

"That's reassuring." So much for small-town living being advantageous in the community coming together to prevent crime. "Guessing you heard what happened at work?"

Trent gripped his hands together and rubbed his palms. "Yeah."

"Then you know I'm off the Palmer case."

"And that you may be leaving PWCPD if what Malone told me is true."

Her head hurt too much to get into what the man thought, and sure, in his place she'd think her actions constituted quitting, but she hadn't come out and said as much in words. "I'm not leaving. In fact, I've got to get back to work."

She jumped up and rushed to the door—and staggered. Her head was spinning.

"Careful there." Trent was quickly at her side, and she brushed him away, but a wave of nausea threatened to topple her and had her returning to the chair she'd been sitting in.

Trent dropped back onto the couch. "Are you going to tell me"—his gaze dipped over every tender spot on her face—"what happened? We're partners."

"Were."

"Don't think you'll get rid of me that easy, and you can also save any speech you might be thinking of about how you're fine and whatever went down here is all fine. Fine is a trigger word for shrinks."

She quirked an eyebrow and that simple action hurt, but she respected this new sassy side to the rookie detective. "And you're a shrink now?" One of the ugly traits that she tended to bring out in her partners.

He stayed silent long enough to draw her out; like a good fisherman who knew how to reel in the line precisely so as not to have his catch break free.

"All right, there was an incident," she admitted, "but I'll be fine."

His jaw tightened, and he rubbed his hands together again, the brushing motion sounding a lot like sandpaper scraping on wood. "I was just an officer with the Dumfries PD," he began.

"Which wasn't long ago," she intercepted.

"Sure, but I was working a case with the FBI."

She was tempted to cut in again, this time with something smart about it being his fifteen minutes of fame that he clung to.

Trent went on. "I might have overstepped and put myself into a situation…"

She found herself leaning forward. There may be more to Trent than met the eye, after all. "Might have?"

"Okay, I did." He tossed out a small smile with the confession. "Anyway, because of that I got shot."

"Come on." There was no way this rookie detective had been hit in the line of duty.

"I'm being serious."

"Huh. I had no idea."

"You'd have no reason to know. I lived, but I take that day with me all the time. Carry it around, but not like a burden or a weight; more as a reminder. I know how embarrassing it can be when someone gets the upper hand, but we're human, Amanda. It happens. Sometimes we're on top. Other times, well, not so much."

She sank back in her chair and studied him, deciding whether she wanted to confess all that had transpired. So much of it was incredibly personal and the fact Trent had shared his story didn't make it mandatory that she share hers.

"You can talk to me. I'm a steel trap," he tagged on and smiled.

"I came home. Figured I'd grab a couple of things and take off... for a bit of a break. My front door was unlocked."

Trent perched forward like he was about to spring into action, but he remained seated. "You should have called it in."

"After I just left my badge and gun behind? No thanks. Anyway, I quickly found out that Palmer's cousin had broken in."

"He hurt you."

"Yeah, he—"

He shook his head. "That wasn't a question. I saw your face before the makeup, and I can still see the bruising and cuts to your lip and cheek through it."

"Wonderful."

"It's barely noticeable."

She narrowed her eyes at him. "Okay, now you're lying."

He pinched his fingers to almost touching.

"Like I told you though, I'm fine. Like you, I survived. I'm alive."

"He threatened your life, didn't he?" Trent's face took on sharp angles.

He was a far better detective than she had ever wanted to give him credit for. "He did." And her father's, but she couldn't bring herself to say that right now.

"We should go pick him up." He sprang off the couch.

She stood and grabbed his arm on a back swing and let go just as quickly. Her head was spinning. "No."

"Why? Why wouldn't we?" He scanned her eyes.

He might as well have said *give me one good reason*. She was catapulted right back to Rick Jensen saying the same.

She blinked slowly. "I first need to know you're on my side."

"Stupid question. You're the first partner I've ever had. Loyalty means something to me."

It was as if seconds ticked off with *clunks* as she held eye contact with him.

Trent stepped back, let out a deep breath. "Talk to me."

"All Rick wants is justice for his cousin."

"He doesn't get that by threatening your life."

"No, you're right, he doesn't," she said to cool him down. "What I tell you next stays between us—remember what you just said? 'Steel trap' and all that?"

"Uh-huh."

"He's holding me accountable for the outcome of the Palmer investigation."

"You told him you're not working it anymore?"

"I did, but he didn't want to hear it."

"So what do you do now?"

She peered into his eyes. How far did his claimed loyalty go? "I plan to keep working the case."

"Oh." Trent raked a hand through his hair. "Just to hear you say it…"

"You're loyal, remember?"

His gaze snapped to hers again.

"There's something I need to tell you. Remember the bracelet I got off Freddy?"

"Yeah?"

"I took it to Digital Forensics last night and it turns out there's evidence on there of a sex-trafficking ring." She probably should have filled him in last night, but she was going to tell him once the files were confirmed on the mainframe server. But Lieutenant Hill happened, then Rick Jensen.

"A— What?" Trent dropped back onto the couch. "Right here in Dumfries or…?"

She realized that Jacob hadn't specified geography. "Probably and Woodbridge, maybe all of Prince William County. Washington, DC, too? I don't know the reach yet."

"Wow. I never would have—"

"I wouldn't have seen this coming either. I mean Palmer was involved with fencing stolen goods. That's a far cry from facilitating the sale of little girls."

"Girls?" Trent blanched.

"Some as young as six." God help any man who might have tried this with Lindsey. Amanda would have disemboweled him and tied his entrails around a tree, letting him bleed out or be eaten by wild animals.

Trent wiped a hand over his mouth. "Wow. So what do we do?"

"We bring them all down. The information from the data chip is already on the server and someone from Sex Crimes has been assigned the case. Detective Patricia Glover. Quite sure that she left me a voicemail, but I haven't listened to it yet."

"Wow."

"Would you please stop saying that?" She realized it was usually her throwing that word around. It was official: she was rubbing off on him.

"It's just I came here thinking I had a good lead to share, but this—what you have—overshadows whatever I could say."

"What is it, Trent?"

"The Caprice was found," he said.

"No, that's good; we might find more pieces of the puzzle." She looked at the front door, then him. "You sure you're okay with me tagging along?"

"I came here to get you, didn't I?"

"Thought you were worried about me."

"That too."

She let him go out first and double-checked to make sure the door was locked—not that it had stopped Rick from getting inside.

She grabbed the passenger door and had one leg in when she saw what was on the seat. Her badge and her gun in its holster.

Trent was sitting behind the wheel, smiling at her. "Sergeant Malone told me you forgot something at the station."

She swiped the items and put them on, looking away so the rookie couldn't see the tears in her eyes, then got into the car. "There's actually something else I need to take care of before we go wherever we're going."

"What is it?"

Her stomach grumbled and he laughed.

"Well, besides the fact that I'm starving…" She hesitated. The next bit wouldn't be easy to say, and it would make the situation more real, but something about having Trent with her, even waiting in the car, made the thought of going to her parents' a little easier to bear.

"Steel trap, remember?" he prompted.

"Rick Jensen took his threats one step further. He said he knows how to get to my dad. He had a picture of him outside my parents' house."

"Tell me where I'm going."

CHAPTER THIRTY

The redbrick two-story was a feature from her past, with its white trim and red shutters, its double garage, its wraparound porch, and the front bay window. She'd skinned her knees and endured numerous bumps and bruises within the confines of those walls and in the yard. She used to love swinging on the tire that hung from the large, majestic oak in the back.

A gray four-door sedan sat in the driveway—the same one from Rick Jensen's photo. It was probably her mother's car, because she'd always preferred monochromatic shades, while her father loved color. Either they had downsized to one car or had started using the garage for more than just storage.

"Are you sure you don't want me to go in with you?" Trent asked.

She saw the curtain in the front window get swept back. Her mother was standing there, a hand on her hip.

"I've got this, Trent. Thank you." She got out and headed to the door, intending to knock, but it whooshed open.

"Mandy!" Her mother threw her arms around Amanda.

It had been so long since she'd felt her mother's embrace. She held her so tightly, Amanda felt pain run down her spine, but she still didn't want to let go. It was only reluctantly that she did so a few moments later. But she had to remember she was there for a purpose, not a reunion, and that Trent was waiting in the car.

Her mother swept a strand of Amanda's hair behind an ear and gingerly touched her cheek. "Oh dear. What happened to you?"

"A long story," Amanda said. "Can I come in?"

"Of course, sweetheart!" Her mother turned and yelled, "Nathan!"

Her father's mumbles reached Amanda's ears, along with footsteps coming through from the back sitting room, which was off the kitchen.

"What is it, Jules?"

"It's—" Her mother clamped her hands over her mouth when Amanda's father stepped into view.

"Mandy," he uttered, eyes full of tears. His face was all shadows.

"I should have called you back, but—"

"Nonsense," her mother said. "This is even better. You're home. Finally." Her mother pranced deeper into the house.

Amanda shut the front door as it seemed her parents had forgotten about it and moved toward her father. She studied the man who'd raised her, who she'd idolized for so long, who she'd wanted to become.

He opened his arms and she fell against him, burrowing her head into his chest. Her father wrapped his arms around her, and all she could smell was the fragrance of Irish Spring soap. It was the kind he'd used for as long as she could remember. His body was warm and comforting, and in this moment, she felt so loved and accepted—like she was home and had never left.

Her father ended their hug, and said, "My Mandy Monkey, it's about time you returned to us."

She sniffled, hating to admit to herself that if it hadn't been for the threat against her father, she probably wouldn't be there now. "I'm so sorry. It's just…" She forced a smile. She was angry and embarrassed and overwrought with guilt. If only she hadn't insisted on getting involved with the Palmer investigation, then her father's life wouldn't be at risk and she could avoid all these uncomfortable feelings. "I can't stay long."

"Nonsense." Her mother reappeared. "I just put the kettle on to make us some tea."

"Someone's waiting for me outside," Amanda said.

"They're welcome to come in."

"No."

Her mother glanced at her husband.

"It's just that we're in the middle of a case," Amanda clarified.

"Why come by now then?" Her mother's brow arched in confusion. "You should have come by when you have some time."

"I just needed to talk to Dad about something."

Her mother's chin quivered, and she crossed her arms.

Amanda went to her; touched her elbow. "I'll be back when I have time."

Her mother palmed her cheeks and met Amanda's gaze. "You promise?"

"I promise."

"You remember that when a Steele gives their word, they—"

"Keep it. And I will." Amanda kissed her mother on the cheek and squeezed her.

"I'll just be in the kitchen." Her mother padded off.

Amanda turned to find her father watching her.

"This a question you have about a case? Want the old man's advice? I've been out of the game for a while, but I'm sure I can still help." He grinned.

"Why don't we sit down?" She sat on a couch.

"Ah, sure." Her father took up in a chair next to a side table where there was a glass with some amber liquid.

"When did you start drinking again?" Her chest pinched just thinking she knew the answer: her abandonment.

"Don't worry your pretty little head about it. I have it under control. So what brings you here?" He leveled his gaze at her, and in his posture and eyes she saw the former police chief still lived on.

She told him about Palmer's murder, the article, snippets of her encounter with Rick Jensen.

"I saw the article—a bunch of horse crap."

"Well, Lieutenant Hill didn't see it that way."

Her father leaned forward. "Sherry Hill as lieutenant. Now that's a miscarriage of justice."

Amanda wanted to ask exactly what her father's beef was with Hill, but now wasn't the time.

"Did she suspend you?" her father asked before she could say anything else.

"No, but she took me off the case."

"Hmph."

"Dad?"

"So what? Are you also here to tell me you're going rogue? If so, you should step away. It's not worth ruining your career over."

She shut her mouth; she couldn't bring herself to tell her dad that things at work hadn't been the same as before the accident.

"But you're not going to back off, are you?" Her father peered into her eyes.

"How can I? Jensen's threatened you."

Her father batted his hand. "I can look after myself."

She thought of Trent's little words of wisdom and how the strong have weak moments. "You just need to be careful, but know that I'm going to do whatever I can—"

"To get that man justice?" Her father shot to his feet. "The same man who—" He snarled and balled his hands into fists.

Amanda put a hand on his back to cool him down. "I know. But you heard what Mom just said: Steeles keep their word."

He tightened his jaw and nodded. "But why you ever got yourself wrapped up in this in the first place, Mandy, I'll never understand."

"I just felt I needed to at the time. And, trust me, it's probably a good thing I did insert myself."

Her father's gaze met hers, and she continued. "There's little girls, Dad. Palmer was booked with a bracelet and there was a hidden data chip on there— Oh, whatever you do, don't say a word of this to Malone. He doesn't know yet. But there's evidence of a sex-trafficking ring."

"An active one here?" Her father dropped back into his chair, his complexion pale. Nothing much shook her father, but it was obvious this news had.

"I assume it's still active. I don't really know, but I intend to find out and to help those girls."

"And to slam the doors on everyone involved."

"Goes without saying." She jacked a thumb toward the front door. "I should get going."

Her father sprang up again, pulled her in for a hug, and tapped a kiss on her forehead. "I have absolute faith in you."

She sniffled and nodded. "Thanks, Dad."

She saw herself out with another hug of her mother. She'd considered going back to her parents over the years, but the longer time had dragged on, the harder the thought of actually doing it was, but now that first step was out of the way.

All it had taken was a threat to her father's life.

CHAPTER THIRTY-ONE

After leaving her parents' house, she didn't feel much like talking at all. It had been unsettling seeing her mom and dad again, like she belonged but at the same time was a stranger. But she'd go back—she had promised her mother—maybe give a reconnection a true chance. Trent got onto highway SR 234 north. "So where are we going? You never said before and I didn't ask."

"The Department of Forensic Science."

"Manassas? And you do realize their regular hours are eight to five Monday to Friday?" The dash read 8:45 PM.

Trent looked over at her. "Sure, but everything that's connected to the Palmer case is to be given priority attention."

She slowly nodded, remembering Malone had told her that. A twinge crept up into her skull with the action. "Who's going to be there?" She wasn't sure she had the tolerance threshold to put up with CSI Blair tonight.

"Blair and Donnelly."

She blew out a deep breath, and Trent laughed.

"I know she's not your favorite person."

"Is she anyone's?" Amanda tapped her fingers on the armrest in the door. "I don't know what her problem is with me."

She let that sit there, but Trent didn't offer any suggestions. She might never find out Blair's issue, but she wasn't exactly feeling like coming out and asking.

She went on. "At least she's putting in OT for— Oh, does she know I'm off the case?"

"Don't know, but I'm not telling her." Trent winked at her.

The guy was starting to grow on her, and she was starting to witness firsthand that loyalty he claimed to have. He might not be as bad as she thought, but she still didn't need a partner.

"They do know we're on our way though," he added. "I called while you were in with your parents." He glanced over at her and she was quite sure she read the unspoken question in his eyes: *How was the reunion?* At least he was smart enough not to ask.

"So where was the Caprice found?" Her jaw ached from talking and her body longed for bed, but it would have to hang in there.

"Hikers found it in the parking lot for Prince William Forest Park. They saw it on Monday morning, then again about two this afternoon."

She nodded. She used to take long walks with Kevin at that park when they were dating and before Lindsey came along. After Lindsey, the walks became shorter. She used to love getting out in the woods during the winter months. There was something invigorating about the brisk air nipping her nose and ears while she burrowed against Kevin's side. She was stuck on why the hikers would call though.

"Just because the Caprice was there two days in a row wouldn't have deemed it suspicious; why did they think something was up with the car?"

"No good reason to be honest, just their instinct. And lucky for us it was right. They've been cleared." He looked over at her. "I was debating whether to rope you into this. The sarge said you were pretty upset, and I mean, you left your badge and gun behind."

When she'd done that, she'd almost felt like she was watching herself from out of her body but also like she was doing exactly what she should have done a long time ago.

"You can understand why I hesitated?" Trent prompted.

"Yep." That's what she said, but she wasn't sure she did understand. Though he was risking his career by keeping her up to date on the case. She looked out the passenger window as Trent passed a slower-moving vehicle.

"It's completely intact too. The Caprice," Trent said. "No one's taken a joyride with it."

"What about any stolen goods in the trunk?"

"Nope. Nothing that obvious, but Blair and Donnelly will be tearing the entire thing apart and we'll be there to watch."

"So let me get this straight: all day while I was, you know, otherwise occupied, what were you doing besides questioning some hikers?"

Trent smirked at her. "I also obtained the warrant for the Happy Time surveillance footage, picked it up, and watched it."

"Did it capture a good image of what happened to Palmer? The gunman?"

"Yep. Well, useful anyway. No direct facial shots, but we now have the height, structure and gait of his assailant. Black hoodie, black jeans."

"George told me about the hoodie."

"I have a still in my phone…" He reached into his coat pocket and handed it to her. "Just in my gallery."

She took the phone and woke the screen. "Pin?"

"One, two, three, four."

"You've got to be kidding me. You're a cop; you should know better."

He laughed. "It's just easy to remember."

"Ah, rookie." She unlocked the phone and found the icon for the photo-gallery app.

"It should be the last ones. I have a couple there."

She studied them both; they were quite similar. The attacker's face was in shadow, but they appeared trim. "What was his height estimated to be?"

"Somewhere between five ten and six one."

"Quite a spread."

"There's actually a little snippet of the video on there too."

"Why?"

Trent kept his gaze out the windshield. "Never know when I'm going to have a minute and want to take another peek; might not be at the station."

"You're telling me you take your work home with you?"

He glanced from the road to her. "Maybe," he dragged out.

She smiled. "You're a brown-noser."

"A what?" he rushed out.

"It's someone who kisses up to look good to authority figures."

He met her gaze and held it longer than she would have liked. She pointed out the front window.

"Eyes on the road please."

He glanced out the windshield. "Do brown-nosers typically work on a case their partner has been taken from?"

"Okay, fair point." She smirked.

"Thank you." He laughed.

She proceeded to play the video clip. It captured the lot from the vantage point that looked down at the perp's back. She watched as the gunman came up on Palmer when he was nearing the Caprice. The perp was carrying the gun in his right hand, close to his side, but his walk showed he was favoring his left knee. She paused the video. "I'd say the gunman's left knee is injured," she said to Trent.

"I noticed that too."

A driver ahead of them tapped their brakes and changed lanes without signaling. Some people didn't know how to drive. She returned her attention to the video. Something caused Palmer to turn around. Maybe he'd heard the perp's footsteps, or the perp had said something. A brief animated interaction followed, resulting in the gun being raised on Palmer. Palmer had his hands up in surrender and it appeared the perp waved for him to put them down. The perp then corralled Palmer to the passenger side of the car at gunpoint, then struck Palmer in the head and hoisted the dead weight into the Caprice.

End of video.

Things played out a little differently from what George had told her in the Happy Time lot, but he had admitted to drinking that night.

She rewound to take a closer look at the stand-off. It was hard to tell, but the gunman seemed twitchy, his arms and shoulders rising and lowering. Either not comfortable holding a gun or nervous. If this was Palmer's killer, she'd say the nerves didn't testify to someone who had killed before. She shared that observation with Trent.

"I wasn't sure what to make of that myself."

"I think we need more pieces of this puzzle." She straightened but every millimeter of adjustment trickled agony down her spine. "So you also watched a video, ate some popcorn… anything else?"

"You're tough, you know that."

She bobbed her head side to side. She could blame that on her father. He'd stressed to her that the only way to succeed and advance rank was to put in the hard work. By passing this "toughness" on, she was really doing Trent a favor.

"And yes, for your information, I did more than just that. I'm quite sure I found out where Palmer got the Caprice."

She jerked her neck so fast to face him, she cried out.

"Whoa. You okay?"

Tears were in her eyes as she met his. "Do people"—she winced—"normally cry out in pain when they're okay?"

"I can take you home if you need or the hospital. You probably should get checked out."

"You take me to either of those places and—"

"You'll what?" He was toying with her; she had nothing she could do to him.

"Just keep driving, rookie. And where did Palmer get the car?"

"A guy named Simon Wheable. He's forty-one, and he's spent time behind bars for robbery, but he's been out and free of parole for a few years now. He works at Eco-Friendly Auto Recyclers." Trent took their exit.

"It's a vehicle salvage yard." Amanda cut through the beautifully painted lingo to the gist of the business model, but she was also familiar with the place from personal experience. It was where her first jalopy had gone, not that she'd thought of the Honda Accord as that when she'd bought it for fifteen hundred with money she'd earned working part-time at a donut shop. Eco-Friendly Auto Recyclers was where vehicles went when they died. Or in the case of her Accord, became more costly to repair than it was worth. She'd ended up with a few hundred in her pocket for the parts.

"That's right," Trent said.

"What led you to Wheable? The plate?" Given the right genius at a computer, the plate could have been enhanced from the Happy Time video.

"Nah, it was stolen and got me nowhere, but I did a little surveillance on Freddy."

"You followed him?"

"Not going to confirm on the grounds it might incriminate me."

"Ridiculous. Go on."

"Anyway, he happened to go to the salvage yard, and I just sort of put two and two together. Would make sense if the car was transporting stolen goods. They'd want to put Palmer in a piece of junk that wouldn't warrant attention."

"And the guy was driving without a license," she mumbled. "Did you talk with Wheable?"

"Haven't had a chance yet."

"I was impressed until then." She smirked over at him and he smiled back, obviously picking up her sarcasm. She proceeded to forward the images and video to her phone and then handed his back to him. She pulled out her own. "I do have a couple of voicemails to check though, if you can entertain yourself while I do that."

"I'll figure something out." Trent tapped his fingers on the wheel to some beat he must have had playing in his head.

She called in and listened to the four unheard messages. The first was from Detective Banks, the lead investigator on the Casey-Anne Ritter murder, basically just saying he was returning her call and when she had a chance to call him back. It had come in that morning; it was probably the blocked number that rang just as she was headed into her house before everything that had happened with Jensen.

The second message was from Malone.

"I understand that you need to cool off. I get it. Trust me. Hill can be a piece of work, but don't throw away everything. In fact, I don't accept your resignation. I never saw anything in writing."

She smirked up at the ceiling of the car and continued listening.

"I'll always have your back…" There was a lengthy pause, then, *"But… whether you're coming back to work or just taking a break, I'll still need your alibi—the sooner the better."*

She groaned and Trent looked over at her.

"Everything all right?"

Amanda nodded and listened to the third message, which was from Becky, touching base to see how she was holding up. The fourth message was from the detective in Sex Crimes.

"Detective Steele, this is Detective Patricia Glover with Sex Crimes. I've been assigned the case referred to me by Detective Jacob Briggs in Digital Forensics. I don't want to leave details over the phone, so please call me as soon as you can."

Her call had come through at 1:03 PM. Glover was probably wondering if Amanda had fallen off the face of the Earth. No to that, but she had temporarily lost her way.

She pocketed her phone just as Trent pulled into the parking lot of the Department of Forensic Science.

CHAPTER THIRTY-TWO

Amanda led the way to the front door, Trent trailing behind.

"Yeah… we're here…" he said into his phone and put it away a few seconds later. He told Amanda, "CSI Blair will come get the front door."

They only had to stand outside the building, a two-story redbrick with generous-sized windows, for a couple of minutes tops, before Blair let them in.

"We meet again," Amanda said.

"Detective Steele," Blair said coolly. She smiled at Trent. "Detective Stenson."

"Evening," he said.

"We've already started processing the vehicle." She headed down a hallway and motioned for them to follow. "There's a lot of potential evidence in prints alone. We still haven't discovered any stolen goods—the ones you alerted us to." Blair looked over a shoulder at Trent. "But we're getting close to ripping out the seats. Criminals will often hollow them out for storage."

Blair opened a door and entered. Amanda stepped in behind her and laid her eyes on Palmer's Caprice in person for the first time. The video had shown her a jalopy, but the video had been taken at night. Here, under the lights, the power-blue sedan was certainly a relic. Rust ate around the wheel wells and the grill.

Her gaze went to the driver's-side back door. Legs were sticking out. Probably belonging to CSI Donnelly.

"Any of those prints lead us anywhere?" Amanda intentionally used *us* to present herself, Trent, and the investigators as being on the same team. A stab at diplomacy.

"No. It's all about collection tonight. Processing in the morning. This is the vehicle number. It was scratched but legible enough." Blair snatched a piece of paper from a table and handed it to Trent.

"Any hits in the system?"

Blair met her gaze. "That I did run quickly, and it was last registered ten years ago."

Amanda turned to Trent. "Sounds like it could be Wheable. He could take cars destined for the compacter and turn them over for cash. No record that way and a quick buck."

"And what's a Wheable?" Blair raised her brows.

"It's a who," Amanda clarified. "Some ex-con we believe sold the car to Palmer or an associate of his for the purpose of carting stolen goods somewhere to fence them. His print could very well pop from some you've collected."

She witnessed the CSI's facial expression tighten at the enclosed request.

"I'll keep you posted. As I said, not tonight or I'll never get home to Derek… That's my husband."

Amanda's heart cinched as she recalled a time when going home had been something she looked forward to, despite loving her job. But at least she'd had Kevin's smiling face and loving arms to help wash away the day, and Lindsey to tuck in or to kiss on the forehead if she was already off in dreamland.

"I understand," Amanda said. The two words scratched from her throat.

She'd probably pushed her luck with the investigator already but there was something else she needed to inquire about. "Did you, by chance, receive a silver chain bracelet connected to the Palmer case? It would have come over to you from Detective Jacob Briggs in Digital Forensics."

"I did."

She'd almost expected that Blair hadn't seen it yet, but, then again, Jacob had got what he needed from the chip. "And?"

"There was epithelial, and before you ask, no hits yet."

"Ooh!" Donnelly reversed out of the back seat and was holding something between two gloved fingers. She was already grinning at her find but beamed brighter when she laid eyes on Amanda and Trent.

Amanda closed the distance to Donnelly. "What is it?"

"A sobriety coin from Alcoholics Anonymous." She flipped it in her palm. "Twenty years. Might lead you to Palmer's killer." Donnelly was still grinning like she'd eaten the last cookie from the jar and enjoyed every last crumb.

Trent stepped up close to Amanda, his elbow brushing against hers.

"I'm cautiously optimistic," Amanda said. "It really could tie back to anyone. Anyone other than Palmer," she added. "Don't think it would be Freddy's or Courtney's. They don't strike me as the type to refrain from drinking, and to reach twenty years sober, they would have entered the program as teens. Wheable as a young adult. You said he was in his forties?" She looked at Trent, who nodded.

She continued. "Maybe someone associated with them. See if you get any usable prints from it," she said to Donnelly.

"Of course."

"Where did you find it in the car?" Trent asked.

"Under the driver's seat toward the back floor mat."

Amanda shrugged. "Who knows how long it could have been there. My guess is it hasn't exactly been detailed in years."

Donnelly chuckled. "Ah, no. The thing smells like a gym locker."

"Any sign of stolen goods or a compartment under the back seat?" Amanda asked.

"Yes to the compartment, but it's empty."

Amanda turned to Trent. "Someone who Palmer turned the goods over to not happy with the deal? Could have come after him?" She dismissed it with a wave of her hand, recalling her earlier thought on the matter. "Never mind. Someone like that would likely just shoot him in the head, not force-feed him alcohol and hang around for hours." As she said this, it sank in how dismissive she was being about the AA sobriety coin. After all, it would seem Palmer's killer had cared about the drinking angle to choose the MO they had.

Donnelly returned to the car and Blair joined her. Amanda and Trent stuck around for a while longer but headed out about ten.

About fifteen minutes down the road, she said, "Why leave the Caprice at the park?"

Trent looked over at her. "Why not?"

She was trying to pin down her thoughts so she could put them into words. She shifted to face him and winced, then held up a hand to Trent. "I'm fine. Okay, Blair said there were a lot of prints. So assuming we believe that Freddy and his crew were involved with Palmer in the transporting of the stolen goods, they wouldn't just leave it for someone to find."

"Okay, I follow. Because they'd be in the system. They'd wipe it clean."

"Right… So that leads me to believe whoever left the car there is someone other than Wheable, Freddy, or his crew."

Trent's mouth started to form *who* and she said, "Don't ask. That's what we still need to figure out."

"I'm not sure—"

"Maybe it's someone involved in the sex-trafficking ring that killed Palmer and dumped the car," she put out somberly. "And/ or Webb and Ritter's killer could very well be back. We should at least consider that as a possibility, but whoever drove the Caprice there had to have had transportation to leave," she said. "They could have walked from the park but unlikely."

"Okay, so the killer drove their own car to the park, left it there, then—what?—took a cab to the Happy Time bar?"

"Why not?" she volleyed back.

"Whoever ended up taking the Caprice to the park could have left their vehicle anywhere and shuttled around town in a taxi."

"Sure. Also possible."

"All this would be assuming that the attacker in the lot was also Palmer's killer…"

She nodded. "One working theory. Only why didn't they shoot Palmer? They had a gun. I keep coming back to that."

"Good question."

A pocket of silence, then she said, "You'll need to follow up with local cab companies and see if they picked up anyone out at the park. It will either lead us to the killer or the attacker, or one and the same."

"I can do that."

"And you should pop by Wheable's, ask about the Caprice, find out if it came from him and inquire about the sobriety coin. And, heck, bring up the bracelet to him too—get his reaction but don't say what was on it. You never know what might come up. Be very cognizant of visual tells. Courtney and Freddy need to be questioned about the bracelet and the sobriety coin too."

"Want us to cover all that tonight?"

She smiled at the "us."

"You're forgetting as it stands right now, I'm not a part of the equation."

"Right…"

"I'm going to talk to Malone though. But calling him right now or showing up at his door isn't going to do either of us any favors."

"Are you going to ask to be put back on the Palmer case?"

"Not exactly. I'm going to tell him about the sex-trafficking ring and pitch it as I'll focus on that and its possible connection to the cold cases of Ritter and Webb while you'll follow leads directly related to Palmer, such as the Caprice, the taxi service, possibly the sobriety coin, etcetera."

"Okay, makes sense. So we'll tackle all that tomorrow?"

"Yeah. It's been a long day."

She leaned against the headrest and ran through what tomorrow morning was going to look like. "Ah, shit."

Trent glanced over but didn't say anything as she pulled out her phone and brought up the notepad app where she'd keyed Motel Guy's plate.

"There's actually one thing I should probably get a start on tonight. My alibi." She turned the keyboard of the onboard computer so she could reach it in the passenger seat and keyed in the tag.

Amanda stared at the DMV results. Motel Guy was legally known as Logan Hunter. She dug a little deeper and pulled up a simple background. *Unbelievable.* He was married! That made Amanda a homewrecker. But she hadn't known he had a wife. No criminal record—a small plus at least.

Logan had lived and worked in Dumfries for the last two years. Before that, a Podunk in Nebraska. His current place of employment was listed as Precise Construction in Dumfries.

She swung the keyboard back in place swiftly enough that Trent looked at her again, but he didn't say anything.

She was going to throttle Mr. Hunter the second she got the chance. She had half a thought to show up on his doorstep tonight and tell his wife all about their night at the Dreamcatcher Inn, but that wouldn't be to Amanda's advantage. She needed Logan to verify her alibi. No, she'd surprise him at work first thing tomorrow morning.

CHAPTER THIRTY-THREE

Amanda's head pounded like a tiny man with no sense of rhythm was playing steel drums in her skull. But she didn't have time to lounge around wallowing in agony. She was a little slower moving than yesterday morning, but she was still out of bed by seven thirty.

She stuck a pod in her coffee machine and, while it got to work, so did she. She called Trent to let him know to carry on with what they'd talked about last night and she'd be in a bit later. She fired off a quick text to Malone letting him know the same and added that she would be getting her alibi sealed up. He came back with an immediate, *Wonderful.*

Next, she grabbed her personal laptop and cracked it open on the kitchen counter. The thing was a few years old, but it still worked for whatever tasks she'd needed it for.

It was still working on signing her in when the coffee machine spewed and sputtered and let out a loud whoosh as it finished topping up her cup. The aroma was intoxicating, and if she homed in on it enough, she might be able to forget that her career was hanging by a thread; that a crazy man could have shot her yesterday; that she'd gone and seen her parents; and that shortly she'd be face to face with Logan Hunter. The thought of those poor girls suffering out there never left her mind.

If she was a drinker, she'd add a splash of bourbon this morning, but she left the coffee unadulterated, blew on it, and took a tentative sip. Perfection. One deep inhale, eyes closed to savor, then she brought up Google and searched Precise Construction.

In seconds she knew their basic business model: construction of residential subdivisions. That information only got her so far though. She had no idea what Logan Hunter did for them. She called the number on the header of the company's website.

"Precise Construction, Barb speaking."

"Barb, I'm Detec—" She stopped there. With her name plastered in the paper, it might be best to use a little deception, and really, she didn't need to give a name. "I'd like to speak with Logan Hunter."

"I can leave a message for him, but Mr. Hunter is on a jobsite today until six."

Did Logan work in the office and was simply out to inspect a jobsite or was he blue collar? She saw the tab for "Meet our Team," that would probably show faces and names for administrative positions—something she might have benefited from visiting before calling, but there was no going back in time. "Oh, I thought I might reach him in the office," she said, hoping to recover.

"I don't see why. He works on jobsites…" There was a leeriness to Barb's voice. "Who did you say this was?"

"I didn't." Amanda quickly hung up. She could have asked the woman where Logan was working, but she highly doubted she'd be getting anything else out of Barb.

She returned her attention to the website. Maybe there was a blog or something to indicate their current projects…

"Aha!"

There was a link to a trade article on the company's media page. According to it, Precise Construction had been awarded the contract for the development of a government-funded, affordable-housing community going up near Interstate 95. It was described as "one of the largest construction developments underway in the area," and Amanda knew right where to find it. Logan might be working somewhere else, but she'd rule out this jobsite first.

Amanda would say the construction project was well underway but far from finished. She recalled from the article that it had been slated for completion at the end of last year. She spotted Logan's Dodge Ram—so he was here somewhere—but she had to hunt for a parking spot.

A sign at the entrance boasted of affordable housing with luxury perks, such as walking trails and a dog-grooming station, and directed interested parties to a trailer clearly marked *Sales Office*. Next to it was another trailer, likely the one belonging to the site foreperson. She found a place to park and went in the foreperson's trailer. Nothing luxurious in there. Purely functional and a no-nonsense work environment with only the staples necessary to get the job done: three cheap, melamine desks, each of which had trays piled high with paper. Blueprints pinned to the wall seemed to qualify as artwork, but no one was home.

She grabbed the door to leave and a man in a hard hat ran right into her. "Whoa!" She lost her footing and faltered backward. He caught her arm, and she brushed free of him. "You should watch where you're going."

"I'm sorry, but I wasn't expect—" He stopped talking and his brow furrowed. His gaze fixed on her badge. "You're a cop."

"Detective, to be more precise."

"Well, we're busy here, so…" He brushed past her to the end of the trailer and tossed a clipboard he was holding onto the desk next to a nameplate that read, *Ross Ford, Foreman*.

"Aren't we all?" She followed, squared her shoulders to appear taller, and solidified her stance. "I need to speak to one of your workers, a Logan Hunter."

"Mr. Hunter is working right now." Ford grabbed papers from a bin on his left and hastily snapped them onto another clipboard.

"I need to discuss an important police matter with him." Not entirely a lie, and she added, "It won't take long."

"Can I ask what this is regarding?" He looked up at her, impatience written all over his face.

"You can, but I can't answer that."

"Then I can't help you." He put his head down, returning to his paperwork, his body language signifying the end of discussion.

How infuriating. She would love to get her alibi sealed up today and over with, but she couldn't push Ford too hard. She wasn't there on actual police business and with that article out there… "Can you tell me when his workday ends?" She just wanted to verify that what Barb at the office had told her was correct.

"Six bells," he said, not bothering to look up again. "But he gets lunch at noon, on the mark."

Okay, that she could work with much easier. "I'll be back."

"Goodie," Ford mumbled.

She shook her head and left. What a dick. She returned to her car, looking around, hoping for some small miracle that Logan Hunter would emerge from the site into view. She wasn't so lucky.

The clock on the dash read just after nine when she got behind the wheel and started her car. She still had the better part of three hours to fill, but it was better than waiting another nine. She really didn't want to see Malone without her alibi, though she might not have a choice.

Her phone rang, and caller ID on the car's heads-up display told her it was Becky. She answered, "Oh, I'm sorry I didn't get a chance to call—"

"No, don't apologize."

"You saw the article." Not a question in Amanda's mind.

"I did."

Amanda sat up at the sight of a man in a hard hat walking from the site to the lot but slumped when she determined it wasn't Logan Hunter.

"How are you doing?" Becky prompted.

"Well, I'm off the case…"

"Probably for the best."

"Yeah, maybe." Except for that tiny little thing—Rick Jensen's threat hanging overhead—that made it necessary to go a bit rogue.

"Don't tell me you're working the case anyway?"

Amanda bit her bottom lip. Her friend knew her too well. "Not exactly." Though it was possible the bracelet and the chip might lead to Palmer's killer.

"No, I can't let you," Becky said.

"I'm a big girl, responsible for my own actions."

"I just don't want to see you get into trouble."

"Too late for that." She chuckled, a case of laugh or cry. "And you don't know what's at stake."

"Your career?"

"No." Amanda shook her head as if her friend could see her. "Something's come up in the investigation that's far bigger than Palmer."

"Oh."

"But I want to talk to Malone about it before I tell you. Make sense?"

"Makes complete sense."

Amanda looked over at the chain-link gate that barred off the parking lot from the construction site. She might be able to get onto the premises, but even if she did, she'd have no clue where to find Hunter.

She wrung her hands on the steering wheel. She couldn't just sit around doing nothing. "I should really get going, Beck."

"Yeah, no worries. Call me when you get a chance."

"Will do. Bye." Amanda ended the call. She'd go to the station, tell Malone about the girls and the sex-trafficking ring, and plead with him to let her work that aspect of the case. She just hoped he'd overlook her lack of an alibi.

CHAPTER THIRTY-FOUR

Amanda hit a coffee shop in Woodbridge before going into the station; it was no Hannah's Diner, but their coffee was decent. And there was something about holding onto a to-go cup that calmed the nerves. She bought one for Trent too, and had the barista stuff a couple of creamers and sugar packets into a small paper bag. She hadn't heard how he'd ordered his coffee the other day and they'd drunk from lidded to-go cups.

But when she reached his cubicle, he was nowhere in sight. Cud was at his desk and did a double-take in her direction, making her feel a little self-conscious about the bruising and cuts to her face. She'd done her best to cover them, but one could only expect so much from foundation and concealer.

"Good morning."

Amanda turned to see Trent, and she smiled at him and held out her offering. "I thought you might like a Jabba."

"Always."

"I didn't know how you took it, so…" She pointed to the bag.

He dropped the bag into his garbage can. "Love it black." He went to take a sip but held it up in a toast gesture. "Thanks."

So he liked it black—interesting. "You're welcome."

"I thought maybe I'd missed you and you were off talking to—"

"Detective Steele."

"Sergeant," she said, spinning to face Malone.

His eyes widened at her appearance, but he regained his composure quickly and pointed toward his office. She dipped her head in acknowledgment.

"As you were," she said to Trent before following her superior.

She sucked in a deep breath as she entered Malone's office and he closed the door behind them.

"I'm not sure I want to know about—" He circled his finger to indicate her face.

"You don't."

"Hmph." He sat behind his desk, and she took the visitor chair.

He said, "From what I see, you and Trent are getting along well. Don't worry, there will be future cases for you two to work together."

She liked Trent, but she still wasn't sold on having a partner. She should plow ahead about the sex-trafficking ring, but instead, she asked, "What's Trent's story?" The question rushed out of her so fast that it surprised her—and given Malone's expression, him too.

"Huh?"

"Well, you must have had a talk with him, told him to take it easy on me. There's no lighting a fire under him."

"He doesn't have enthusiasm for the job?"

"Not what I meant."

"Ah, you've done your best to provoke him and it hasn't worked."

She smirked and hitched her shoulders. "Maybe."

"Why am I not surprised?" He laughed, which somehow after yesterday's events sounded sweeter than ever. "I think it's a Steele family trait. Your father, as much as I like and respect the man, made me want to punch him more than once."

"I'm pretty sure you actually did once." She buried her smile in the lip of her coffee cup.

Malone held up an index finger.

Amanda went on. "Well, if you didn't talk to Trent, he's got to be the most laid-back rookie ever. Usually they're all gung-ho and eager to go in guns blazing— Oh."

Malone seemed to watch her as her own realization struck.

"He told me he was shot."

He held up two fingers. "Twice. One round to his shoulder, another to his chest. He was damn lucky."

"I'd say." It would seem Trent had a way of downplaying his incident with a gunman too.

"That changes a person."

She simply nodded, remembering how he'd told her that he carried that day with him.

"But enough about Trent. We need to talk about yesterday, Amanda."

She'd figured the diversion wouldn't last forever. She drank some coffee and tried to gather her thoughts. "It's just… Hill got me so mad." So much for articulation.

"I can't have my detectives tossing their badge like that. I need to know I can count on them to do their jobs."

"You have my word."

Malone clasped his hands on his lap, wet his lips, and nodded. "Very well. Now, do you have your alibi for me?"

"Not quite yet. But should be very soon."

Malone sighed. "I don't know what you expect from me."

"Actually," she started, "I need to talk to you about something very important and urgent."

"Why do I get the feeling you're going to try to sweet-talk your way back onto the case? I can't let it happen. You know that."

"I know, but what you don't know is Palmer was booked with a silver bracelet when he went to prison."

"And the big deal is…?"

"There was a data chip in the clasp that contains an inventory of girls."

Malone's eyes widened. "Girls? A sex-trafficking ring? No." He shook his head. "I don't see Chad Palmer being involved with that."

"Neither do I, but Trent's going to poke around, talk to a few of Palmer's associates again and pressure them."

"Okay, what do you want?"

"I want permission to look into the cold cases. I can't help but wonder if there's not something there that might be tied to the network. There's already a detective in Sex Crimes who's been assigned—"

"Hold up." Malone held up his hand. "This is already moving and you're telling me after the fact?"

"I'm sorry. It all happened so fast and…"

"That happened." He pointed to her face.

She was hoping to eternally avoid needing to tell him about Rick Jensen, his assault, his threat, and the fact she'd just let him get away with it. As a long-time friend of the family he might understand, but she couldn't take that risk.

"Yeah. Anyway, I'm fine, but those girls are not. They need to be helped and whatever degenerates are involved need to be brought to justice."

Malone's lips twitched and there was a sparkle in his eyes—one she hadn't seen for her in a long time. He was proud of her and it made her sit up straighter.

"So? Can I work the cold cases?"

"You really don't think there's any true connection to Palmer?"

She got comfortable and laid out what she was thinking. "It could be a leap, and I have no way of knowing until I dig into it, but do you remember the stripper who was murdered in Georgia five and a half years ago?"

"Yeah. What about her?"

"Well, we haven't been able to figure out a connection between the girl and Webb—not that we've had a lot of time to focus on that. But we know enough that Casey-Anne Ritter seems to be an assumed identity and living off the grid. That tells me she either had something to hide or she was hiding. So was her connection to Webb an involvement in the ring or was she a victim?"

Malone chewed on his thumbnail. "Huh. Just assure me again that if any of this starts leading to Palmer's killer, you'll back off and turn whatever you have over to Trent?"

"Does that mean that you're letting me—"

"Hold up. There's still the matter of your alibi. I'd feel a lot better if I had that. What seems to be the issue anyway?"

It would be easier if she could convince herself to come clean about the one-night stand, but she wasn't ready to go there unless she had no choice. "I should have it in a couple of hours." She glanced at his clock on the wall. "Less than," she added with a smile.

"Hmph. Fine. Get it, then get to work."

"What am I supposed to do until then?"

"Not my problem, Detective." He swept his hand in a brushing motion. "Shoo."

She returned to her cubicle, but Trent wasn't in his and his coat and coffee were gone. *Atta boy, he's following a lead,* she thought.

She sat at her desk and downed the rest of her drink and stared at the partition. What a waste of time just sitting around waiting. Surely there was something she could do that wouldn't give Malone a fit. She recalled Detective Patricia Glover's voicemail. One phone call couldn't hurt anything. She called but got voicemail, and it sure felt like the universe might be conspiring against her too. She didn't leave a message.

Next, she tried Detective Banks from Georgia. He answered on the second ring.

"This is Detective Steele," she said. There was a pause on his end, so she reminded him. "I called about a case you worked over five years ago. Casey-Anne Ritter."

"Oh right. Yes. How can I help? You said you thought you might have a related case? You referring to Jackson Webb—the guy killed with the same gun a few days later? Has new evidence surfaced?"

"Yes, and no, I guess." She filled him in on the data chip and the sex-trafficking ring. "I think it's possible that Casey-Anne was either involved or a victim."

A huge sigh traveled over the line. "I wish I could say that surprises me."

The hairs rose on the back of Amanda's neck. "Which—victim or perpetrator?"

"Definitely the former, and I'd say she lived in fear. It was just the starkness of the girl's apartment, you see. She had a beanbag chair in the living room and couple of hardcover books. Her bedroom was a used mattress and second-hand dresser. Ask me, she was ready to run whenever she needed to. She paid for her rent in cash. She worked at a strip club, dancing." He paused there as if he wasn't sure if Amanda was aware of that.

"I read that in the file." Casey-Anne was more likely sex-trafficking victim than perpetrator.

"Well, when she showed up to rent her place, she'd banged on the building manager's door, saying she was responding to the paper in the window advertising the studio apartment. She had a wad of bills in hand, enough to cover first and last month's rent."

Pawning the bracelet on its own wouldn't net "wads of bills." Assuming they weren't completely off base with their theories about Casey-Anne, it would seem she'd exchanged other items for cash too.

"Did she provide references?" A stretch, no doubt.

"She didn't have any, but she had cash. That was something the manager repeated often."

A ball of rage knotted in Amanda's chest. All it took was a wad of cash and some members of society could overlook a young girl who was obviously running from some sort of trouble.

"How did the manager describe Casey-Anne?"

"Said she was jittery, but she was clean—another thing of importance to the man. He wanted a building free of druggies."

"At least he had some standards," Amanda lamented. "My part— another detective in my unit happened to search for Casey-Anne Ritter and came up empty. He was under the impression it was a fake name."

"I found the same, but she had ID that pegged her as Casey-Anne Ritter, twenty-one."

"And that's what you ran with?"

"Yes and no."

"It's the no part I'm interested in."

"I did consult the missing persons database for Atlanta to see if anyone had reported her missing. To me, she barely looked eighteen."

Amanda glanced at her monitor, her mind on the files waiting for her on the mainframe, all those young girls. Would she find Casey-Anne Ritter among them? "I'm taking it nothing hit for you?" she said to Banks.

"No. You think she might have had ties to your city—"

Dumfries wasn't exactly a city, but… "Was thinking Prince William County as a whole, maybe farther out." Once Amanda started digging in, she'd check the local missing persons database and see what she could find, but the more specifics she could gather on Casey-Anne first the better. "Did she have any distinguishing markers?"

"Besides the gunshot wound?"

Banks paused there and she wasn't sure if he was being sarcastic or had a warped sense of humor. He cleared this throat and continued.

"She had a cherry birthmark the size of a quarter on her lower back. Beyond that she was a natural brunette, though she was a platinum blond at the time of death. She had brown eyes and a small dimple in her chin. She was five-seven."

Amanda scribbled all this down for quick reference when she got off the call. "What about any leads in the case?"

"Didn't get far. I mean, obviously, given that the case went cold."

She didn't respect how easily it seemed Detective Banks had relieved himself of any obligation in that regard. He clearly wasn't the see-it-through type.

"What about friends, coworkers at the club where she stripped?"

"Georgia's Peaches. Yeah, we spoke with all of them. Oh— There was one dancer who went by Ginger, who saw Ritter just before she left what was her last shift. She said that Ritter was in a hurry to get out of the club."

"Did she know why?"

"She said she seemed spooked but pressing that didn't get me anywhere."

Probably because Ginger had her own secrets that she didn't want being probed, and getting too involved in a police investigation had a way of making that happen. But the fact that Ritter was "spooked" made Amanda wonder if Casey-Anne had spotted someone from her past and that's why she'd been high-tailing it out of the club that night.

"There's also something else that might help, though it hasn't so far." Spoken as if Banks had continued working the case. "A neighbor in Ritter's building said she saw a man in the hall outside her door."

Amanda sat up. "Was this around the time of the murder?"

"No," Banks said. "That's why it was dismissed as irrelevant—or should I say, my sergeant told me that it probably wouldn't get me anywhere."

Amanda strongly disagreed. Every lead in a homicide investigation had to be seen through until it either produced the next step or hit a dead end. "When was it?"

"During the day."

"The day she was murdered?"

Banks didn't say anything, but Amanda heard him sigh.

"That day? And you didn't pursue the lead?"

Banks remained silent, probably tired of defending his boss, and hopefully feeling shame for so easily backing down himself.

"Did this neighbor talk to the man?"

"She said 'hi' to him and asked if she could help him. He told her that he was Casey-Anne's uncle, in town visiting. The neighbor lady accepted that and went back into her apartment, but she said the man gave her the creeps."

Amanda bit her tongue so as not to jump down the detective's throat—an eyewitness saw a man outside the vic's apartment who gave her the creeps on the day of the murder, no less, and that still wasn't a lead worth pursuing?

She wanted to throttle something. "I think we both know—"

"It wasn't her uncle? Yeah."

"Uncle" was probably there for the bracelet—assuming Amanda's earlier speculation held merit. The more she could gather about this guy the better. "Did this neighbor have anything else to offer about this 'uncle' guy? What he looked or sounded like?"

"She said that he had a bit of a lisp and a very slight limp."

The gunman in the Happy Time surveillance video favored the left knee—a coincidence or had "Uncle" returned to kill Palmer?

"What about hair color, eyes, height?"

"Strong and lean, black hair, and he was short for a guy. If I remember only about five ten."

That height would also fit with the perp who'd assaulted Palmer. "What was he wearing?"

"Jeans and a black sweater."

"A hoodie?" She just thought she'd ask.

"She didn't say that."

"Okay, you've given me a lot. Thanks for all your help."

"I hope you find her justice, and if there's anything else I can help you with on this end, I'm just a call away."

"Actually… Back closer to when this happened and after the murder of Jackson Webb, did you speak with anyone from Prince William County PD?"

"I did. Can't remember the detective I spoke to now, but it was a man."

"Detective Dennis Bishop sound familiar?"

"Yeah, I think that's it."

"Did you tell him about this "uncle" guy?"

"I did, but he didn't seem too interested. Told me he had no eyewitnesses for his case, and unless I got somewhere with "Uncle," he didn't think it was related to the murders."

She looked over her partition and could see the top of Cud's head. She'd be asking him about this. "Okay, thanks," she said to Banks.

He ended the call, and she cupped her phone in her hands and got up, fully intent on questioning Cud about what he was thinking back then.

The sound of someone snapping their fingers had her looking over a shoulder. She groaned internally at the sight of Malone.

"You have that alibi?"

She opened her mouth and—

"No? I didn't think so." He looked at her sternly, and she consulted the clock—*11:30 AM.*

"Going to get it right now!" She ran out the door. She had thirty minutes to get back to the construction site in Dumfries.

CHAPTER THIRTY-FIVE

Amanda pulled into the construction lot at five to noon. Three food trucks were there now, no doubt eager to satisfy the appetites of the hungry workers. Logan's pickup was in the same place as it had been earlier, and now there was an available spot two down from it. She parked and would wait there. It was convenient if Logan was going to leave the premises for lunch and it afforded her a good view of the gate.

She pulled down the visor and looked in the mirror. The bruises weren't that noticeable, but they weren't exactly invisible either. She didn't have a powder compact in her car, but she had some lipstick in a pocket, so she smeared some of that on and finished primping by fluffing and sweeping her hair over her shoulders. She examined the final product and clued in. What the hell was she doing? She flipped the visor back up.

This guy was her alibi, nothing more. She didn't want anything more out of this. After all, he was married, and the other night it was quite clear he was screwed up. Then again, wasn't everyone who went to bed with a stranger? Surely most had an emotional need or issue they were dealing with or wanted satisfied. She should know.

Workers started filing through the gate into the lot. The majority seemed on track for the food trucks. She scanned the crowd for any sign of Logan, and just when it was starting to feel like the possibility of seeing him was on par with a unicorn sighting, he walked through the gate. He was headed right for his pickup.

She got out of her car and approached him. He was holding a hard hat in his hands and wearing sunglasses. He slowed his stride at the sight of her.

"Logan, I need to talk to you."

"Should I even ask how you found—" His gaze had landed on the badge she had clipped to her waist. "Never mind. Cop?"

"Detective, but yeah."

They were standing face to face now, and he didn't seem in any hurry to move on so that was a good thing.

"Just a second of your time is all I need," she said. "I need to talk to you."

"We tried talking the other night, but it didn't go too well."

"We?" She scoffed laughter. "No, *I* tried to talk. What was going on with you anyway?"

He took a few steps back at the personal question.

"Never mind. None of my business."

He stopped and faced her. "You're right about that," he said and resumed walking.

"You're giving me such a hard time considering you're the one who's married," she spat.

He returned to her, his stride quickly eating up the bit of distance he'd put between them. Pain danced across his face. "Must be nice to have a badge. It makes stalking a whole lot easier."

"I'm not stalking you, but enough. Listen, we had our thing the other night, but I need your help. There's a case… I can't get into the details, but—"

Logan's shoulders lowered. "You said something about needing an alibi?"

Given how drunk he'd been, she was surprised he remembered.

"Yes. I need you to testify that we were together this past Sunday from seven until eleven." The time-of-death window started at six, but she'd been with Logan starting at seven.

His gaze went past her, and it was enough to tell Amanda what he was probably thinking.

"Your wife doesn't need to find out," she said. "I just need you to give your statement to my sergeant."

"What happened during the time of seven to eleven?"

"There was a murder," she said.

"And what? You're a suspect?"

"Not exactly, but if I'm going to be allowed to continue working cases, I need this alibi."

A smile toyed the edges of his lips.

"I'm glad you find this amusing."

"I find it interesting."

She stiffened. He was on some sort of power trip, though he didn't know about the poor girls out there, or that the longer he kept her tied up, the longer they remained prisoners.

"Well, will you testify that we were together or not?"

"What sort of details do I need to hand—"

She scowled and he laughed. The playboy she'd seen in his eyes at the Tipsy Moose the night they'd hooked up was back, alive and well. She briefly considered asking him to make it sound like they were more than they were, but, really, Malone probably wouldn't care about her having one-night stands. "You just need to speak to my sergeant. Stick to saying we were together at the time."

"Enjoying each other's company." He smirked and she shook her head. He added, "And if your sergeant asks what we were doing?"

"I highly doubt he will." She viewed Malone almost as a second father sometimes, and if he felt at all the same, he wouldn't want details about her sex life anyway. "If he asks, just tell him the details of our outing are none of his business—that it's personal."

"Sure. I can do that."

She breathed with relief. "Thank you. I'll have him call you, but I'll need your number."

"Surprised you don't have it already."

She wasn't about to admit that she'd pulled a background report on him and none showed on record. She took out her phone and created a new contact named *Alibi*. "Ready when you are."

He rattled off the number and she keyed it in. "What kind of detective are you, anyway?"

"I'm with Homicide." She put her phone in a pocket.

He squinted behind his shades, small lines forming around his eyes. "Cool."

"Cool? I investigate murders. That means people have died. There's nothing cool about it." That's what she said at least, but honestly, the Homicide Unit was where she belonged.

"Sure, okay, but I'm going to need you to do me a favor before I—"

"You're blackmailing a cop?"

"Detective, isn't that what you said? I'd like to start over. Don't think I'm asking for much."

"Start over... what?" Her heart bumped off rhythm, her instinct telling her he was going to ask her out. But there was a huge problem with that. He was a married man, and she didn't get involved with them. Well, not *after* she found out they were married anyway. She slept with guys once. One night. One time. One and done.

"I want to go out for dinner with you," he said. "The whole deal: appetizers, drinks, main course, dessert."

Her impulse was to correct him; she didn't drink. "Think you're forgetting the part where you're married."

"Separated, actually. Have been for a couple of years. Well, two years, eight months, sixteen days, but who's counting."

"Sounds like you are."

"Maybe a little, but it's only because she pisses me off. Look, sorry if I was a real prick the other night. It's hard to serve divorce papers to someone you can't find. I hired a private investigator and he'd just followed what turned out to be yet another dead end. But maybe you could help me with that. You seem to have a way of finding people, even if they don't want to be found." One corner of his mouth lifted in the beginnings of an arrogant smirk. "So what do you say to dinner?"

She crossed her arms and jutted out her chin. Her heart was racing at the fact she was considering his proposal. "You give my alibi to my sergeant and then we'll talk."

"Nope."

"What do you mean—"

"You tell me right now that you'll go out to dinner with me and then I'll talk with your sergeant."

She felt like she'd just jumped into a swirling whirlpool and was being sucked down to her ultimate demise. "Fine. One dinner."

"All I'm asking for. We can take it from there."

"Take it from—take it from—" she stuttered.

"Ah, you're cute."

He brushed the back of his hand to her right cheek and walked around her to his truck. He opened the door and turned around, stepped back to her.

"I will need you to shake on this arrangement of ours though. Figure you're a detective and should keep your word, but—" He held out his hand and she took it. "All right. Have a good one. Talk soon."

She watched him drive out of the lot. Her legs felt stuck to the gravel. What the hell had just happened, and what had she gotten herself into? Her cheeks were warm, and she palmed them, hating herself for the way her body responded to him. The last time she'd felt anything close to this way, it had been Kevin heating her core. Her chest tugged. She'd felt like she was betraying him by sleeping with other men; how could she ever forgive herself if she started to move on?

Her hands clenched into fists and she resolved she would never let that happen. It was just one lousy dinner, and nothing had even been scheduled. But it was the damn handshake and her word again. She jammed the heel of her right boot into the ground.

Her phone rang, the caller ID blocked. She braced herself and answered firmly, "Detective Steele."

"You'd be wise to back off." The caller was using a voice modulator, so it was hard to distinguish whether it was a man or woman.

"Who the hell is—"

Click.

She held out her phone and stared at it, confused. Rick Jensen would have no reason to call and threaten her like that, but it left a chilling question. Who did?

She burrowed into her coat, feeling like eyes were crawling over her skin. Could it be someone associated with the data chip and the sex trafficking? If so, they were going to find out that she didn't scare easily. Rather, they should be afraid because she was going to do everything in her power to save those girls and bring the ring and all those associated with it down.

CHAPTER THIRTY-SIX

Amanda called Malone to let him know that she had her alibi and gave him Logan's number.

"I'll call him," Malone said.

"So can I work the cold cases?"

"I still need to call… Oh, fine, you can work—"

"Thank you! The girls will thank you too."

"Just stop everything if any evidence gets you close to Palmer's murderer, run it by me, and I'll let you know whether to back off or proceed."

"Yes, of course." She hung up and connected her phone to the car's Bluetooth system and called Trent. His line was ringing over the speakers as she pulled out of the construction lot.

"Detective Stenson," he answered.

"Trent, how did you make out with Wheable, Freddy, and Courtney about the bracelet?" She should feel bad that she'd just hung up with Malone and was already prying into a case she was banned from, but there was still the matter of Rick's threat hanging overhead. Guilt over lying to Malone would be nothing compared to letting anything happen to her parents.

"I'd say all of them are telling me the truth when they say they know nothing about it. Well, beyond Freddy saying that Palmer gave it to him."

"Did you tell them what was on it?"

"I might be a rookie, but I'm not an idiot. Why would they confess knowledge of it if they realized what it had on it?"

Amanda smiled, not that he could see it, but she was pleased to witness Trent growing a backbone. Maybe being out on his own had been the best thing for him. He'd probably become a better detective than he would under her shadow. Then again, he might have already picked up some of her sass. Though he must have possessed some already given that he'd run ahead at a crime scene and got himself shot.

Trent continued. "They were really lost on why I was so interested in a stupid bracelet. And, trust me, I pressed all of them hard and none crumbled. I believed them. Now, Courtney did give me something that might be useful. I was getting ready to call you about it as I just finished speaking with her. To start with, she was at Denver's Motel from Saturday afternoon until Sunday morning."

"She lied to us. Why am I not surprised? Also explains the extra towels Palmer requested."

"Yep."

"If someone lies once…"

"I know, but I'm sure she really doesn't know about the bracelet."

"You said I might find something useful; she's a liar, is that all?" She stopped for a traffic light a few blocks from Central.

"Nope, it's that I think she might have seen Casey-Anne Ritter at the pawnshop the day of the accident."

They hadn't been able to make the connection without conjecture. "She saw her pawn the bracelet?"

"Can't be certain."

"Okay," Amanda dragged out. "But I'm struggling with why Courtney remembers this from over five years ago. What was so special about Casey-Anne?"

"Apparently she was flirting with Palmer while she was pawning some of her things."

Some women were more prone to jealousy and possessiveness, and it wasn't too far a stretch to imagine Courtney could have remembered the interaction.

"Let me guess, she doesn't remember what she was turning over?"

"Would be nice, but she was too blinded by the green-eyed monster. I did show her Casey-Anne's picture though, and she was quite sure that could have been her."

The light turned green and she hit the gas.

Amanda ran through the interview she and Trent had conducted with Courtney in her mind. They'd asked if she knew Casey-Anne and Courtney had said no, but that was explicable if she'd just been a random customer to her. They hadn't thought to show her Casey-Anne's photo.

"Okay, so what about our other leads?" She realized she'd said *our* after it was out.

"I asked Wheable about the empty compartment in the back of the Caprice. He claimed not to know anything about it. He did say Courtney's the one who took the car from him. Stands behind 'what happened with it after that wasn't on him' and that he has no idea."

"Like hell. He would be who Freddy was fearful of, I bet. You told me Wheable served time for robbery. I bet he's back in the game. And Courtney was at Denver's Motel, the same day Lorraine Nash saw the Caprice. She was probably delivering the car to Palmer that day."

"Could very well have been. She didn't admit to that, but I have reached out to the Property Crimes Unit and passed along Wheable's, Courtney's, and Freddy's names with our suspicions. What they do with it from here is their business."

Amanda turned down the street where Central was located. Trent had filled her in on the bracelet and the car, but one piece she was interested in had been missing from his update. "How did you make out with the coin?"

"It's not Freddy's, Courtney's, or Wheable's."

"Well, it was just a thought. Now following the coin might not lead us to Palmer's killer—but let's rule it out first. Look up local AA groups and see if they'll give you a list of everyone who was issued a twenty-year sobriety coin. There can't be that many."

"Guess we'll find out. I'll keep you posted."

"Hey, I'm just about to pull into Central. You there?"

"No, I'm following up the taxi angle still. Figured I'd visit the companies in person."

"Talk later."

"Bye." Trent beat her to hanging up.

Realizing he had the investigation under control set her mind at ease about Rick Jensen. As long as Trent was thorough, she could focus on the cold cases, with specific attention on Casey-Anne Ritter, without too much worry.

She parked in the station's lot and headed for the door when her phone rang. The caller ID was blocked. Unbelievable. People thought by blocking their number they couldn't be found, but people with tech skills like Jacob could get past it. She'd be calling Jacob for a favor as soon as she had a chance.

She swiped a finger across the screen to accept the call and said nothing.

"Hello?" It was a woman's voice.

She breathed easier and said, "Detective Steele."

"CSI Blair."

Amanda's chest tightened.

"I got a couple of DNA hits on the epithelial that I pulled from that silver bracelet."

Amanda stopped walking and a cool breeze circled her. She pulled her coat tighter around her.

Blair went on. "It ties to Chad Palmer, but also to a murder case in Georgia five and a half years ago. The victim, more specifically—"

"Casey-Anne Ritter." Goose bumps pricked on Amanda's arms.

"That's right." A pause, then, "How did you know that?"

Amanda would like to say she was psychic, but sadly that was far from the truth. "You're probably also about to say her murder was tied to the Jackson Webb murder case in Woodbridge three days later."

"Yes. But how— When I told you about Webb's murder, I didn't know about the link to the previous one in Georgia. But the same gun was used to kill both Webb and Ritter."

"I'm aware. I'm actually starting to pry into both cold cases."

"I wish you success."

If Amanda's feet hadn't been grounded firmly on the pavement, she might topple over. This cordial side of Blair wasn't one she was used to seeing, but Amanda suspected the reason for that, and it didn't mean Blair suddenly cared for Amanda. "You heard what was in the bracelet?"

"Yeah, like I said, I wish you success—both with solving the murder cases and rounding up those poor girls."

"Thank you. But just one question, how much would you say a bracelet like that is worth?"

A few seconds then, "A few hundred, nothing too substantial."

Just enough to get a bus ticket out of town. So there had to be other items Casey-Anne had pawned or another way she'd earned money between Dumfries and showing up at the building manager's door. "That's what I would have guessed. Thanks."

"Uh-huh." With that, Blair hung up.

"All righty then." Amanda smiled, looking at her phone in her hand. What CSI Blair might not have known was that she'd just confirmed for Amanda Casey-Anne's link to Dumfries and the pawnshop. For her DNA to be on the bracelet—a miracle after all this time, though it had spent a bulk of the last several years untouched in lockup—she had to have had it around her wrist at one time.

CHAPTER THIRTY-SEVEN

Malone was walking toward Amanda as she was headed to her cubicle. He had an enormous grin on his face. "What's up with you?" She raised her brows and proceeded to put her jacket on the back of her chair and sit down.

"I'm just happy for you."

"Happy for me?" She was obviously missing something.

"Logan Hunter."

She already didn't like the direction of this conversation. "What about him?"

"He sounds like a nice guy. And the way he tells it, you two hit it off on Sunday night and spent a lovely evening together. Not sure why it took so long to nail down your alibi. Were you embarrassed to tell me you have a love life?"

Love life? She could choke on that.

"You don't have to be, you know," he went on. "I wouldn't expect a woman your age to be sitting at home all alone."

Wow, he actually went there…

He had stopped talking and was looking at her expectantly. She had to think quickly. "I just didn't want you to make more of it than it is. It's really nothing."

"Not the way he tells it. Guess you guys are going out again. He told me he plans on taking you out for a nice dinner."

"Did he now?" She smirked. Logan Hunter must have been sure to plant that in there to remind her of her promise.

"Uh-huh." Malone's face fell more serious. "There's something else I'd like to talk with you about though. Let's just slip into my office for a minute."

She glanced at the clock on the wall and discovered it was after one now. Time was getting away from her, and with every second those girls were suffering. "I really need to get to work."

"One minute." His earlier comment had been more directive than an invitation.

Behind his closed door, he sat at his desk, and she in his visitor chair.

"You never did tell me what happened to you," he said.

"What—"

He flicked a finger toward her face.

"It's nothing." There was no way she'd be coming forward about Rick Jensen's visit. She just needed to get back to work.

He dipped his head and leveled his gaze at her. "This is me you're talking to. I know that something—"

"Trent told you."

"No. If he had, would I be asking?"

"Maybe just to verify what you heard," she volleyed back.

"He told me nothing, but now I'm wondering if he should have."

"It's nothing—don't worry about it."

"Okay. That's not what I need to talk to you about anyway. I didn't want to bring it up earlier, but I need to. Can you tell me why Courtney Barrett threatened to sue the department for harassment because, left to my imagination, it sounds like you spoke to her on your own? She obviously knew exactly who you were."

"Not that she let on to me that she did, but I suppose everyone in this frickin' town knows too much—or at least thinks they do."

"Did you speak to her alone?"

"No."

Malone made eye contact with her. "You're telling me the truth?"

"Of course."

"And you let Trent take the lead with the interview?"

She wrung her hands.

"You were to be Trent's shadow. What am I supposed to tell Hill?"

"Just tell her I was there with Trent. That's not a lie."

Malone worried his bottom lip. "Might work. I wish I could say you weren't in the room."

Her sergeant didn't need to say as much, but it was clear he regretted ever letting her near the Palmer case. But she didn't have time to sit around talking. She glanced at the clock again. She'd lost another fifteen minutes.

"Are you in a hurry, Detective?"

"Matter of fact, yes."

"I know you said you'd back off the cold cases if what you uncover is a direct tie to Palmer's murderer. I want to see your eyes when you tell me that."

"I promise. I'll back off if it becomes necessary." She wondered how many more times she'd have to assure him before he believed her.

He leaned back in his chair and studied her. "Guess that's the best I'm gonna get. If you were anyone else—"

"I know. You'd have kept me off the case from the start. I appreciate that you trust me enough."

Malone mumbled something incoherent, then, "Do you think the sex-trafficking thing is going to lead to Palmer's killer?"

"I'd need to be clairvoyant like Trent's sister."

"Clair— Never mind, and don't get smart with me."

She smiled. Malone couldn't be any further from new-age ideology than a Catholic priest. "Sorry. Didn't mean to be. But I don't have any reason to believe that's the case yet. Obviously, the bracelet with the girls on it was the one on Palmer at the time of his booking and release, but I really don't think he knew what was on it."

She proceeded to fill him in on CSI Blair's call and Casey-Anne Ritter's connection to the bracelet and the pawnshop where she would have crossed paths with Palmer. She empathized that was all: crossed paths. She almost told him what Courtney and the others associated with Palmer had to say about the bracelet, but she shouldn't know any of that.

"Palmer must have liked the bracelet, tried it on, and that's where it stayed," she added. "I believe that whoever killed Palmer was a different person than who took out Ritter and Webb based on the murder method."

"Hmm." Malone rubbed his jaw.

"Sarge?" she prompted.

"Okay, go. Get to work."

She hopped up.

"Oh, Detective, be careful not to step on any toes either. I know you're rather focused on the girl's murder, but Detective Bishop worked the Jackson Webb case. So if you're going to him, just play nice."

His warning might have come a little late as Cud hadn't taken too kindly to her asking about the Webb case the other day.

"You bet."

She left Malone's office and hurried to her desk, not wanting to pass another second chit-chatting. It was time to get some real work done.

CHAPTER THIRTY-EIGHT

Amanda had just sat down when her cell phone rang. "You've got to be kidding me." She answered without consulting ID.

"Detective Steele?" An unfamiliar voice.

"Who is this?"

"Detective Patricia Glover from Sex Crimes. Most people just call me Patty."

"Oh, I tried reaching you, but I didn't leave a message. I intended to try you again."

"No worries. Life can get a little overwhelming, but I just wanted to touch base."

"Do you think those girls are still out there to find or the players involved?" Amanda found herself spewing her greatest concern.

"It's hard to say. The records date back seventeen years, but—"

"Seventeen?" Amanda gasped.

"Yep, and I'd bet whoever's behind this ring is still active. These types keep doing what they do until they're stopped."

"Guess we better stop them then."

"I like your optimism." Patty's smile traveled the line.

"Did you hear about the history of the files—how they were in a bracelet that's now been connected to a cold case in Georgia?" Amanda thought it best to make sure that Patty was just as informed as she was.

"Yeah, I heard. Also, it's linked to a murder in Woodbridge a few days later."

"That's right."

"I really believe that Casey-Anne Ritter had been a victim of the ring and that she escaped." Amanda laid out her reasons: the assumed name and living off the grid.

"Makes sense to me. If I were her and got free, I'd run as far away as I could. It's sad that it would seem her past caught up to her."

Sadder still that Ritter had nothing to bargain for her life with as the bracelet her killer was probably after was in possession of the county while Palmer was behind bars. "I'm going to say whoever killed Ritter and Webb were mixed up in the ring."

"Could be. Not sure how much you know—or if you've had a chance to look at the files yet—but there were records of bank transfers on the data chip."

"Yes, Jacob—Detective Briggs—told me."

"Okay, good. Well, I've started on obtaining subpoenas, so I have the right to track those to the banking institutions. I can see if the accounts are still active and from there see what I can get. Hoping to get some names."

"I haven't accessed the files yet, but I take it there are no names mentioned?"

"Nicknames are assigned to everyone, but that's normal—even when the files are encrypted and hidden on a chip in a bracelet clasp."

"They have a lot to lose," Amanda lamented, sadly considering that included innocent children. "As I said, keep me posted. I'm going to start with trying to see if I can track down more information on Casey-Anne Ritter, whoever she was."

"Makes sense. Let me know if you need any help."

"I should be fine on that front."

"What's the plan?"

Amanda bristled a bit at the micro-managing. "Jacob said there are pictures. I was considering scrolling through them to see if any resemble Ritter."

"Just a warning: it's not easy to look at those type of pictures." Patty's voice turned grave. "I've been at this for five years now, the longest in this unit actually. It's definitively not a unit where most officers pitch their tent. Most transfer out after a year."

"So what keeps you around?"

"The days I actually get to take these creeps down make it worth it. The wins, as you could say." A lightness was back in her tone.

"I get that." Amanda was ready to get on with things, but there was something a bit clingy about Patty. She professed to like her job, but she didn't seem eager to return to work.

"I better get going," Amanda said. "Lots to do. There are hundreds of pictures from what I understand."

"Yes, there are. Again, call if you need anything. You have my number from the other day still?"

"I do."

With that, Amanda ended the call and set her phone on her desk. She hadn't laid out her entire plan to Patty, but she was going to look at the photos and files and cross-reference what she found with local news. She'd also try Missing Persons and see if she had more luck than the detective in Georgia had with his search. But he said he'd limited his search to Atlanta.

She took a few deep breaths and accessed the mainframe. There were three files right where Jacob had told her they'd be, and she clicked on the first one. It opened a spreadsheet listing contacts in one column, with their preferences and bids in columns to the right. As Patty had noted, the contacts were codenames, and to Amanda appeared to reference characters in literature and movies. It churned her stomach to see the list contained two hundred perverts, all with a lust for young women, a few with a desire for six-year-olds.

She opened the next file, which was pages long of scanned bank transfers.

The third file was a database—or catalogue—of girls. The girls were assigned nicknames too, and their profiles included age, ethnicity, hair, eye color, with photos attached.

She clicked on the picture attached to the first girl, and when it popped up, she shut the window down as fast as she could. The profile noted she was only ten years old and the photo depicted her— Bile rose in her throat. No wonder people transferred out of Sex Crimes. Once you saw an image like that, there was no going back, and the one Amanda had just seen would be burned on her brain for life.

CHAPTER THIRTY-NINE

Amanda would let Patty Glover scour the files and do her thing, while Amanda would do all she could to work around the disgusting files. She brought up the missing persons database for Prince William County and searched for girls aged between six and nineteen but didn't set any limitations as to when the reports were filed. She added *cherry birthmark* under identifying markers. Sadly, there were far more than Amanda would have imagined or than she had time to investigate.

Maybe she was going at this from the wrong angle. If Casey-Anne Ritter had gone missing as a young girl, it would have been big news. If she had been taken within Prince William County, she would have likely heard buzz about it firsthand through her father and the community, even if Amanda had been a young woman herself. But she didn't remember any of that happening. So it might be prudent that she extend the search geographically. And maybe instead of looking in a missing persons database, she'd consult the worldwide web.

She keyed in *missing girl state of Virginia age six to nineteen* and watched as the screen filled with news articles.

She started the search and sat back, sipping on another cup of coffee—she'd lost track of the number now. She'd been at this for hours and a glance at the clock told her it was now after three in the afternoon. Her ass was numb, and her head throbbed from staring at the screen so hard, wishing for it to provide answers.

Trent entered her cubicle with a grease-stained paper bag. "I'd put it on your desk, but…"

"What is— Oh, you didn't need to—"

"I know I didn't." He looked at her desk and seemed to be trying to figure where he could set the bag down.

"Here." She took it from him with a smile. The smell of bacon, cheese, and onion wafted up and had her stomach rumbling. After seeing the picture she had, and contemplating the horrible evils in the world, she was surprised she had an appetite.

"You are a prince."

She opened the bag and dug out the bacon cheeseburger, then cleared a spot on her desk and set it down. Grease marks—who cared. She unwrapped it and took a bite. A glorious, heavenly, devilish bite.

"Oh… my… God," she said between chomping. Grease dripped from the corners of her mouth, and she snatched a tissue from the box on her desk and dabbed it away. "Thank you so much."

"You're very welcome. I figured if I've gotten to know you at all in the last couple of days, you'd probably be slaving away with no regard to your body's needs."

"How did you know you'd find me at my desk though?"

"I didn't. Figured if you weren't here, I'd just have it later. Hence the onions. Hopefully, you like—"

"Love." She tore off another chunk of cow and gluten.

"Good." Trent chuckled and sat at his desk.

She desperately wanted to press him for updates, but with all the ears around and Malone down the hall, she thought better of it. She held her burger in her left hand, scrolled down the headlines with her right. On page three, an article from fifteen and a half years ago caught her eye.

Had her gamble actually paid off?

She swallowed the last bit of food in her mouth, set down the burger, and clicked on the article. It told the story of eight-year-old Phoebe Baldwin from Williamsburg, Virginia, who'd gone missing. There was something vaguely familiar about the name, but Amanda paused to do the quick math. Phoebe, if she was Casey-Anne, would have been eighteen—the age Detective Banks said she looked to be when she was murdered.

She returned to the article and gleaned takeaways. Phoebe's parents were Wes and Tanya Baldwin, married at the time of the report, and wealthy as God. Wes was a thoracic surgeon and his wife was an aristocrat and hailed from old money. Phoebe had gone missing from a playground in the city while under a babysitter's care. The babysitter was noted as a Rhonda Osborne, age twenty-five. That would presently put her around forty.

Amanda opened the missing persons database again and keyed in Phoebe's name. The report quickly filled her screen. There were pictures. She hovered the mouse over the photos attached to the file. The first picture showed a bright-eyed young girl sitting on a concrete step in overalls and a T-shirt, a doll on her lap and an ice cream cone melting in her hand.

But it was the doll that tore Amanda's heart and had tears pooling in her eyes. Lindsey used to have a doll just like that one. Maybe there were worse fates than death. But no matter how quickly and briefly that thought had passed through her mind, she felt a jab of remorse so deep, it might as well have been a stab wound. She hadn't been able to save Lindsey, just as she wouldn't be able to save Casey-Anne, but maybe she could save some of the other girls.

She didn't want to return to the database on the mainframe, but it could be one way of confirming if Phoebe was Casey-Anne. She opened the catalogue of girls and found a search option and looked for eight-year-olds. Several came back, but the nickname of the third one down had her attention. The name was *Colonial*. As in Colonial Williamsburg? And she was marked as "Sold."

Amanda took a jagged breath and clicked on the picture. She gasped but forced herself to focus only on the face, not the lurid act the cameraman had her performing on herself. She closed the image, having seen all she needed—and more than she wanted. Colonial was Phoebe Baldwin, a.k.a. Casey-Anne Ritter.

She returned to the internet browser, opened another window, and typed in *Phoebe Baldwin, Rhonda Osborne, Williamsburg, Virginia.* Suspicion always fell first on the person who had last been with the child or tasked with their care. In this case, the babysitter.

Pages of results returned. Phoebe's disappearance had made nationwide headlines. The most recent article was one that had been written on the tenth anniversary of the date she went missing. That put it just a few months before Casey-Anne Ritter's death.

Amanda clicked the article and before she could read a thing, she was arrested by the photo of a young Phoebe with an artist's rendering of what she'd look like present day. That being about six years ago.

She changed windows and brought up the image of Casey-Anne Ritter as photographed in the morgue. Even in death, it was plain to see Phoebe Baldwin and Casey-Anne Ritter were one and the same.

Her eyes fell to her half-masticated burger and the smells that had originally enticed her now tossed her stomach. She wrapped it back up, tossed it in the bag, and put it in her garbage can. The pile of grease left on her desk would require soap and water.

She got up to get what was necessary to clean it and dried off the area quickly. She didn't have time to procrastinate. It might have been too late to save Phoebe Baldwin, but she could bring her justice and her parents closure.

She sat back down and read the anniversary article.

Phoebe Baldwin went missing from a park where her babysitter Rhonda Osborne had taken the girl.

"I just looked away for a second," Osborne claimed while in tears.

Amanda scanned down further and plucked out tidbits such as no ransom demands were made and that it was like little Phoebe had just disappeared into thin air.

She went on to wade through several other articles and none came out with suspects, but there was an opinion piece written about Osborne.

She was new to the family, only working with them for a couple of months before Phoebe went missing, but she came with good, solid references. Police say they've investigated Osborne but have cleared her of involvement in the abduction.

Amanda scribbled Osborne's name on a notepad and scratched a circle around it.

She pulled a brief background on Osborne and found she didn't have a criminal record. Conveniently if Amanda wanted to speak with her—and she did—her current address was in Woodbridge. But she'd prefer to start by speaking with the Baldwins. She wanted to know what they had to say about Osborne firsthand. While some of the articles had alluded to a man passing through having taken the girl, the Baldwins may have their own opinion on what had happened to their daughter.

A quick search told her the Baldwins were still married and living in Williamsburg. It was a two-hour drive and she was certain would be well worth her time. Her dad had drilled into her that solving cases often required starting at the beginning. While Phoebe might not have been the first victim of the ring, she could get Amanda closer to Phoebe's and Webb's killer.

She shut her computer down and grabbed her jacket. The clock on the wall told her it was 3:45 PM. If she left now, she'd be at Williamsburg about six.

CHAPTER FORTY

Amanda had forgotten to account for traffic when she was thinking about the straight run from Woodbridge to Williamsburg as two hours. Before running out, she'd updated Malone on her findings, and he'd approved her travel to see the Baldwins and Osborne. He suggested that she take someone else from the unit with her, but that's all she viewed it as: a suggestion.

She'd called Patty on her way and told her to flag "Colonial" as a priority in tracking down who'd purchased her. Thinking of a person being bought and sold was outside the realm of humanity and tread upon the path of demons as far as Amanda was concerned.

She pulled into the Baldwins' driveway closer to seven thirty and found the house was lit like a showpiece. A Jaguar and a BMW were parked in the triple-wide lane. She had called Wes and Tanya before leaving—that was an order from Malone—so they were expecting her arrival.

The front door opened before she reached it and she was greeted by a handsome couple in their late fifties.

"Mr. and Mrs. Baldwin?" Amanda said.

"We are. Detective Steele?" Wes studied her and his gaze settled momentarily on her badge, which was clipped to her waistband.

"Yes. You can call me Amanda."

Wes's lips twitched in an attempted smile. "How about Ms. Steele instead?"

Very formal but… "Sure." She smiled at him, and let the expression carry for Tanya.

"Please come in," Tanya said. Her voice was high-pitched, but her demeanor pleasant and slightly more casual than her husband's, which was surprising as she was the aristocrat and he went to work.

The home was a showy display full of centuries-old charm, but it also held a modern, updated feel. It had clearly been renovated properly and in accordance with heritage guidelines.

The Baldwins saw her to a parlor, and Amanda sat on a salmon-pink sofa while the couple perched in wingback chairs.

Shortly after everyone was seated, a woman in a black-and-white maid's uniform entered the room with a silver tray, holding a tea set and milk and sugar.

"I hope that I was not presumptuous, Detective," Tanya said, "to assume that you might be interested in a spot of tea."

"Sounds lovely." Amanda would do whatever necessary to set the Baldwins at ease. She couldn't help but feel a knot in the pit of her stomach whenever she really looked at their faces. She couldn't begin to imagine the horror of what they faced every day.

The maid prepared the tea to order and, once the cups were distributed, she left the room.

Tanya lifted her teacup, her pinkie pointed out, and took a generous draw. "Oh, I should tell you that it's a perfect drinking temperature."

Amanda took a drink of her tea and set the cup down. She didn't handle the china anywhere near as delicately as Mrs. Baldwin—and she wasn't much of a tea drinker.

"We were pleased to have you reach out to us, Ms. Steele," Wes began. "Do you have information about our daughter?"

Hope marked his voice and it sliced Amanda's heart. Malone had ordered her to keep quiet about the murder until she had absolute proof that Casey-Anne Ritter was the couple's Phoebe. She'd argued him on that point because the Baldwins deserved to know, but he hadn't budged on his decision. Not even after showing him the photos and the striking similarity between them. He was looking for forensics or other indisputable evidence. Maybe, if she could get a hairbrush or toothbrush—something with DNA. The investigating detectives should have collected such things and/ or Phoebe's prints, but if so, they hadn't sparked a match when Casey-Anne was murdered.

"I do have some questions," Amanda put it out there tenderly, then sat back and crossed her legs. She suddenly felt somewhat self-conscious in this formal house in her jeans and sweater.

"Ask us whatever you would like," Tanya encouraged, "if it brings our little Phoebe back. Though, she will be twenty-four next month."

Tanya still referred to her daughter in the present tense after all these years, but Amanda could understand her desire to hold out hope.

"I'm sorry for all that you have suffered these years," Amanda offered.

"It's our Phoebe we think about," Wes said firmly. "Just getting some kind of closure would be better than not knowing."

Curse Malone and his directive to hold back on Phoebe's fate. It was obvious the Baldwins relived their daughter's abduction every day. Instead of it tearing them apart though, it seemed to bond them with a purpose. By letting them know Phoebe was dead, it might be the worst thing for their marriage. She'd seen and heard of couples divorcing after the death of a child.

"As I told you on the phone, I'm from the Prince William County Police Department, and during the course of an investigation I was made aware of your daughter's disappearance." Amanda felt phrasing it as an abduction might disclose too much.

"And you work with what unit?" Wes asked.

"Homicide."

Tanya gasped and covered her mouth.

"I apologize for my wife, Detective."

Amanda noted how she'd gone from Ms. Steele to Detective now that murder had come up.

Wes stiffened and stretched his neck. "How did you come to find out exactly?"

"Before I get into that, I have some questions for you, as I mentioned on the phone." Amanda put it as delicately as possible, but it still had Wes scowling and his wife frowning. She couldn't say she blamed them. If she were in their position and some detective from out of town showed up wanting answers and avoided hers, it would be grating, but she'd endure if there was any chance it could bring her daughter back.

Tanya said, "Please go ahead."

"How well did you know Rhonda Osborne?"

Tanya glanced at her husband and proceeded to answer. "She came with good references. I called all of them myself. She really seemed to love Phoebe, and Phoebe took a shine to her."

"I understand she only worked with you for a couple of months before Phoebe's disappearance," Amanda said.

"That's right," Wes interjected. "We hired her because caring for a young child day to day became too much for my wife."

Tanya's gaze went into her teacup.

"Not that I'm implying that Phoebe's not being here is in any way my wife's fault." Wes looked apologetically to Tanya, who ended up nodding acceptance. "But Rhonda did seem good with Phoebe, as my wife said."

"And did Rhonda have a lot of friends in the area?" Amanda might have gotten some of this from the detective investigating Phoebe's disappearance, but that would have meant more sitting around.

"She had one lady she seemed to be good friends with. I know police spoke to her about Rhonda when she was suspected of being involved. But there were no ransom demands. We waited for one, certain it would come." Tanya took another drink of her tea.

"What was this friend's name?"

"Elise Pierce," Tanya told her. "I probably have a picture of her around here somewhere. Rhonda left some photos in a drawer in her room."

Tanya set off and returned not long later. She handed a small stack of pictures to Amanda and leaned over her shoulder as she shuffled through them.

"There!" Tanya pointed at a snapshot of Phoebe with two women and a man and proceeded to indicate who was Rhonda Osborne and who was Elise Pierce.

"And the man?"

"I don't know who he is. Probably either Rhonda's or Elise's boyfriend. I'm just guessing."

"Could I take this one with me?"

"Sure, if you think it would help."

"Thanks." Amanda tucked it into her coat pocket, not sure if it would or not. She was going to add Elise Pierce to her list of people to visit though. She might have information on Rhonda Osborne and know who the man was. She was aware that police had cleared Osborne of suspicion, and she hoped there had been a solid reason for it, but sometimes after time passes, things that were buried resurfaced. Osborne could have been involved and good at covering her tracks, and, if so, she might have grown lazy and careless over the years. It was also possible that more memories would shake loose that might lead to the identity of Phoebe's abductor. Amanda would also like to see a background on Elise.

"What's always eaten away at me," Tanya began, "is that Rhonda took Phoebe to a different park than she normally did that day."

"Did she say why?"

"Just that she wanted to give Phoebe a change of scenery."

It was something Amanda probably didn't have to tell Tanya, but an eight-year-old wasn't so interested in the scenery as she was the play equipment.

"Now, this might be a hard question to answer, especially after all this time," Amanda started, "but what do you think took place that day?"

"I think it was the wrong time, wrong place," Wes said. "Someone from out of town probably took her. We see lots of tourists all year."

"And you, Mrs. Baldwin?"

Tanya trembled and hugged herself. She met Amanda's eyes. "I have nightmares. Not as bad in recent years, but I still get them from time to time. I think that she's… dead." Her chin quivered, and her gaze shot to her husband. "I think she's been dead for several years. I think that some pervert scooped her from that park and did—" She gasped and covered her mouth as tears fell down her cheeks.

Amanda's chest pinched and she swallowed her own tears. Wes was staring blankly at his wife, but it was probably something he'd heard her say many times.

"What happened to our girl, Detective?" Wes asked, and it had his wife sniffling and her sobs taking pause.

Malone had told her not to tell them, but what was she supposed to do? Just leave without giving them any indication as to what she was certain had happened?

"I can't say just yet." She put it out there firmly.

"But you know something." Tanya perked up.

"I may, but it might help if there was any way I could get a sample of her DNA."

The Baldwins paled and matched gazes and nodded in unison as if some greater being had pulled a string and made them do so.

"We haven't touched her room since that day," Tanya eventually said, and invited Amanda to follow her through the house and up the stairs.

CHAPTER FORTY-ONE

Phoebe's bedroom would have been any little girl's dream. The walls were pink, the bedding was pink, some of the furniture was pink. Any adult and antique pieces that were spread about the rest of the house had no place within these four walls. This space had unmistakably belonged to a princess.

Amanda would have loved to ask if she could be left there alone for a few minutes, especially after her gaze settled on the doll—the one in the photograph. It was sitting on a bench beneath the window next to a bookcase full of children's books. She walked over but didn't touch the doll, though she desperately wanted to do just that. She looked outside to the beautiful backyard. Only illuminated by the moon, she could see it would be an absolute retreat in the summer with its gardens, stone statues, and tiered fountain.

She tried to keep her mind outside, off the effects in the room, off the fact that it had all belonged to a little girl who'd lived a horrible life at the hands of evil, perverted men and how she'd met her end with a bullet to her head.

Amanda pinched her eyes shut. Yes, there might be worse evils than death.

Tanya walked up behind her and stood next to her at the window. "We set up a memorial for her out there, not really a grave, but someplace to visit and think of her."

She stopped talking, as if she expected Amanda to speak, but she was having a hard time not falling apart.

Tanya went on. "Phoebe loved it when we'd sit here, and I'd read to her."

She looked over at Amanda and Amanda forced herself to look at the grieving mother.

"I'd just gotten so busy with setting up fundraisers… I missed out a lot on my daughter's last couple of years with us. Do you have children?"

"Yeah." Amanda wasn't getting into the fact that both were dead—one before she'd even got to know them.

"How nice? What are their names?"

"Lindsey and Nathan." She'd named her unborn baby after her father despite not knowing its sex. "Lindsey had—has—a doll just like that one." She gulped roughly when she realized her slip and then her awkward correction.

"Is your daughter…"

She looked back out the window as she answered, "Five-and-a-half years ago."

Tanya put a hand on Amanda's shoulder and squeezed. No words were spoken, but none were needed. In that moment there was an unmistakable bond between the two women made of pain that no one should ever need endure.

"Ah, I guess I should be hitting the road," Amanda said and turned.

"You were looking for a brush or something that might have Phoebe's DNA," Tanya reminded her.

"Right." Amanda smiled at her. "It's been a long day."

Tanya didn't speak, though her eyes seemed to say that it had been a long fifteen and a half years.

"I can get you her toothbrush." Tanya disappeared for a few seconds and returned. "I can put it into a plastic bag for you."

"That would work. Thank you." Amanda's heart ached that Tanya still had her daughter's toothbrush after all these years. She went to leave the room and spotted a framed casting. She stopped in front of it.

"That's Phoebe's toes and fingers." Tanya's voice took on a wistful tone, as if she'd been transported back to pleasanter times when there was still excitement for the future.

"Could I take it too?" Amanda asked. Sometimes DNA degraded and wasn't viable, so having her prints could help. She was surprised that the detectives investigating Phoebe's disappearance hadn't taken it with them.

"Sure." Tanya took it off the wall and said, "I'll put it into a bag too. But please be careful with it. I'd like to get it back."

"I understand."

Tanya dipped her head and blinked softly. Again, no words were needed.

Amanda thanked the Baldwins for their time and promised them she'd pass on whatever information she could, when she could. They expressed their appreciation at her offering, but there was a darkness in their eyes that made her think they'd heard such assurances before to no real avail.

She got in the department car and looked up Elise Pierce, Osborne's friend. She figured if she was in Williamsburg, she'd just get a hotel room and pay her a visit in the morning, but it turned out Elise was in Woodbridge, just like Osborne.

Were the friends still in touch and, regardless, what had brought them both to Prince William County?

CHAPTER FORTY-TWO

Even hours down the road when Amanda was taking the highway turn-off for Dumfries, she was thinking of the interactions she'd had with the Baldwins, and Tanya in particular. Also of the little girl who had been robbed of her innocence. In the days after she'd escaped her captors, Amanda hoped that Phoebe Baldwin had experienced the best time of her life. She didn't want to dwell on the strong likelihood her horror had never been far from her mind. And how the life of a sex slave had her turning to stripping and using her body to earn money. Sadly, it was the only thing she'd known.

She'd filled Malone in on the drive back as to how she'd made out with the Baldwins. Tomorrow, she'd pay Elise and Rhonda a visit.

It was nearing midnight when Amanda got home, still in the department car, and she found a Mazda in her driveway, and someone was in the driver seat.

What the hell?

She pulled in next to the car and got out with her hand on her hip, ready to draw her service weapon if necessary. Her visitor got out of their car.

"Steele, it's Bishop."

She could see him now, at least enough between the moonlight and streetlights.

"What are you doing here?" She relaxed a little, but she was still on high alert.

"You have to stop looking into the cold cases. Just walk away."

Forget relaxing. Her body tensed. "Why would I do that?"

They got to within five feet of each other, but neither of them made any move to get closer. Cud kept shifting his weight from his left to right, and he raked a hand through his hair. For the first time in her memory, he wasn't chewing gum.

"Listen, I know about the bracelet, the sex-trafficking ring," he said. "Word gets around."

"Why do you care if I'm looking into it?" She'd asked the question out loud, but the answer in her head sent chills right through her. She put a hand on her weapon. "Are you involved?"

"No," he said quickly.

"Then why show up here, tell me to walk away?"

"Because if you don't, someone could get hurt."

The skin on the back of her neck tightened, but she set aside her fear. "People *are* getting hurt, Bishop—have been for years. Girls," she stressed. "Innocent girls."

"I can't do anything about that."

He seemed to believe his claim, but she wasn't having it. "You knew that an eyewitness spotted a man outside Casey-Anne's apartment, but you didn't latch onto that lead."

"It meant nothing. He was her uncle."

"You and I both know he wasn't her uncle," she snapped back.

"You know what?" He flailed his hands in the air. "I tried to warn you, but—"

"You threatening me?"

Cud's eyes pierced hers in the relative darkness. "You'd be wise to back off. All I'm sayin'." With that, he returned to his Mazda and drove off.

She stood there, her entire body shaking. What the hell had just happened and what had Cud threatening her? Was he involved in the sex-trafficking ring? She didn't know the guy much outside of work, but she couldn't imagine that—but then sometimes it was the people you didn't see.

She walked to her front door, and it took a few stabs for her hand to calm enough to get the key into the lock.

You'd be wise to back off. His words replayed in her head.

They were the same ones her blocked caller had told her, and there was something in the way he'd annunciated the words. Was Cud her mystery caller? It was time to call Jacob and ask for that favor.

Once inside her house, she called him, knowing he'd be at work. He answered on the second ring and she told him she needed him to track a couple of calls made to her phone. She gave him the time and date of the one when the caller had spoken and the other times it had just been breathing followed by a click. "How long do you think it will take?"

"A day; two tops."

"Thanks."

"No problem. Night."

She ended the call, dropped her keys in the bowl, shucked off her shoes and jacket, and headed for the master. But she found herself stopping outside Lindsey's room. She cracked the door and inhaled. She was hoping to smell something that would remind her of her daughter, but it was just stale air. It had been a long time since she'd stepped foot in there; it simply hurt too much.

She flicked on the light and took in the space. Lindsey didn't have parents with a limitless budget, so it wasn't as decked out as Phoebe's had been, but it was apparent that Lindsey had been loved. Still was.

Her bed wasn't a canopy, but it had a bookcase headboard, and, just like Phoebe, her sweet Lindsey had also liked being read to. She could never pick a favorite among the classics that Amanda and Kevin had from their childhoods, but she had a slight preference for Curious George.

The bed was still made as if it were waiting for its owner to return. Barbies were in the corner of the room, some of them sitting at a picnic table. They'd been having that picnic for the last five and a half years.

Amanda walked over to the window, where there was a small desk she and Kevin had picked up for Lindsey. On it were her crayons, some of them strewn across an open coloring book, her daughter's last strokes staring up at her.

She wailed, so violently her body convulsed. She'd worked so hard to suppress her feelings, to will them away, and they had returned with a bitter vengeance. They say time heals all wounds, but she had yet to experience that for herself.

She sobbed and sniffled. There would be no holding the doll her daughter had valued above all her toys, no tactile experience that way to bring her closer. That doll had long ago been destroyed. It had been in the car that night and had likely been stained with her baby's blood.

Another gut-curdling cry hurled from her and she doubled over. Sheer, raw pain, so intense—as if the loss had just happened—overcame her. Rage also pulsated through her and she just wanted to throw something, to hurt something, to feel better.

She dropped onto her daughter's bed and burrowed onto her side, snuggling in and wishing that night had never happened. That if there was a God, she'd just awaken and it all would have been a bad dream. It was something that she had clung to in the first few months—and years—but at some point she'd realized there would be no waking up. This was her reality and her nightmare.

She just lay there crying, heaving for breath.

CHAPTER FORTY-THREE

Amanda woke up to sunlight coming in through the white daisy curtains. Her head pounded and there was a kink in her shoulders. She grumbled as she turned slowly to her back. Her hip was tender too. She must have slept on her side all night without moving.

"My sweet, sweet Lindsey," she whispered to the walls.

There was an emotional ache in the middle of her chest that was far more painful than her physical discomforts. She forced herself from bed and realized that she was still wearing yesterday's clothes. She'd slept from— She looked to the clock on Lindsey's dresser, but it was blinking. She hadn't reset it since the first power outage after their deaths. She didn't want to think about how long the clock would have been winking at nothing, serving no purpose.

She pulled her cell phone from her pocket and squinted at the brightness of the screen. It was after eight in the morning.

She'd slept for the better part of eight hours, without a sleeping pill. That was the first night that had happened since she'd been released from the hospital.

She wandered down the hall and took care of business in the bathroom and got freshened up for work. Twenty minutes later she was out the door, and shortly after that pulling into the parking lot of Hannah's Diner. A coffee and a muffin would hit the spot.

She went inside and May helped her out. She gave her an extra-large and only charged her for a medium.

Amanda said, "You don't have to—"

May batted a hand. "Amanda, I know I don't have to do anything, but I want to."

Amanda gave her a large tip and grabbed her blueberry muffin. Its top was devoured well before she reached Central.

She passed Cud's cubicle and was happy that he wasn't in. She'd want to confront him and call him out in front of the department, but then she might never get to the bottom of what was really going on. The same went for reporting his threats to Malone. The question was, though, was Cud trying to protect himself, as she'd considered last night, or trying to protect someone else?

She sat at her desk, slurped back the rest of her coffee, then tossed the to-go cup in her garbage can. Her mind was juggling the unknown man in the photograph she'd collected from the Baldwins, and Cud. That's if her trip to Williamsburg had sparked his visit. And if so, what was his connection to any of this?

She tapped her fingers on her desk and an idea came to her. There was one link between Cud and Ritter—the detective that Cud had worked the case with. But who was he again? Jonah... something.

She pulled up the file on the Ritter investigation and got the full name. Jonah Reid.

But now what? She had no way of accessing human resources records, but the internet had proved invaluable in her finding Casey-Anne Ritter's true identity. She keyed in the name *Jonah Reid* and seconds later had several links to social-media profiles showing Jonah Reids of all ages and nationalities. She typed in *Jonah Reid, Virginia*.

Far fewer results, but she realized she could narrow it down further. She added *PWCPD* to the search bar.

Bingo. Only five images to look at it, but it was the first one that had her attention.

She pulled the photo that Tanya Baldwin had given her from her jacket and held it to the screen, angling her head this way and that. It didn't take long for her to make a conclusion. The Jonah Reid on her screen was the man in the photo with Elise Pierce, Rhonda Osborne, and Phoebe Baldwin. What the hell?

She clicked the link that took her to his LinkedIn profile. Her stomach twisted at his occupation.

"Hey."

She looked up at Trent. "Hey," she replied absentmindedly.

"How are you doing?"

"Fine." She kept her gaze on the screen, not believing what she was seeing, but there it was in black and white: Jonah Reid had gone on to become an aide to Washington congressman Eugene Davis.

She got up and walked outside the station. Fresh air might be the only thing that could help her right now. What should she do? Was a current congressman's aide involved with sex trafficking? Or was she leaping to a conclusion based on his brief stint at PWCPD combined with Cud's strange behavior and his face in a picture with Phoebe Baldwin? Surely there could be some reasonable explanation.

She paced the parking lot. Her thoughts weren't settling. Take the blip at PWCPD. Sure, not everyone was cut out to be a cop, but the pieces weren't assembling unless… What was she even thinking: that Reid had been planted on the Webb investigation? If that were true, how entrenched was the ring and was it those deep connections that had Cud fearful and spewing threats?

She had to see Reid and confront him, and she'd have to go it alone. If she laid all this out for Malone, he'd rattle Cud and it would sure as hell get back to Reid and the other cohorts in the ring, and they'd go so far underground, there'd be no way of finding any of them. Whether she liked it or not, whether it was wise or not, she had to go this alone.

But when?

What would be the best time to approach Reid? The answer presented immediately that she'd need to get him alone. She couldn't exactly go into the congressman's office and demand time to speak with Reid. She'd have to find him at home, and Washington kept long hours.

She returned to her desk and brought up the background on Jonah Reid. No criminal record—not that she'd expected one given that he'd served as a detective. Reid lived just outside of Woodbridge, and she scribbled down his address and left the station. She then keyed off a quick text to Malone, who wasn't in, that she wasn't feeling well and was going home to rest. What he didn't know was that she'd spend the rest of the day likely splitting her time between home and gathering intel. Then, as soon as night fell, she'd show up at Reid's door. Hopefully he wouldn't be expecting her.

CHAPTER FORTY-FOUR

It was nearing midnight when she decided to head out to Reid's house. She figured she'd find the aide home from Washington and still awake. She'd driven by the address earlier in the day but hadn't managed to get a good look at the place from the road as it was nestled in the woods. All that peeked out between branches and evergreens were sections of the roofline. Noting the seclusion, goose bumps pricked her flesh at the thought that the isolation would serve the purposes of a sex-trafficking ring well. Especially if Reid was holding girls here.

She was armed with her service weapon, but she'd also grabbed her Beretta and had it in an ankle holster. Just to be safe.

She pulled the department car she'd signed out into the driveway and slowly crept toward the house. She watched the woods on each side closely for any sign of armed guards.

A two-story, older house sat in an open patch and was bathed in moonlight. Lights were on in a few rooms and shone through the closed curtains.

She parked next to a couple of mid-level sedans and got out.

Loudly cooing mourning doves and a towering sycamore with its wide, outstretched branches gave the property a sinister feel and had shivers trickling down her spine.

She talked her imagination back and knocked on the front door.

It took doing it twice before footsteps headed toward the door. The curtain in its window was pulled back and a woman's face was looking out at her. The deadbolt clunked as it was unlatched. The door slowly cracked open.

"Yeah?" It was a woman in her forties and Amanda recognized her immediately as Elise Pierce, but she kept her expression neutral—revealing that she knew who Elise was wouldn't help the cover story she'd devised.

"Sorry for the late hour, but I'm Detective Steele with Prince William County Police Department. I'm looking to speak with Jonah Reid. I understand he lives here."

"What's it to you?" Elise crossed her arms.

"I have concerns about a former associate who used to work within the department." She planned to feel Reid out while making him think she considered Cud a suspect.

Elise narrowed her eyes. "What sort of concerns?"

"Kind of something I'd like to discuss with him."

"Fine, step inside."

"Thanks." Amanda stopped short at the sight of the place.

To call it a sty would be unfair to pigs. Takeout containers littered every available surface, along with empty beer bottles. Framed movie posters covered most of the wall space. Her stomach knotted as she remembered the contacts in the spreadsheet were all named based on literary and movie characters.

"Maid hasn't shown up yet," Elise said. She must have sensed Amanda's disgust.

Amanda gave her a pressed-lip smile. "No worries. I wasn't expected."

Elise took Amanda to a living room, cleared a cushion on the couch, and pointed for Amanda to sit. She did so, and Elise dropped into a wooden rocking chair.

"You must be Jonah's wife? Girlfriend?" Amanda said. She'd been surprised by Elise's presence, but she was also uncomfortable by the fact that Elise hadn't offered to go get Jonah.

"Girlfriend." A few seconds then, "Name's Elise."

"Nice to meet you," was what Amanda said with all the pleasantry she could muster, but just being in this place was nauseating. Did they keep any of the girls here or did they pass through here? Either way.

"Could you go get Jonah?" she asked lightly, as if Elise not already doing so had been an innocent slip, but everything was telling Amanda that Jonah Reid was already aware of her presence.

"I'm sure he'll be along— Oh, there he is." Elise smiled smugly, her gaze going behind Amanda.

Amanda turned and found Jonah Reid standing there, a gun trained on her.

"Whoa, wait, what are—" Amanda put her hands up.

"You aren't here to talk." He was about five-nine, with dark hair, dark eyes, and a slight lisp.

Uncle! She screamed in her head, recalling the eyewitness account Banks had told her about.

He was the right size to be the man in the video from Happy Time—so had he also struck and killed Palmer?

"I had a bad feeling you'd end up at my door," he said.

"Why?" she tried to play it cool.

"Let's just say I'm an informed person, Detective."

The way he said *Detective* it felt like tiny spiders were scurrying along her arms. "I'm just here to talk about your old partner, Dennis Bishop."

"Oh, please, you must think I'm an idiot."

She went to reach for her service weapon.

He clicked back on his shotgun. "I wouldn't."

"No one needs to get hurt." She put her hands up. "I just came to talk."

Jonah nodded toward Elise. "Take her gun and get her to the basement."

Amanda was questioning her earlier decision to go on this mission without backup. She'd underestimated Jonah.

Elise grabbed a gun from a drawer in a table next to her and approached Amanda. Each step she took, Amanda ran through scenarios in her head, but none of them resulted in her walking away.

"Gun, now," Elise barked and held out one hand, her other holding the gun trained on Amanda.

Amanda moved slowly so as not to startle them and her phone rang. Shit!

"Ignore it and give her your gun!" Jonah barked over the trill.

"I should probably answer or—" She really had no idea who was on the other end of the line, but whoever it was might be able to get help here.

"Shut up." Jonah pushed the gun harder against her skull. "Give me a reason," he said.

She raised her arms again. "We can work something out."

"I don't negotiate with cops. Elise!" he barked.

Elise took Amanda's phone from her coat pocket. The entire time it kept ringing, only drilling into Amanda's head that help was so close yet so far away.

Elise stuffed it into a pocket of her pants. "Get up and do as I say," she said.

Amanda stood, and Elise prodded her in the back.

"Take the first door on the left and go down," Elise told her.

Amanda might be able to play Elise and get her to turn on Reid, but they had been together for at least fifteen-plus years if the photo Tanya had given her was any indication. "You don't have to do as he says." Amanda spoke just above a whisper, not certain if Jonah was following them.

Elise said nothing but applied more pressure with her gun on Amanda's spine.

"No one needs to know about this if you stop now," Amanda dangled out there.

"Turn right at the bottom of the stairs." Unfazed.

Amanda reached the bottom and gagged. The reek of shit and urine was overpowering. A few dim bulbs fought the shadows that clung in the corners, but she could still make out numerous steel doors. Most of them were shut, but one about ten feet away was open. There was no more doubt: the girls were being held here.

"Move!" Elise nudged her toward the open steel door, and when they were within a foot, she shouted, "Get in!" and pushed Amanda forward.

The force was unexpected, and she'd been mid-stride. Amanda toppled forward but caught herself on the doorframe. Her mind was screaming. There was no way she could allow herself to go into that room or it would be over. But then, maybe, just *maybe* she could see Kevin and Lindsey again.

All in a flash, her father's voicemail also replayed in her mind, *It's over, sweetheart.*

Completely out of context, but a tiny part of her almost welcomed the comfort of defeat if that meant a brief meeting of the darkness followed by a walk toward the light. Being with her family again would be a marvelous reunion, something that she'd dreamed of for many years. But it had also been great seeing her parents the other day and how would they cope if something happened to her now?

Her phone started ringing again. Maybe it was the same person again, desperately trying to reach her. She could only hope that someone would look for her and track her whereabouts.

"Get in the room!" Elise kicked Amanda's legs.

Only then did Amanda realize they had been preventing the door from closing. If she went into that cell, she could only guess her future would be torture, rape, and murder. And she couldn't serve the girls in the other cells if she was dead. She had to fight.

She put her arms under her and lifted herself up, then stood and spun to face Elise. Her gun was level at her solar plexus. In that second, Amanda didn't want to die, but she wasn't afraid of it either. And at least there was no sign of Jonah.

In a swift motion—an act of reckless abandon—Amanda wrapped her hand around the barrel of Elise's gun and swept it to the side. A hail Mary, let-the-fates-decide move.

A bullet fired and the sound was deafening. Elise screamed and the gun went flying.

Amanda kicked Elise in her ribs, and she let out a strangled cry.

"Elise!" Jonah was thumping across the floorboards above them and nearing the top of the basement stairs.

Amanda had less than a second to decide on her next step. She needed to rid Elise of her gun if she was to stand a chance. She ducked to the ground, throwing herself on her side. Her fingers played on the handle; the weapon was just out of reach.

Elise was clawing at her legs and pulling her back. Amanda stopped her struggling and let the woman advance on her. When she was within reach, she wound up and punched her as hard as she could in the nose.

Bone and cartilage crunched, and Amanda's knuckles were likely bloody and throbbing, but she felt nothing. Adrenaline had kicked in and she was ready to go down fighting if she had to, but she sure as hell wasn't going down without one.

Jonah's steps were getting closer, then they were on the stairs.

Elise resembled a deranged animal as she lunged at Amanda again.

Amanda held up her hands to thwart her attack when there was a thunderous crack, and Elise's body collapsed against her—her head had a gaping crater where her brain had been.

Amanda's ears were ringing, and her vision was hazy, but she still made out Jonah standing across the room with a smoking shotgun.

Amanda reached for the gun in her ankle holster. If she had to, she'd use Elise's body as a shield.

"Stop fucking moving or you're next!" Jonah yelled.

He hadn't even hesitated to kill his girlfriend; she would be less than nothing to him. She could scream at the top of her lungs, but it wouldn't matter. Even the shotgun firing wouldn't have been heard by anyone. They were in relative isolation.

"That bitch cost me far more trouble than she was worth!" he spat.

"Wh-Who?" Amanda asked, not sure if she'd heard him correctly.

"Little Miss Colonial!" He advanced on her and her body became lead.

"Did you kill her?" She tried to articulate the revelation as a shock.

"What the hell do you think?" He stopped moving, and Amanda took a deep breath, still paralyzed by fear.

Fear—a feeling. She had to survive, if only to bring this shit down and free those poor girls!

"I think you did," she said defiantly. "I also think that you killed Jackson Webb."

"Ding, ding, tell her what she's won, Bob. None of this was supposed to track back to me, so how the fu—"

"You're not the smart and glamorous man you think you are, you piece of shit!" She scrambled to her feet, managing to get her Beretta free of the ankle holster in the process. She held her gun behind her back. "You sell young girls for a payday, probably play with the merchandise yourself."

"You don't know anything," he bellowed, but her talking to him, challenging him, and his enormous ego seemed to be keeping him from pulling the trigger on her.

"I do, actually. You took Phoebe Baldwin from a park in Williamsburg. Ah— nah, that was probably Elise who did that for you right? Little girls would be far more trusting of a woman than a man. Though maybe Rhonda, the babysitter, was in on this thing you've got going too. Or should I say *had* going."

"Shut up!"

"You couldn't have gotten the little girl to go with you."

The man snarled and he raised the shotgun on her.

"Go ahead. Shoot." She stared down the man with the gun, her hand holding hers still behind her back. "Take the coward's way out, but know that if you kill me, you'll never live another day of your life without looking over a shoulder. If I found you, someone else will too."

"I've been looking over it all my life," he hissed.

"It must have been worse when Phoebe stole your bracelet. You know, the one with all your organization's players on it." She smiled smugly at him.

His eyes bored through her.

"But you killed her, and you still didn't recover your property, so you tried to torture it out of Jackson Webb, only he didn't have it either. You must have been shittin' your pants." She gave a forced laugh. "But see, if you had found it, then I wouldn't be here now. We never would have met."

"What a tragedy that would have been," he said drily.

"You killed Chad Palmer too—just changed up your MO."

"No," he pushed out, the shotgun lowering slightly.

"You're really not too bright. He had your bracelet all these years—well, the county did. He was wearing it when he was arrested."

Jonah's eye twitched—

She raised her gun and fired off two consecutive rounds just as Jonah was raising the shotgun again.

The first struck him in the arm that held the weapon and it clattered to the basement floor. The second bullet embedded in his shoulder.

"You bi—" He lunged toward her, and she popped a third round in his left kneecap. He crumpled to the floor.

She quickly kicked his shotgun out of reach and aimed her gun at him. "What's it gonna be? Want another hole in your fucking body or do you surrender to a girl? Now, give me the key for the other cells!"

"Fuck you!"

"Now!" Screw him. There was no way she was getting any closer than necessary. He might be injured, but he wasn't unconscious and adrenaline had a way of muting pain and infusing strength.

He writhed and wailed as he twisted his body to access his pocket. He eventually withdrew the key and tossed it at her with his good arm.

"Now, get in that cell!" She nodded toward the one she'd almost been locked in. "I don't care if you crawl or if I have to drag you! Get moving!"

Jonah flashed her another murderous glare, and she cocked her gun.

Her turn to say, "Give me one good reason."

He started to move, and she kicked him the rest of the way into the cell and shut the door, locking it behind him. She set about freeing the girls, then she'd call it in.

Fifteen in total, all of them somewhere between ten and fifteen, and sharing three small cells.

The sound of approaching sirens was as melodious as an angels' choir and just as miraculous. She hadn't called for help.

CHAPTER FORTY-FIVE

The next afternoon Amanda was sitting across from Malone, running through her entire thought process on going to Reid's solo. It had made sense in her mind, but on speaking her reasoning out loud, it fell flat. She should have trusted him to keep her play on the down-low.

"We've had this conversation before, Steele," Malone said, the formal address never a good sign. "You have to stop acting like a one-man show."

"Woman. One-woman."

"Whatever." Malone batted his hand in the air. "You're missing my point. We work with partners for a reason."

"Didn't benefit Bishop much." She fought the smirk that so desperately wanted to come to fruition.

"Don't be using that partnership as a model. At least he ended up doing the right thing," Malone said.

She tilted her head. "What do you mean?" One of the calls she'd missed while fighting for her life had been from Jacob Briggs. He'd tracked down the source of the blocked calls. Two numbers had come back. Her silent caller had been Rick Jensen, and—as she'd suspected— Cud had been the one to use the voice modulator.

"Bishop's the one who sent cars to Reid's house."

In the flourish that had transpired after other officers had arrived on scene, getting the girls sorted out and provided for, she'd forgotten all about the backup coming before she'd had a chance to call. Today would be a happy day for a lot of families as their girls would be going home. Tears filled Amanda's eyes. She'd saved them! But there were still so many more out there. "How did he know I was there?"

"Said that he'd been keeping an eye on you. Anyway, he admits to burying evidence in the Webb case," Malone offered.

"Why would he do all that though? He isn't… tell me he isn't part of the ring?"

Malone shook his head. "Not at all. Never was, but like you he was starting to get close to the truth—had his suspicions anyway and they were too strong for Jonah Reid's liking. Reid threatened Bishop's sister, and he believed him enough to turn the other way."

Amanda could understand a bit how that could happen but wasn't saying that much to Malone.

"You did good, but I can't stress enough that next time—"

"I know, go with backup."

"At least with your partner."

"Kind of hard when I didn't have one at the time."

"Nah, no, you're not flipping this back on me."

"Well, there has to be some accountability." She smirked.

Her phone rang and the caller ID was blocked. *Not again*, she thought. "I should probably get this."

"Go ahead."

Amanda answered on her way out of Malone's office and headed for her cubicle.

"Detective Steele, it's Patty—ah, Detective Glover."

"Yes, Patty?"

"I heard you found the girls. That's marvelous."

"At least some of them will be going home."

"Some more too, hopefully." Patty paused a few heartbeats. "I have more good news for you. Now, I haven't been able to track anywhere near all the clients yet—and sadly, I might never be able to. The money transfers are deeply rooted and hard to track.

I was able to find that the deposits tended to go to a few different bank accounts and they always came back to a few names. Arrest warrants are in the works."

"Great news." Amanda would have loved to be there when they brought those miscreants down, but let those trained in that handle it. Speaking of…

"How did the interrogation go with Reid? And did you bring in Rhonda Osborne?" Amanda had got a signed confession from Jonah Reid that he'd killed Casey-Anne Ritter and Jackson Webb and then Amanda had handed him over to Sex Crimes.

"Reid will be going away for a long time. He's still refusing to give up anyone he was working with," Patty said. "These types never operate on their own, but we'll do all we can to get him to speak, and if not, well, we keep working. Rhonda Osborne was brought in and questioned, but there's no evidence to indicate that she was involved or facilitated Phoebe's abduction. She was genuinely horrified when she found out that her friend had played a role."

Amanda accepted that Patty and her team knew what they were doing, but she still had a niggling in her gut about Osborne. Then again, people don't always truly know those closest to them. "Were you able to find out who purchased Phoebe Baldwin?"

"Unfortunately, not yet. Still working through the maze on the wire transfer."

"Too bad."

"We'll get him."

She would celebrate the day that man—or woman—got what was coming to them. "Please keep me posted on the girls I found, who bought them, etcetera."

"Absolutely. I hope to keep in touch. I know you cleared the murders you were looking at, but…"

"I'd love to stay in touch. Thank you."

Amanda ended the call. She was looking over at Trent's cubicle, but he wasn't there. As Patty had noted, she'd solved the cold cases, but she still had to see things through with Palmer. Reid had told her he wasn't involved, and she believed him. She was just about to call Trent when the phone on her desk rang.

"Detective Steele," she answered.

"This is Lily; Lieutenant Hill wants you to come to her office."

"Right now?"

"Yes." Hill's assistant hung up.

Amanda got up and made her way to Hill's office, and it felt like she was making her way to the guillotine. Lily told her to go on in and that the lieutenant was waiting for her.

She let herself in, but Hill wasn't waiting alone. There was a man with her: mid-fifties, graying hair, still dark at the temples. Handsome and wearing a suit. He rose from a couch Hill had in her office when Amanda entered.

"There she is." Hill grinned. It had Amanda wondering if she'd fallen and hit her head.

"Here I am," she parroted and feigned a smile.

The man came over to Amanda. "I wanted to personally thank you for bringing Jonah's crimes into the light and serving justice to those poor girls."

Amanda glanced from him to Hill, who was striding over, back to the stranger. "And you are?"

"Detective Steele," Hill said, "this is my brother-in-law, Congressman Eugene Davis."

Amanda's eyes snapped to the congressman's eyes. *Brother-in-law?* Jonah Reid had worked for Davis. Some pieces were starting to make sense—at least how it might have been possible that Reid pop into PWCPD and out so quickly. But was Amanda really thinking that Hill had facilitated that for a darker, more sinister purpose—that she was somehow involved with the ring? That was ludicrous.

"Thank you," Davis repeated. "I truly mean it." He held out his hand to shake Amanda's and the cuff of his jacket sleeve lifted enough to expose a bracelet, much like the one that— Her head went light.

"Detective?" Hill prompted.

"Oh, sorry." She touched a hand to her forehead. "I'll be fine. Just a little off balance still with all that happened." She offered a tepid smile to both the lieutenant and the congressman.

"Understandable," Hill said. "Maybe take a day or two off."

"I just might." Amanda eyed the door. "Can I—?"

"Yes, of course. That's all I'd wanted you here for."

Amanda staggered back to her desk, sometimes brushing against the walls. She had to have imagined what she'd swear she'd seen. A bracelet, just like the one with the recovered data chip, around the congressman's wrist—the lieutenant's *brother-in-law's* wrist. Was Eugene Davis part of the sex-trafficking ring with Jonah Reid? And did Lieutenant Hill know about it or worse was she involved herself? *Ridiculous*, she concluded, and just further proof she needed some time off. After all, there were a lot of silver bracelets out there.

Amanda made it back to her desk and dropped in her chair. Trent was sitting at his.

"Congratulations on solving your case," he said to her.

"Thanks, and I'm still alive to talk about it. Ah, how's the Palmer investigation going?" She swallowed roughly, smiled at Trent.

"Actually, I've been waiting for a good time to talk with you." Trent's eyes darted around. "Maybe we could grab a Jabba."

She could tell he'd said the word as a stab at joviality, but something was bothering him. "Sure."

She let him drive, but he didn't go anywhere for coffee. He drove a few blocks from the station and parked on a side street.

He angled toward her. "I know I'm not supposed to… Well, you're not supposed to touch the Palmer case, but…"

The way he was looking at her had her stomach twisting like he was going to tell her someone died. "What is it?"

He pulled a piece of paper from his inside jacket pocket and handed it to her.

She took it, tempted to ask what it was, but the letterhead was stamped with a local chapter of Alcoholics Anonymous.

"It's a list of names of those who have been issued twenty-year sobriety coins in the last ten years," he said.

"Okay and…"

"You might want to look at page five."

She eyeballed him, holding his gaze for a few seconds before flipping the sheets of paper. On the fifth line was a name she knew far too well. She let go of the report.

"I'm sorry, Amanda, but it looks like—"

"I— I know what it looks like but, no, he wouldn't have done this." Her mouth was pasty, and she felt like being sick. She looked back down and there it was in black and white: *Nathan Steele*. The coin had been issued the week before the accident; she'd been so caught up in the whirlwind of her life, she'd had no idea, but then how could she have?

"I thought you might like to know."

She looked at him, blinked tears, found her voice. "Did you follow up the other leads? A cab that could be tied to the perp or…"

"Not successfully." He wrung a hand around the steering wheel and didn't say anything.

"You shouldn't have shown me this." She stiffened, no longer wanting any part of the Palmer investigation. She'd figure out how to handle Rick Jensen and his threats another way. "And there's no way…" But in her memory there was a flicker of the amber liquid in her father's glass… His choice of drink was whiskey. Could he have made that slip when killing Palmer?

"He'd have a motive," Trent said softly.

She couldn't get herself to speak. Her father did have a motive, and he'd been quick to call to tell her it was over and that she could come back home. Had he killed Palmer to get her to return to her family? As a way of getting closure for Kevin and Lindsey too? Or had the injustice of Palmer's measly prison sentence preyed on her father? She'd heard the rumors coming up through the department about him and how he'd toed the line. Some said he crossed it, but she'd always shut those people down. But what if they had been right all along? What if her father was the type of man who made his own justice?

"You have to let me talk to him," she blurted out.

"I can't... You're not supposed to—"

"I know, and I'll take complete responsibility if it all turns to shit, but this is something I need to do." When she'd promised Jensen she'd find justice for his cousin, she'd never have dreamed that might mean taking down her own father.

"I need to do this," she stressed. "You can be on standby, and, if need be, there to make the arrest. But let me talk to him. He's my father." She met his gaze and eventually he nodded.

"When do you want to—"

"Right now. Let's clear this up *right now.*"

"You sure?"

"Nope," she admitted and faced out the windshield.

A few seconds later the car was moving in the direction of her parents' house.

CHAPTER FORTY-SIX

Amanda's mother was all smiles and hugs when Amanda showed up at the door.

"I hope you have time for a real visit this time," her mother said. "But it would have been nice if you'd called ahead."

"Is Dad home?"

"Yeah, he's—"

Amanda went into the living room and found her father with his feet up, a rocks glass in his hand, watching TV.

"Mandy, what's going on?" Her mother had trailed into the room behind her.

"Nothing, Mom; why don't you go put on the kettle?" Amanda tried to calm the surge of emotions rolling through her. She had no intention of having a tea, but it would let her speak to her father alone while her mother was busy in the kitchen.

Her father kicked the leg rest down on his chair and muted the television program he'd been watching. "Twice in one week? Guess you're back, Mandy Monkey. I love it."

"Thanks, Dad." She sat on the couch close to him. "It's hard for me to ask this…" Emotional torment had physical pain spiking through her abdomen. "When did you start drinking again?" She'd build up to her reason for being there. She just couldn't bring herself to attack the situation, even though it might be nice to get it over with.

He cleared his throat and glanced away.

"I'm going to guess," she started. "Not long after the accident?"

He chewed on his bottom lip, his eyes welling up with tears.

A wave of guilt threatened to engulf Amanda. "I know you loved Lindsey so much, and Kevin."

"It wasn't then," he said, his voice husky.

"When?"

"When we realized that we'd lost you too." Her father hiccupped a sob and it tore right through her.

"I'm so… sorry." She sniffled as her heart broke, something she never thought it would be able to do again. She took a deep breath. "Before that though, you hadn't had a drink in a long time, had you, Dad? What, twenty years or so?"

He scowled. "I don't want a lecture."

"No, Dad, no lecture. I was just so proud of you."

The sunlight streaming through the front window caused her father's watery eyes to sparkle. He had his hands balled into fists on the arms of his chair.

"That's amazing. And all one day at a time." She was stalling, but this would be one of the toughest things she'd ever have to do in her life. "You called me after Chad Palmer's murder."

"So? I figured maybe you'd finally be able to put the past behind you and return to your family. Your mother encouraged me, but I'm wondering if I did the right thing given the way you're looking at me all disappointed." His gaze cut to the window.

She followed the direction he was looking and watched a cardinal perched on the porch railing.

Her mother came into the room holding a plastic, lime-green tray with three mugs. "I hope you still like it the way you used to? Two sugars and milk?"

"Yes," Amanda told her. Tea was exempt from the "drink it black" philosophy.

"Good, good. Take that one there." She indicated with a jab of her chin for Amanda to take the mug closest to her. "Nathan," she prompted when she moved in front of him. Her mother set the tray on the long rectangular coffee table and sat on a reclining chair. She lifted her mug in a toast, blew it, and took a cautious sip. "That horrible man finally got his due, wouldn't you say, Nathan?"

Her father was back looking out the window again. Amanda's heart nearly stopped in her chest just thinking about the question she had to ask him.

Her mother rubbed her knee and continued. "He was a drunk and took out two of the sweetest people that had ever walked the planet, and you—he ended up taking you away from us too. I might never understand why you pulled away, but I respected you enough to let you have your space." She looked at Amanda as if seeking an explanation now.

"It's just… It hurt too much to be around you." She pointed to her mother's massaging hand. "What's wrong with your knee?"

"Oh, it's nothing. Just my arthritis acting up these days." Her mother tossed that out like it was nothing of consequence, but it had Amanda's mind whirling.

The perp who had attacked Palmer in the Happy Time parking lot had favored their left knee. Surely her mother's ailment had to be a coincidence. That along with the fact her mother was the right height to be the person in the hoodie. Maybe they'd been wrong to assume it had been a man. And her father would have seen the accident report and known that Palmer's drink of choice had been vodka—unless it slipped his mind like it had hers temporarily. But Amanda didn't think that was the case. Her throat stitched together when she asked, "Mom, is there something you should be telling us?"

Her mother bit her bottom lip and shook her head, her gaze drifting about as if she were lost in her thoughts. "Just such a horrible man. He certainly got what he deserved."

"And that was?" Amanda squeaked out.

"Well, the papers are saying he was murdered. Hogwash, and to slap a defamatory spotlight on you, the Steele family. Disgusting. That man likely drank himself to death, choked on his own vomit."

Every bit of Amanda's body sparked. It had never been made public how Palmer had died. "How do you know he drank himself to death?"

Out of her peripheral vision, she caught her father turn toward her mother.

"Mom," she prompted.

"Well, it makes sense to me. He was a drunk." Her mother's face knotted up and turned a bright red. "Probably drowned himself with whiskey."

"Palmer's preferred drink was vodka, but Dad's is whiskey." She looked at her father.

"Don't go accusing your father of anything," her mother hissed.

"I'm not, Mom." Amanda's heart pounded in her chest as she leveled her gaze at her mother. "Did you kill Chad Palmer?"

"Why I— I can't believe—" She rubbed at the back of her neck.

"Julie," her father moaned with heartbreak.

"He took everything from me," she spat. "And I'm not sorry he's dead!"

"What did you do?" Nathan cried out. "Is that where you were last weekend? You didn't spend it at Fee's?"

Her mother's older sister, Fee, lived in Charlotte, North Carolina, over five hours away.

Her mother twisted the hem of her shirt and wouldn't look her husband in the eye.

"Mom." That's all that would come out of Amanda's mouth.

"I'd been following him since his release from prison last Friday afternoon. I knew he was going to drink and drive again—and sure enough I was right. The night I killed him, I stopped him. He wasn't going to hurt anyone again." She tilted her chin up.

"You wanted some time with your sister," her father mumbled, chewing on his wife's betrayal, seemingly wanting to avoid her confession.

"I only lied because it was necessary."

"It was—" Her father clenched his teeth.

"Where did you go, Mom?" She didn't want to hear any more; every word from her mother's mouth was another stab to her heart. And the way she had so callously tossed out "killed him" stole her breath.

"I stayed at a hotel in Dumfries last weekend, starting Friday night, and had it booked through until Monday morning. I figured it wouldn't take longer than that." Her mother drank some of her tea. "It wasn't as difficult as I thought it might be."

Amanda swallowed roughly. Killing a man hadn't been difficult…

Her mom continued. "I planned out what I was going to do and just waited for the right moment."

"Shit, Jules, that's premeditated." Her father's face contorted in anguish.

Her mother continued as if she hadn't heard him. "I bought the whiskey and kept it in the trunk of my car. I also had one of your dad's guns with me, along with his sobriety coin."

"Why?" her father asked.

"To remind me of what else I'd lost all those years ago. I lost my husband." Tears fell, but she didn't stop to weep. "You're not the same person when you drink. You've got a short temper; you're distant."

Her father's gaze hardened and blanked over.

Amanda's chest was in a knot. She'd made everything worse by taking off at a time when family should come together.

"And I lost the coin." Her mother met her gaze. "Guessing maybe you found it and that's what led you here?"

Amanda briefly pinched her eyes shut. "Just tell me what happened."

"He came out of that bar and I confronted him. The fast and dirty version is I thwacked him on the head with the butt of the pistol, drove him to the crap motel he was holed up in, and forced whiskey down his throat. I wasn't going to shoot him; your father's gun would probably be in the system. But it worked to coerce that sack of shit into doing what I told him to."

Maybe to get him back to the motel… "How did you force Palmer to drink?" Amanda went numb. Her mother had been the up-until-then faceless psychopath hanging around waiting for a man to die.

"At gunpoint. I had him zip-tie his ankles and one wrist to a chair in the room. I tied his last one, while keeping my eye—and the gun—on him." Her mother paused and inserted a tiny smile. "It was a good use for some zip-ties that were just sitting around here."

"How did you get him to drink?" Amanda repeated, feeling like she was watching this all unfold from outside herself. Her mother had fully planned and executed everything.

"I stuck a funnel in his mouth, something I'd grabbed from here too, and taped it in place. I squeezed his neck, held his head back and just kept pouring. He bucked a bit at first, but his fight died really fast. He probably believed he deserved to go out that way. When he passed out, I dragged him onto the bed—that part wasn't easy. Dead weight is no joke." She met Amanda's eyes—searching for empathy or understanding?

She went on. "I staged the room and hoped it would just look like he'd drank himself to death. Maybe I should have just waited it out, let him do it to himself, but he was going to drive drunk again! Just seeing him, knowing what he intended to do…" Her mother paused and clenched her jaw. "Set me off."

"You stayed by his side for hours waiting for him to die, watching him… choke… and…" As Amanda spoke, she felt for what Palmer would have suffered. "I don't know what you expect me to do here, Mom."

Her mother shook her head and fired a glare at her husband. "You just taught her too well, Nathan. She saw through the scene, knew he was murdered."

She couldn't take all the credit as Trent had obtained the AA records that had brought her to her parents' door, but she had been the one with the idea to get the records in the first place—little had she known…

There was one other piece from that night that needed clarity though. "Mom, his car, your car, the logistics. How did you—"

"I assume you found it?"

"Yes."

"Well, I took my car to the park and took a driving service from there to a couple of blocks away from the Happy Time bar. Walked the rest of the way. See, I'd already followed him to the bar just before doing that, so I knew where to catch up with him. And, sure enough, he was still there warming a stool."

"Driving service? You mean a Lyft or an Uber?" Amanda asked.

Her mother snapped her fingers. "A Lyft, yes."

That would explain why Trent hadn't got anywhere with the taxi companies.

"Then after you killed him, you took his car to the park and drove off in your own?"

"Uh-huh."

"What are you going to do?" Her father's voice was gruff, and he looked at Amanda.

Both of her parents were watching her, and it would have been easy in a lot of ways to turn her back on this, but it really was out of her hands. And to see her mother so full of rage was unsettling—she'd always been a rock and one of the kindest, most gentle people she knew. But her grief and her hatred, her inability to forgive, had murdered her soul, her moral compass, her morality. And reflected in her mother's eyes, Amanda saw herself. She'd been heading down the same path, but the victim would have been herself.

"I have no choice but to turn you over—"

"No." Her mother thrust out her chin. "If I'm being arrested, it's by you. It will clear your name of that awful accusation made in the paper." Her mother looked at her father, who raised his hands.

"I'm off this case, Mom, but I will be by your side every step of the way. My partner is in the car and he'll be the one to bring you in. As far as our conversation, your confession to me, none of it happened."

Amanda got up, her feet like lead as she headed to the front door.

EPILOGUE

A week later...

Amanda reluctantly left a reunion at her parents' house late afternoon. She hadn't been able to get enough hugs from her brothers and sisters, nieces and nephews. Everyone was happy that Amanda was back but coming to grips with what Julie Steele had done, and there were moments when Amanda felt she may have imagined it all, but the horror of it was too much for her to have simply created. Like grief ebbed and flowed, so too did her mother's actions play out in her mind as surreal, an alternate and imagined reality. If Amanda hadn't heard her mother's confession with her own ears, she never would have believed it, but the truth was there, not only in her words, but in her eyes. And the entire family would be the subject of county gossip for a long while to come—or at least until the next big thing. Right now, all anyone could talk about was the arrest of former police chief Nathan Steele's wife in the murder of Chad Palmer. In the media, Detective Amanda Steele had been credited with the arrest, but officially it had been Trent.

The toughest reunion had come with her sister Kristen and niece, Ava. Amanda hadn't realized just how much it had hurt to distance herself from them until she was holding on to them again. When she'd made the choice to cut them out of her life, it had been too painful to look at them because all she saw was the accident, the funeral, the lowering of the coffins... that little one that had housed her baby girl. At the sight of Kristen and Ava today, her heart had opened up like it hadn't in years, and she let them in and soaked up their love and poured hers on them.

"I'm so sorry," she'd whispered in Kristen's ear when they hugged and wept.

"Me too. I never should have stopped fighting for you." Kristen sniffled and stepped out of the embrace. "I just…" She palmed her wet cheeks.

"I know." It hurt her and her sister and the rest of her family. But now they had a chance to at least inch toward healing old wounds, though it was shadowed by their mother facing prison time. Amanda had pulled her sister in for another hug and didn't let her go until their baby sister, Sydney, who was twenty-five, nudged them apart.

The entire day had been somewhat bittersweet, but Amanda was happy to be reunited with her family again. She only wished she'd done it sooner. If she had, maybe her mother wouldn't have murdered Palmer.

She pulled into the cemetery and walked across the lawn to the knoll and planted the bouquets she'd brought for Kevin and Lindsey in the holders in front of their stones. She crouched next to their graves and let the tears fall as she spoke to them from her heart and didn't leave a detail out. It had been early evening when she'd arrived, and the sun had sunk in the sky by the time she was getting ready to leave.

She pressed a kiss to her palm and passed it to the stones. "Thank you, to both of you, for having been a part of my life and helping me through this…" She hiccupped a sob. "The worst pain I've ever experienced. I will love you always and I will always, always do everything I can to make you proud of me. Thank you, Lindsey, for helping Mommy keep her word."

Amanda headed home, wanting nothing more than her bed and pillow, and she had some time to catch up on her sleep. Malone had granted her a week's leave and Amanda was taking it. She'd use much of it visiting with her family, but she was also fulfilling her promise to be by her mother's side through the judicial process. They'd hired Hannah Byrd out of Washington as her mother's attorney and she'd got her mother out on bail. Hannah was optimistic she could get the sentencing down to fifteen years and, with good behavior, parole in seven and a half, but nothing was certain in the world of law. Nothing was for certain in the world period. Amanda didn't miss the irony that her mother might not spend much more time than Palmer had behind bars, and how she'd always viewed the sentence as unjust and measly. And, sure, Palmer hadn't deserved to go out the way he had, and her mother had to pay the price, but this was her mother. They'd fight for her.

Yesterday she had driven out to Williamsburg and returned the cast of Phoebe's toes and fingers to the Baldwins. She'd also broken the news to them about their daughter. There'd been a lot of emotion and tears had fallen, but there was also a sense of relief that came with closure. Tanya had even commented that at least her daughter was no longer in pain. Amanda wasn't so sure she could have seen the positive so quickly, but she supposed the Baldwins had been preparing themselves for this type of outcome for many years.

Amanda let herself in her house and dropped her keys in the bowl by the front door. She padded down the hall, and realized before she could drop into bed that there was something she should take care of first. It could wait until tomorrow, but by then she'd probably have come up with a slew of excuses.

She pulled out her phone and tapped a number in her contacts. With each ring, she prayed that her call wouldn't be answered and then she could excuse herself and say that she'd tried.

Third ring, then, "Hi."

She stopped breathing, then, "Logan?"

"That's me."

"Detective Steele."

"Who?" There was a smile in his voice.

"Cut it out. You know exactly who I am."

He laughed, and she rolled her eyes and smiled. He was going to make her work for this. "I was calling to see if you'd like to join me for dinner this coming Friday night."

"Oh, Friday, I'm not sure if—"

"All right. Well, I tried—"

"I'm just pulling your leg." He laughed again. "Friday will work great. Where are you thinking and what time?"

"Rein back the hundred questions." She found herself giggling and named a place and a time.

"I'll see you there."

"Yep." She hung up, smiling. With all the hell of the past couple of weeks, it was as if something had jarred loose within her, a faint impression of the life she used to live coming through in cracks of light.

She got ready for bed and opened the top drawer in her nightstand. She was going in for a sleeping pill but there was something else in there. The six Xanax pills and Freddy's card.

She'd kept her word to Palmer's cousin and brought him justice—even at the expense of herself and her family. She took the baggie from the drawer, no longer drawn to pop one of the pills and dumped them in the toilet. Then she tore up Freddy's card into a million tiny pieces, dropped them in too, and flushed.

When she returned to her room, there was a lightness in her steps. She closed the drawer without taking a sleeping pill, crawled into bed and fell into a deep slumber.

A LETTER FROM CAROLYN

Dear reader,

I want to say a huge thank you for choosing to read *The Little Grave*. If you enjoyed it and would like to keep up to date with upcoming releases in the Amanda Steele series, just sign up at the following link. Your email address will never be shared, and you can unsubscribe at any time.

www.bookouture.com/carolyn-arnold

There's nothing quite like that feeling of finishing a good book. Even as a writer, it's hard to put it into words. There's definitely a sense of satisfaction but also sadness at ending a journey with characters you've become attached to. I hope you feel this way after reading *The Little Grave*. If so, I did my job at bringing you a story that sucked you into its pages and let you escape reality for a while.

I first met Trent Stenson and Becky Tulson when writing *Silent Graves* in my Brandon Fisher FBI series. When it came to pitching a new series idea to Bookouture, I decided I wanted to return to Dumfries, Virginia. And, yes, there's a story in there as to how that location made its impact on me, but let's save that for another day.

But if you're familiar with Prince William County, you'll know that I took some creative and literary license and, hey, that's what authors often do. There's no Hannah's Diner, but I'm sure there's a place the locals love to go for their coffee and a woman like May Byrd—though maybe not!

If you loved *The Little Grave*, I would be incredibly grateful if you would write a brief, honest review. Also, if you'd like to continue investigating murder, you'll be happy to know there will be more Amanda Steele books. But I also offer several other international bestselling series and have over thirty published books for you to enjoy in everything from crime fiction, to cozy mysteries, to thrillers and action adventures. One of these series features Detective Madison Knight, a female kick-ass detective who will risk her life, her badge—whatever it takes—to find justice for murder victims.

I love hearing from my readers. You can get in touch on my Facebook page, through Twitter, Goodreads, or my website. This is a good way to stay notified of all my new releases. You can also reach out to me via email at Carolyn@CarolynArnold.net.

Wishing you a thrill a word!
Carolyn Arnold

carolynarnold.net

Carolyn_Arnold

AuthorCarolynArnold

ACKNOWLEDGMENTS

I'm grateful to everyone who helped me through the process to get this book published. My husband, George, to whom this book is dedicated, is my best friend and has stood by my side for over twenty years. I love talking murder and bouncing ideas around with him. He has a way of calming me down and keeping me level-headed even as deadlines loom. He's also my favorite celebrating buddy!

I want to thank First Sergeant Jonathan Perok of Prince William County Police Department for answering my emails, helping me understand the organization, and even for his insights inside Central District. I hope he forgives and overlooks the times I took creative license with building layouts and possibly on some procedure that may be specific to the area.

I also thank a sergeant (who'll I'll leave unnamed) with the Dumfries Police Department who was only a call away.

Yvonne Bradley, a former coroner in Georgia, came to my rescue again and helped guide me through what the scene at an ethanol poisoning would be like and the effects of alcohol on the body. When she told me it was often an accidental death, she probably thought that I wouldn't be happy about that, but this suited my plot perfectly. I wanted there to be initial doubt as to whether Palmer had been murdered or had just drank himself to death.

I thank Emily Gowers for believing in me and this series idea. I'm also grateful that she worked on this project with me as a partnership, considering my ideas and respecting my opinions.

I also thank my publisher, Bookouture, for helping me bring Amanda Steele to the world.

Last but not least, a shout-out goes to all those who serve the badge with honor, whether it be in Prince William County or anywhere in the world.